THE KILLING

C. P. CLARKE

Cover design by: The Smithy Creative
www.thesmithycreative.co.uk

ISBN 13 -: 978-1505586794
ISBN-10: 1505586798

Other titles by the author:

Life In Shadows
Stalking The Daylight
Vicky Rivers

POV – A Personal Perspective of the Bible
A Question of Faith
Stories on a Wall

THE KILLING

C. P. CLARKE

The soul is a terrible reality. It can be bought, and sold, and bartered away. It can be poisoned, or made perfect. There is a soul in each one of us. I know it."

The Picture of Dorian Gray
Oscar Wilde

C. P. CLARKE

PART ONE

C. P. CLARKE

"I never used to hear the demons in my head, now I do and they frighten me."
Jonathan Rivers

'Sin, death, and hell have set their marks on him,
And all their ministers attend on him.'
King Richard III
William Shakespeare

"Therefore keep watch, because you do not know the day or the hour."
Matthew 25:13

C. P. CLARKE

1

The handover was rushed as per usual. The traffic had been awful for a Friday night, usually it would have been clear with most trying to knock off early for the weekend and spreading out the rush hour so that its trunks of traffic were thinner by the time he'd left the office, but instead he had spent a good extra twenty minutes pumping the clutch and riding the break praying the line of devil eyes ahead would clear so that he could get home to relieve Vicky of her charge. The travel report on the radio omitted any news of any major hold-up in the area, which was a good thing, but nevertheless he'd found himself galloping the horses against the steering wheel as he tried to crane his neck around the crawling cars ahead to see what the hold-up was. It had turned out in the end to be a faulty temporary traffic light set up by some road works on one of the minor rat runs; actually he hadn't done too badly as they couldn't have been out for too long, had he been a few minutes later he'd have been caught in the snarl-up which snaked back onto the High Street and beyond, its tail rattling with frustrated horns behind him as drivers lost patience and frantically turned three pointers in the middle of the road in an attempt to flee the raging furnace of exhaust fumes. He was going to be late no matter what and she had already called twice to find out where he was.

Vicky had rushed out the door as soon as he pulled the car up onto the driveway. There was a quick exchange of the relevant information: the kids are both asleep, your dinner's in the oven, your mum phoned – can you call her back, I'm off, I'll see you later; the exchange ended with a brief kiss on the lips as he stepped out of the car and she jumped into the driver's seat. He wished her a good evening as she readjusted the rear view mirror and he closed the car door as he stepped away backwards to allow her to reverse out.

An hour later and he was getting undressed in the bathroom. He had popped in on the kids when he first came in and found to his amazement that they were, for once, both sound asleep. They must have had an exhausting time at school for them to have conked out so early in the evening; usually there was a battle of wills as to how many times they had to be lovingly yelled at to get back into their beds as they sought any excuse to stay up a bit longer. He had gone into both their rooms and with a quietly practised action checked on them in the dark.

Lisa, at nearly nine, the eldest by three years and quite tall for her age, was fast asleep with her right thumb in her mouth and one foot sticking out from under covers. He gently tucked the foot back in without waking her before checking on Jack. The just turned six year old was lying on his back under his Spiderman duvet with his arms held high over his head as though worshipping God or hypnotised by the lights and sound at a rave.

Jack's room wasn't as dark as Lisa's so he was easier to see. Vicky as usual, knowing Jack to be afraid of the dark, had left his bedside lamp on so that he didn't freak during the night, something he often did having the most dreadful night terrors which scared mum and dad just as much as they did him, with his screaming and wide open eyes and the occasional sleepwalking, all whilst still fast asleep and with no recollection of events when day dawned. On one or two occasions Jack had awoken with screaming and David had gone into him to reassure him to find Jack sat upright wide eyed and grinning, the grin would turn to an uncomfortable chuckle before the crying began again, followed by the chuckle and a brief cry before he flopped back on the bed in a deep and unshakable sleep. Those were the worst, the ones that sent a shiver up David's back; they were so unnerving that he would make a point of asking Jack about them the next morning, but of course Jack had no recollection of any of it.

Without a doubt he loved his kids and would do anything for them. He was proud of what he had produced. They were both good kids and they generally got on well together, with the exception of the standard bickering expected between brother and sister. They played well together and mostly looked out for each other. He felt blessed to have such a great family.

In their ten years together he and Vicky had rowed rarely, their few big arguments coming at times of clear stress were quickly remedied. They kept a good balance of home life and work life and always made time for each other, keeping date nights and family times a priority and trying to model it well to their kids. They were also sure not to live in each other's pockets by making sure that they kept their individual friendships; he had his pals both in work and out of work whom he met up with regularly for drinks or to play golf, and she had her friends, some of whom were old school mates and some she'd made through the kid's school friends at the school gate. Vicky probably had more of a social life than he did but that was okay, he didn't resent her for that, in fact he thought it was healthy and actively encouraged it, often racing home so that she could go for a night out – tonight she and two friends were meeting at the cinema to see some rom-com that he barely knew the title of; she'd have fun and tell him all about it when she got home if he was still up, otherwise she would relay all the gossip to him in the morning whilst he was having breakfast.

He'd eaten a hearty dinner that she'd slaved over and left him warming in the oven, a big portion of spaghetti bolognaise which he took his time over and washed down with some orange juice. He had a plan for the evening, it was pretty much his normal plan, his routine to chill out in his own space and veg in front of the TV with a cool beer in one hand and a big bag of crisps in the other. Deep down he knew the routine, along with his wife's good cooking and the lack of motivation to do any form of exercise, was the reason that over the past year he had put on so much weight; the chiselled jaw was now rounded and his ripped torso was now bulging with rippling loose tyres. He had let himself go a fair bit but Vicky didn't seem to mind, if she did then he would do something about it; he didn't want to cause her any unhappiness, and so far there had been no complaints.

Before he could relax though he needed a shower; he hated sitting feeling the grime of the day still lingering on him. Sitting in front of a computer screen all day always made him feel oily, he didn't know why, it was why he tried to avoid cramming the reports late at night on the company purchased clunky truck of a computer that sat in the corner of the dining room, he would always feel the need to wash afterwards if he sat up staring at its flickering blue screen which seemed to also wire his brain so that he couldn't get to sleep easily, leaving him always regretting not just sitting to crash for a couple of hours of mindless TV.

He stripped off his clothes and turned on the shower, opening the sliding door a fraction and putting his hand in to test the temperature before stepping in and letting the hot water pummel him, gently massaging his scalp and shoulder blades as he closed his eyes waiting a few moments before reaching across for the shampoo from the wire rack suctioned to the tiled wall. He allowed the water to fill his ears as he rubbed in the thick cold gel of the lime green shampoo. Had it not been for the torrent brushing over his ears he'd have heard the bathroom door open. Had it not been for the lather of the shampoo now dripping down his face and covering his eyes he'd have seen the figure peering at him through the steamed plastic of the shower screen. As it was he felt a chill from the door being opened followed by the uncanny feeling of being watched. He tried to open his eyes quickly without thinking first to rinse off the shampoo, a costly mistake he realised as immediately his eyes began to sting as he tried to peer down at Jack on the other side of the shower door.

"Aaah!" David yelled to himself as he put his face back under the shower head, his thumb and forefinger of his right hand pushed to his eyes as he pulled at the door of the shower with his left. "Jack, are you alright son?" he asked as he got the door open and finally cleared part of his vision enough to see that his son had a wild crazed smile on his face and his eyes, though open and seeing, weren't quite focused and awake.

Jack stepped forward. He had something in his hand. David couldn't make it out but was sure that his son wasn't totally aware and in full knowledge of what he was doing. He reached forward to stop his son from entering the shower and getting wet, half thinking that he should reach up and turn off the water before his boy got a shock awakening and a drenching of his pyjamas. David caught the glint of the object in Jack's hand and automatically reached out to grab it with shock streaking across his face but the forward motion caused his foot to slip on the wet plastic shower base and he fell forward onto the large black handled kitchen scissors. The blades of the scissors, which were held in a feeble grip, separated as they collided with his shoulder causing the top one to slice no more than a deep scratch through the skin which sent his body into reflex trying to jolt backwards against the forward motion, his feet still slipping and eventually giving way so that he spun awkwardly with his back to the shower door as a thin line of blood oozed into the flow of water.

David's head hit hard against the plastic base but his concern was on his son. He didn't feel the pain as he tried to pull himself up in the confined space of the cubicle.

He didn't feel the pain of the stab as the twin blades were poised together in a purposeful strike into the upturned right side of his back just below the shoulder blade. Initially there was shock. Was that really what he'd felt? He rolled himself around to see Jack, calling out to wake him, but it was too late, David's hand rose in awkward defence as the scissors found another target between the ribs of the right side. And again. And again. And again they came down upon him. By the time the scissors fell to the ground David was already laying in a pool of more blood than water.

He was still alive but the pain was too much for him to move, being that he was wedged in to the enclosed space, the bathroom door now sliding back to close behind his son who left the room and returned, he hoped, back to bed. He tried to call out a warning to Lisa, along with a cry for help, but the scissors had punctured his right lung and the attempt to draw in breath to raise his voice pinned him down, his breath spluttering out in a raspy whisper.

2

By the time the police arrived the world was spinning in a kaleidoscope of nauseous colour, everything moved but her. The children were gone; taken into protective care, not that she knew for sure why or where, she wasn't sure she wanted to know, wasn't sure she trusted her senses and the reality of what was going on around her. Surely she was dreaming, a nightmare more terrible than she could imagine and one she was desperate to wake from.

She was numb. The police had tried to talk to her but she was clearly in a state of shock and the paramedics were making preparations to take her to the hospital. The upstairs of the house had been sealed off, in fact the whole house was now a crime scene and would remain so for some time as the scene of crime officers did their job and the murder investigation team made their enquiries. She wasn't a suspect, which was a shame; she so desperately wanted to be the guilty party, it would be so much easier to accept than the alternative of what it appeared.

She tried to rationalise how Jack had all the blood on his hands, but even in her unqualified and inexperienced deduction of the events it was hard to imagine any other way that her son hadn't been the one to stab her husband, his own loving father, to death.

For at least an hour now (was it longer? she couldn't tell, her mind having lost track of time) since she'd stumbled downstairs and sat down on the living room sofa to call the police, her whole body shaking uncontrollably with shock as she made the call, she'd been sat virtually comatose playing back a lifetime of events in short synapses of past, present, and an impossible future as she battled to swim against the downward pull of the spiralling whirlpool pulling her uncontrollably away from what she held secure and safe, planned and predicted, wished and longed for - a future alone and too terrifying to imagine. She had got up only once in that time, reacting zombie-like to the blue lights and the bang on the door. She'd opened the door not even seeing the two uniformed figures in front of her as she stepped aside to let them in and pointed upstairs and mumbled something about him being in the bathroom. Both the children were still asleep, they'd not awakened to her muffled screams, not even when she'd followed the trail of blood spots on the carpet that led to Jack's room and entered and pulled back the covers to see the blood and scissors cradled in his hands.

When she first got home she had gone into Lisa's room fulfilling her promise to pop in and see her as soon as she got in, finding her fast asleep she kissed her cheek gently goodnight for the very last time and gently pushed her foot back under the covers from where it had been protruding. Curious to the trail of blood spots she had gone into Jack's room and immediately saw the blood on his pillow and on the duvet cover that showed up as a dark patch under the dim light of his bedside lamp. She assumed he'd had a nose bleed, and that David was totally unaware of it; it wouldn't have been the first time. Jack had a bad habit of picking his nose in his sleep recently which often made his nose bleed especially if his nails needed cutting. She was about to wake him to clean him up, pulling the covers back first to see how much needed clearing up, that was when she saw the scissors which he held lovingly in his hands as though cuddling a soft toy, his hands were caked and his pyjama top was wet, not just from blood but something else, water she thought, what's more his face had very little blood on it. It slowly dawned on her as she stared at him, still innocently wondering how to wake him, that he hadn't had a nose bleed and that the blood was possibly not his. She watched his chest rise and dip gently in a deep sleep and then cocked her ear to the bathroom.

How long had he been in the shower? She had been home nearing fifteen minutes now, having pottered about downstairs checking the kitchen cupboards trying to weigh up whether she needed another trip to the supermarket again in the morning. She'd assumed that he had watched his film and was taking a late night shower and so hadn't disturbed him but had instead waited patiently for him to emerge from the bathroom – but that was a long shower!

The girls had gone to a late night showing of the movie, it being a Friday night and none of them had work in the morning or needed to get up for the school run, which allowed them plenty of time to catch up and gossip over a couple of drinks in the pub first. Cathy and Sue had argued over which bar to grab a drink in before seeing the film leaving Vicky with the job of defusing the situation by suggesting an alternative, a buzzing bar a short distance walk from the cinema, forcing both sides to compromise. For a brief moment it looked like the evening was going to be cut short with the film being abandoned and the girls turning for home and an early night with their partners, alas the girls had conceded and admitted it wasn't worth falling out over and accepted Vicky's suggestion. The film was average and forgettable, the sort David would have hated, though the girls enjoyed it enough to hang about afterwards discussing the funnier scenes, all of which delayed her further, not that she felt the need to rush back knowing how much David liked his own space and his alone time, she knew she'd probably walk in to find him sitting with an empty bottle of beer watching the tail end of a movie, most likely an action flick that he'd seen countless times before, she'd creep in and try not to interrupt him until the credits rolled and then she'd plonk her rounded frame next to his on the sofa and snuggle up while she filled him in on her evening and he recounted his day at work. She had been fairly surprised to find him in the shower on her return but alarm bells hadn't rung anything out of the ordinary at that point.

All these images and more filed through her mind refused to let her see the room around her and the circus that it had become. Her daughter, Lisa, was far from her mind, a distant thought barely recognizable as part of her life as she assaulted her consciousness with the horror of seeing her husband laying wide eyed and naked with water splashing down, having washed off any blood so that his open wounds were clean and obvious at first glance. She hadn't returned to the children's rooms, instead she had backed out of the bathroom trying to stifle her screams, barely making it down the stairs into the living room. She thought she knew what must have happened, but couldn't bring herself to accept it.

How could he?

Why?

How would he react when he awoke?

She knew Jack loved his dad, they got on fantastically together; there was no way he could have done it intentionally. How would he ever recover? How would she ever recover?

She played through every possibility of a family life but in every scenario it failed to materialize completely as a picture in her head. The only pictures that seemed to stick were the one of David lying dead in the shower and the calmly content son laying soundly asleep in his bloodied bed snuggling tightly to the scissors that had torn their family apart.

She had glimpsed the children when they were led out, dazed and confused and ignorant of the truth. She wasn't conscious of seeing them but she would recall it a few days later as she lay bleeding in the locked bathroom of her mother's house; that vague image flashing through her mind of the last time she saw them, and the last time they would see their mother alive.

3

The location on the screen read France and that was okay with him, it was convenient although not intended, it could have read Timbuktu for all he cared so long as it didn't give him away. His uncluttered screen, lit bright in the gloom before dawn, also told him he had a text message and the time in large numerals taking up most of the three inch display yelled that it was ridiculously early to be getting a message from anyone, not that he minded, he was up anyway.

Not only was he up but he was stretching his legs across the hilly streets on route out to the point, his usual routine when he was sleep deprived in the early hours when the sun was yet to wake from its slumber over the flat edge of the world. It was a long old trek into the dewy mist that left the air constantly moist over the peninsular and under the slates of clouds lofting the sky above, not one that he'd ever measured out in distance and cared little for the preciseness of, but of marathon proportions it unquestionably was. It was the personal challenge, the aggressive pounding into the headwind as his lungs sucked in and heaved at the cold sea air as he climbed where mostly only cars bothered to exceed, and even then not at this hour.

The land would flatten out eventually as he reached the ascending head having passed the Fairview Cottage and the Pulpit Inn inland (a stopping point on the rare occasions his legs failed to carry his slender muscular figure all the way round – there would always be someone he could hitch a ride back to town with as the day broke over the water). He kept to the Southwest Coastal Path mainly, meandering round the headland's two lighthouses as he circled the open fields that rose above the cliffs, eventually beating back down into the sand as he reached Pebble Lane where, if the weather allowed, he would sink his burning feet into the sand, or the sea, and walk the short distance back to his narrowly compact two bed semi where the wall of his house rose steeply with the pavement, but unlike the houses opposite he had a driveway to park his car and his motorbike, and a covered porch to leave his shoes and coat, there was even space for his green wheelie bin, the basics of which were the envy of those whose living rooms hugged the traffic squeezing by the precariously parked cars kissing the stone walled boundaries of the narrow street. Each brick house that rose on the slope of the hill was painted brightly or clad in its original stone, leaving a clean and countrified village setting which echoed of neighbours who always got on and met down at the local pub regularly to socialise.

If only that were true.

These days people were too busy to bother with their neighbours, something for which he was thankful, a polite hello when passing was mostly as far as it went, and a few did even meet up at the pub, but mostly the young were professionals who kept to themselves and the old were too infirm to haul themselves out of the tombs they'd built for themselves; the only times you would see them was when they were being picked up or dropped off at the nearby Weymouth and Portland Hospital. Most of the older generation had lived here all their lives but were now having to give way to those pushed out of the city centre or just wanting to escape it. Either way he cared not for those that lived in his locality, and only once had to conduct business here – an old soldier not too long ago who'd become a loose end for someone else's problem; an easy enough job, knock on the door, wait for him to answer, do the deed and ride off back to Charmouth where he had a lockup, ditch the bike (not his own obviously, his was sat on his driveway – this one was permanently borrowed without permission) leaving it deeply sunken to rust on the river bed before driving back home the next day to the scandal he'd created, and boy did it create some; it was a hotbed of press for days to come.

Business was business and he didn't batter an eyelid when the call came. He was always available, always willing to travel, and all jobs were considered, if not always taken.

The wind picked up and blew at his cheeks not yet warmed to the adrenalin of his morning uphill run to the Portland Bill Lighthouse. Two things he carried: his house key, which was zipped tightly in his sweat top, and his mobile phone from which he never parted and now gripped tightly in his left hand whilst the cold index finger of his right scrolled across the touch screen. He read the message then took a moment to deliberate; it was a job, he was needed in London and by the eagerness of the timing he assumed it was urgent. He sucked in the sea air and decided he had time; he needed the run to clear his head. He'd taken on a lot of jobs recently and they were beginning to take their toll – he couldn't afford to get sloppy. He let his feet pick up the pace again. A couple more hours of obscurity off the grid would do him good before he crossed the Portland Beach Road back to where the network welcomed him home from Cherbourg across the Channel.

He would stop at one of his lockups en-route and pick up some tools for the job, then drive up to London and check in, get the job spec, do the background checks, make a plan, do the recon...

His mind worked the numbers as his legs worked the uphill pace. He hummed as he ran, the familiar tune working into his step until it bubbled into a mutter from his fluttering lips ...*tic tac toe, that's the way to go, Mamma said stick ya fingers to ya head. Flat cap snap chat...*

4

He felt inside the rim of his nostrils with his thumb and forefinger, not obviously but slowly and subtly with the concentration of someone watching an intense thriller or reading a gripping novel, their mind focused as their eyes dived into the swimming pool of a reality that wasn't their own. His eyes though, separate to the goings on around the rest of his face, read his surroundings, and more importantly the people within them.

He let his hand fall gently to his lap before lowering his eyes to examine the tips of his fingers. There were little specs of black as he had expected. He sucked at the saliva behind his teeth as the skin around his jaw drew in showing his mild annoyance.

He hated trains, well not so much trains but rather the tube. The overground tended to be cleaner and less congested in comparison to the London Underground with its claustrophobic pack 'em in like sardines mentality and the breath in my armpit odour or the grope my crotch invasion of personal space, and not to mention the heavy dust that tasted musty and settled on the skin and added to the grime on the collar of the pristine white shirt that sat beneath his suit. This was the dirt he looked at now with disgust as he took his eye momentarily off the woman opposite.

She hadn't noticed him at all, no one had really, except maybe the middle aged professional woman in the conservative skirt and blouse who was trying desperately not to notice, or was trying to be polite by avoiding a rude stare by peering across the seats using the reflection in the window as the darkness of the tunnel bounced the light back at her. He caught her glimpse a couple of times as she dared to look round directly at the woman adjacent to her, her eyes catching his with a slight embarrassed smile as she acknowledged where his attention was drawn. Other than her none paid him any attention. They were all too captivated by the woman opposite him.

The object of his fascination, and that of most of the crammed-in carriage, was oblivious to the attention she was receiving, or else she knew but cared little, of this he couldn't judge for she was clearly too much in a world of her own to even try to fathom her thoughts.

He brushed off his thumb and finger on the edge of the seat and immediately regretted it. The seat felt grimy like the grease of a frying pan had been smeared upon it and left to dry. He made a mental note to find a public washroom at the earliest convenience and freshen up. If there was one thing he despised it was uncleanliness, and the mess left by others infuriated him. He reached for the other end of the free newspaper he'd picked up on boarding the train, reaching for the pages he'd let go of to breathe in his own skin in favour of the stew of air that floated around him. He raised the pages up high again, his elbows tucked in so as not to infract on those to his sides pushing their thighs and knees up against his. He made to read the open pages, but in truth had no interest in them, he could read them later or not at all.

She shuffled her things again, reorganising her handbag for the umpteenth time since boarding the train, only this time she also moved her rather wide butt and spread her thighs a little too wide for anyone's comfort, her short skirt riding a little too high, high enough for any red blooded man watching to avert his eyes quickly to avoid the not so pretty sight. She wore a yellow skirt and ripped tights down to bright red high heels that would have been fitting on a Soho hooker. Her top half consisted of a brown corduroy jacket spotted with a montage of stains all of which he was sure had their own sad story as to the abuse that had led them to be there. Beneath the jacket lay a low cut orange vest that showed more than ample cleavage bursting forth from a pink lacy bra. In truth there was more of her than her clothes could contain for surely she was a well-built girl, but her clothes did her no justice and her age was hard to judge as her jet black African skin hid the seams of time that would normally show on lighter flesh. Her scraggly hair hung down across the dark brown glitzy D&G sunglasses that hid her eyes, a few clumps tied up in brightly coloured wide bands. There was a silver charm around her left ankle and a couple more around her wrists on varying shades of silver and gold bracelets. On her left wrist there was also a large diamond encrusted watch of a make he couldn't read across the distance of the aisle, and besides, another passenger was stood rocking back and forth disturbing his otherwise clear view with the raised brown edge of his overcoat as his arm that was held high to grasp at the handhold above his head. On her fingers sat rocks of blue and green and flat golden sovereigns, all of which he would have taken for fake had he not glimpsed the contents of her handbag.

   She'd be moving soon and he could feel the pull of temptation running through him. He fought it as he felt

the train begin to slow towards the next station. He'd
have to be quick. Hesitation could cost him everything,
but right now a huge part of him wanted to hesitate,
wanted him to sit and not move.

She was mad, no doubt about it. The whole carriage
could see the lunacy of attention seeking that was
parading before their eyes. All could see, but all
pretended not to. Like so many she was just another of
today's crazy victims of society that had been screwed
up by poor parenting and then abandoned by a poor
health service who found her falling into a too difficult
box and so was allowed to manage her mental illness in
the openness of a population that had grown
accustomed to it and now cared little for their
neighbour sitting next to them on the train, or in their
office, or in their street, or in the bed next to them in
their own homes. As if there were any doubt, one only
had to listen to her rant and swear at the top of her
voice as she yelled into her mobile phone chattering
gibberish to someone on the other end who apparently
cared and agreed with her odd and outlandish
comments cast out in her foul bloke-ish tone of east end
London/African mix, all the while sorting through the
contents of her handbag, taking things out, reshuffling
them, putting them back, and starting again.

He closed the newspaper and folded it; he'd use it
for cover. He tightened his tie, pulling the shirt collar
from his throat as he did so before brushing off a speck
of fluff from the shoulder of his suit blazer. He could
feel a cold sweat beginning to form on his forehead and
tutted to himself with gritted teeth. It wasn't nerves
that made him sweat but annoyance at himself for what

he knew he was too weak to resist. Despite himself he knew he would give into the temptation.

She shuffled her bottom forward in the seat as the darkness of the windows gave way to the lights of the platform as the train pulled into the underground station. He could see the money, it was loose in the bag and the bag, amazingly, was still open. It was one of the things she'd been rearranging in the sparkly silver handbag that sat on her lap. Three hundred and fifty pounds he'd counted, and she'd just flung it back in the bag after openly showing it to the world. She was a walking target, an easy target. One with a mouth that would batter you senseless in a verbal assault and send you running for dear life from the pounding she'd give you if she caught you trying to rob her no doubt, and for most they wouldn't even dare try, but he wasn't most.

He would have to time it right. Rise with her, sway on the brake, use the paper and the passenger stood in the brown coat for cover, collide but not enough for her to feel under pressure, dip in, dip out.

She stood. He stood. The crazily dressed loud lunatic and the sharply suited professional facing each other. The train braked, as expected. She was still talking on her mobile phone. He made his move. She didn't notice as he grabbed for his falling paper allowing her to continue passed him on the way to the exit doors. The doors opened and out she went onto the platform with all around giving her a wide berth. He fell in step behind, mingling silently into the crowd, his hand calmly placing his cache of crumpled notes into his trouser pocket.

Did he feel guilt as the empty space of the outgoing tube train filled the void behind him? Hell yes! He'd promised himself he wouldn't give into it anymore. But he still had it didn't he, oh yes! One hundred per cent still in the game! As he made his way out of the station the feeling of guilt quickly turned to pride as the edges of his mouth smiled up at the light of the sun bearing down on him.

5

It had been a clear run into Sunbury, that was until he'd hit the bottle neck at the M25 turn off and the fifty zone immediately after it. Still he was thankful it wasn't worse as he knew how congested it could sometimes get on the way into town, but he'd purposely avoided the early morning rush which he would have hit if he had left straight away.

It was early afternoon and he'd decided to pull off the motorway at junction 1 instead of continuing directly onto the A316 into London. There were things to do before he hit town: lunch for one, refuelling the car for another, and, of course, making the all-important phone call.

He turned left off the Sunbury Cross roundabout, he knew the area well as a regular route into town, and headed for the nearby Tesco superstore, one not unlike the one in Swaythling, just along from the Southampton University Campus, where he'd picked up the Prius He had parked a couple of miles away where he knew he could leave his own car indefinitely and had caught the bus (laboured down with his black kit bag) straight into the superstore's car park and sat there and waited for his car to arrive. It hadn't been a long wait, black Prius' were fairly common cars. He waited for the driver (a balding middle aged man with a slight limp and wearing a green Barbour jacket) to get out and commence his shopping, watching him from the bus stop where he sat pretending to wait for another bus, ensuring his victim selected a large trolley for a full shop and not a smaller half sized one or a basket – he would need as long as possible to get out of the area before the theft was reported. There were no cameras in the supermarket car park so sliding alongside the car and slipping the drivers lock was made as casual as a tropical fish grazing stopping to inspect the coral whilst the passing of other finely colourfully dressed fish swam about the parked anemone, he then moved round to the rear to pop the boot and place his bag inside, slapping on the false plate above the bumper as he did so, and then moved to the front to do the same, the magnetic strips attached to the pre-stolen plates smacking into place perfectly, and then he was in amongst the coral rock starting the engine and bringing it to life to leave the reef en route to another ocean.

As he pulled into the Sunbury Tesco and parked he wiped down the steering wheel, the handbrake, and the gear stick. He didn't intend to be long and there was little chance of the car being spotted but he did it as a precaution anyway; it was a habit every time he stole a new car, one that wouldn't last as he got more familiar with the vehicle and knowing that at some point in the near future he would burn it out somewhere far from where he stole it. No one would was likely to be looking for it anyway; who steals a Prius? It wasn't exactly high on the agenda of car thieves, and it was for this exact reason that he took it, having stolen the plates from a similar model a month or so ago and kept them at the lock up ready for use; it was a car that blended in and with its quiet engine was one that benefited him greatly for night time stalking.

There was a public phone box on the main road away from the store, he bought a sandwich and then walked to it to make his call, eating his lunch en route to save time, aware that he had flitted away most of the day just getting here, even though he'd made good speed on the run up.

'*Jack,*' the voice on the other end of the line had said, '*this one's different,*' and indeed it had been. He hadn't expected to be called for this type of job, it wasn't what he did, but under the circumstances he accepted it, and he guessed they knew he would.

He made his way back to the store and refuelled the car, paying cash, and then headed for Acton. It wouldn't take long and he knew exactly where to find him.

A few minutes later and he was manoeuvring the lanes onto the Sunbury Cross roundabout once again to re-join the road he'd left not twenty minutes earlier. Someone was tooting their horn. The lanes on the roundabout were confusing enough without having to look round to see who was tooting who. To his astonishment he realised that it was he who was being tooted. A mid-set Asian man with heavy dirty looking stubble and a small child in the rear of a battered white Peugeot who didn't appear to be buckled in. The man was waving his fist angrily and accusingly as if he'd been cut up. Jack swiftly double checked his positioning on the roundabout and the other vehicles around him, checked the road markings on the tarmac and the signs near the traffic lights – he was in the right, no doubt about it.

The driver of the Peugeot was persistent, stubbornly so as he pulled alongside the Prius with his window wound down shouting something Jack couldn't quiet hear but getting the general gist through the intonation of the still waving fist. The lights on the roundabout changed and the driver of the Peugeot raced passed him at an angle to cut up in front of him and then floored it onto the slip road back onto the A316 into London.

Jack, who up until this point was calmly going through the motions of his day, suddenly pulled across a curtain to block out all around him other than the car in front as a red mist descended and his right foot punched the accelerator pedal in pursuit of the Peugeot. He caught up to him as he reached the end of the slip lane, overtaking him and swinging round his off-side so that Jack took control of all traffic joining the faster flowing road. He could sense the panic in the other driver as he had no choice but to allow Jack to pull round him onto the outer lane, jerkily reducing his speed at the challenge he hadn't been expecting a few moments ago; his cocky initial anger now depleted he was probably hoping that he could avoid a major road rage incident by just backing off – but with Jack there was to be no such luck.

There was a slip road only a few hundred yards further on from where they had joined the main road, it was a truck stop and rest point complete with roadside burger van hidden behind an island of trees separating it from the road, and then off to the left it fell away to a dense tree line fenced in with broken metal railings. Of the cars that parked here few were here to rest, most were men hoping for a quick grope and bugger as they left their cars and made their way through the broken fence in the trees; a well-known cottaging site for gay men, or straight men lying to themselves as they hid their secret from their blind misguided wives. It was into here that Jack swerved his car from the middle lane in front of the Peugeot forcing it to do likewise at the last minute to avoid a collision so that both cars careened into the layby. He could see the panic on the Asian man's face as he wildly looked at him in the rear view mirror, stopping abruptly so that the car behind had nowhere to go.

Jack stepped out, foolishly so did the other driver. In the blink of an eye Jack was at the door of the Peugeot, his left hand around the collar of his opponent whilst his right reached for the small blade he kept tucked into the waistband of his trousers. His eyes flittered over to the back seat. He didn't say a word. The child was screaming and cowering in the far corner of the car. He could smell the fear on the father's breath over the strong odour of spice, and could see that he knew the intention in his eyes. He begged, a simple, heavily accented word: *'please!'* Then followed it up for emphasis: *'please, for me child's sake, please!'* Still Jack didn't let go, but he did do something he wasn't akin to doing - he hesitated. *'I'm sorry,'* mumbled the man with his eyes lowered to his fate, and then without a word from Jack the grip on his collar was released and Jack was walking away back to his car.

Jack pulled his car over to the side of the layby as the Peugeot, without hesitation, took the opportunity to flee, no doubt aware of how lucky an escape he'd had. Jack could see that as he was driving off he was yelling at the child to put on her seatbelt.

Jack sat and turned the engine off confused. What just happened? He thought initially that it was the kid in the back that caused him to stop, but that had never stopped him before; or maybe it was deep down a reasoned logic about having to adapt plans for the job at hand to cover his tracks and disposing of an unsightly roadside mess – he hadn't stopped to think about who was watching, looking now it appeared his was the only car parked in the rest stop – fortunately, but then that didn't mean that there weren't a couple of fagots blowing each other back deep in the bushes staring out from the trees. He'd taken someone out here before, in both senses of the phrase, letting himself be played with and blown before snapping the neck of the middle aged city accountant who'd cooked the wrong books, leaving his family to face the humiliation of a homophobic death broadcast across the news. It had made the previously little known rest stop a local talking point and no longer a respectful place to park up your car without a knowing eyebrow being raised; if you drove a truck you could get away with it, but even then it was questionable. That was long ago; the council had changed the fence since then, replaced it with high metal slats that ended in a sharp point, but he could see from where he sat that part of the fence has been yanked from the ground and hung wide enough to squeeze a person through to the darkness and debauched and disreputable activities beyond.

He thought back to the little girl cowering in the back of the car, maybe the same age or slightly younger than the girl in the house that time.

Damn what was happening to him? It was a bit late in his career to be growing a conscience. Suddenly he felt the age of his years unlock as though they'd been in a time capsule, now released and free to catch up with him, to slow him down, to overtake him like a moron on the motorway tailgating, forcing him to pull over to the inside lane so that he could be overtaken by the shaking of his fist, or more abusive finger, but instead of rising to the bate and the red mist of anger tempting him to tear after him with road rage (as he had just done) he simply resigned himself to defeat and pulled onto the hard shoulder to cry.

How many times had he raced through this scenario? How many times had he reacted, snapping instinctively and without thought, lashing out, and without care of the consequences? So as he imagined so he did, watching the white car drive away safely as he sat by the roadside with tears streaming down his cheeks.

6

Abigail Henderson got off the same stop at the same time every day. Every day she would look out for him, hoping to catch a glimpse, hoping that one day she would build up enough courage to talk to him. He wasn't there every day, if fact he didn't seem to have a regular pattern, and she sometimes altered hers just in case he'd caught an earlier or later train. She figured in the end that he must work shifts or flexitime for she had seen him often enough over the past year for him to be a regular city worker but not regular enough for him to have a set daily pattern.

There had been a growing desire growing within her regarding this elusive figure she too often shied away from speaking to. She had an opportunity once, he'd bumped into her on the train just before they got off, he had apologised in his deep, rather posh and not at all fitting with his appearance, London accent; it had been just the one word, a brief 'sorry' as he stepped back to allow her to step off the train before her. She remembered how she had flushed crimson and lowered her eyes, her throat swelling nervously, words wanting to rise up but her champagne syllables caught by the cork of her flustered bottleneck.

He wasn't married, he wore no ring at any rate, so that was a good thing she hoped. He looked too manly to be gay, although it had crossed her mind how naively stereotypical she was being, still he had caught *her* eye on more than one occasion, admiring, if not lustful looks stripping her up and down, not that she minded, indeed even approved if not welcomed them. He had smiled at her also, so she imagined, not directly but coyly, having looked away with a slight smirk; once she even thought he had nodded a greeting to her. She had never heard him speak, other than the one time, but she imagined his voice to be commanding, stern yet gentle and compassionate. She pictured him as managerial, he was too solid a frame to be of a demure personality, not fat but muscular, tightly hidden beneath his crisp business suit, his chiselled jawline and immaculately shaven cheeks rising to sunken and mysterious dark brown eyes that webbed out to tidy but greying cropped hair that put his age in his mid-forties, a good ten years her senior.

He made her feel like a little girl, a teenage hottie with a burning crush, kind of like she'd had on Paul Sizemore, her lecturer at Bristol University. He had been easier to tempt; she still had her figure back then and hadn't been burned by a string of bad relationships and a failed and abusive marriage that left her penniless and childless and full of regret for her life. Paul Sizemore hadn't treated her good but that hadn't mattered back then, she hadn't wanted a relationship just a good exciting fling in a locked corner of the campus, had even consented to a threesome with him and a girl she'd seen around but had never shared a class with. It had been an adventurous romp made all the more exciting because she knew it was wrong and knew there could be terrible consequences if they were found out, more so for Paul she guessed. Still, she had allowed herself to fall for his charms as she had so many others until one by one she became known as the university bicycle, ridden often and by many but never taken in to the bike shed, instead always left abandoned outside in the cold rain. When she eventually broke free of her spiralling lifestyle and pitiful reputation she returned home to London to find she had lost the ability to socialise and get ahead without flaunting herself, her self-worth now embodied in her sexual desire, or rather her need to be accepted through the sexual desires of others. Her relationships from then on all fell shallow and even the ones she felt were deep held only murky water below the surface, mostly containing a broody current that rose up in a torrent with violent waves whipping up and slapping viciously until she became accustomed, even expectant, of the abuse. Her eventual marriage, Alder had been the name she'd taken on then, had lasted only three years; it had taken her longer to lose the name and even longer to rebuild her life and stop allowing herself to be the proverbial doormat to every man she encountered. By the time she gained her independence, if not the confidence of her own self, she looked worn and haggard and unshapely. She tried her best to be presentable but in truth she was mentally beaten and had all but surrendered any chance of finding true happiness.

There hadn't been much interest in recent years, and not much she'd been interested in. She satisfied herself with power tools and images of those she wished in another life she could have, often the devoted and loving husbands of her friends and work colleagues, secretly desiring the lives they had. Of her fantasies of late was this enigmatic figure she longed for on the way home every day. Sometimes he had been there on the way to work but he often seemed to get off at different stops so that she couldn't figure out what area of town he worked. On more than one occasion she had tried to follow him out of the station only to lose him in the crowd, frustrating in itself and more so for the delay it caused her in getting to work having to get back onto the tube to get to her own stop.

Today she had walked through the carriages, as she often did, looking for him, hoping to get a glimpse of him. He usually sat midway along the tube where it was busiest, but if it was congested elsewhere then that was often where he would be found. Today he was stood, his free Evening Standard in hand whilst holding onto the cold metal of the bar with the other. He was squeezed between a young smartly dressed white woman with long straight blonde hair with facial features that gave away her eastern European heritage and a tall black youth with the hood of his jogging top above the rucksack that hung low behind him, he had his back to her so that she couldn't see his face but his hand on the bar gave away his ethnicity.

He raised his eyes above his paper and looked around studying the people around him, as she had noted he was in the habit of doing. Often he would clumsily bump into people, sometimes it would almost appear on purpose but in her dreamy mind she never saw anything odd about the way he did this. As he looked around his eyes caught hers and the corner of his mouth raised ever so slightly.

Was that a smile? Did he just smile at me? I think he did. His head just dipped! He just nodded to me, I'm sure of it.

She could feel the skin of her pale face filling up like a thermometer, the mercury rising steadily with no intention of subsiding as her embarrassment grew.

Only three more stops until they reached Acton Town. She had lowered her eyes, now she raised them again and tried to catch his. He was still looking! He looked away towards his paper and she waited with the intensity of watching a fast paced sport, or more likely for her the unblinking focus of Saturday night in front of the television watching Strictly Come Dancing, not wanting to miss one dance move as she judged for herself and dreamt of the days when as a teenager she had moved so gracefully across the dance floor in the classes her parents had paid for. She watched and waited and eventually it paid off: he raised his eyes above the paper and peered out at her.

She sucked in her breath and prepared herself. Today would be the day. She couldn't get close to him now for the carriage was too congested, and anyway how would she approach him, what would she say? She pictured herself shrinking back into the laughter and sniggers of the other passengers as she tried to make small talk, her tongue tying in knots as she tripped over her words. No she would wait until they were off. She knew which way he would head when they left the station and how the crowds petered off as they walked away towards the park. She would wait till then when he was on his own as she could minimise any embarrassment that should come her way.

The last three stops passed way too quickly. She wanted to linger her eyes on him much longer but other passengers had shuffled their positions and blocked her view. A coy nervousness had dried up her mouth and she hunted through her handbag for some mints or other sweets, anything to moisten up her mouth and freshen her breath; oh how many times had she been through this!

Acton Town rolled into view and she stepped off the tube train and onto the platform pushing aside the crowd with her thoughts as she watched him fumble with something in his hand and then place it in his pocket before two-stepping the stairs up towards the exit onto the main road. He didn't go through the barrier she noticed but flashed a Travelcard at the guard; she'd seen him use an Oyster Card before to touch out but every so often he seemed to buy a ticket.

He turned left, as expected, out of the station and walked passed the parade of shops and the used car showroom on the left up towards the traffic lights that crossed Gunnersbury Avenue as it drove down towards the Chiswick roundabout to the left and the Hanger Lane gyratory system to the right. If they continued straight on they would walk to South Ealing but she knew he wouldn't wander that far for he'd have stayed on the train for another stop if that were the case. The houses, she recalled, were rather large and wealthy properties the far side of the Gunnersbury Avenue surrounding Gunnersbury Park, a much nicer area than her single bed flat behind her to the right of the tube station. She walked a fair way behind him, enough to look casual but not so far that she would have to run to catch him up - she could walk fast if she needed to but would feel silly run-skipping to chase him down.

Very few other pedestrians walked as far as the lights and most of those that did turned left towards Chiswick.

Now was her chance.

The traffic lights changed and he had hop-skipped across them just on the cusp, leaving her stranded to await the tidal wave of cars racing each other off from the lights to jostle for position in the lanes of heavy rush hour traffic that would clog up before they hit the roundabout further up.

She watched him quick pace it towards the park and then quickly nip in through the gate on his left towards the park's museum entrance. By the time she had gotten across she had lost sight of him. She dithered as to whether to continue her pursuit, standing at the gate unsure, eventually deciding what the hell – what did she have to lose?

She walked into the park and noted that the museum, a large white 19th century building which housed a collection of local historical finds including pottery, paintings and photographs, and a selection of vintage vehicles, was closed, it of course being beyond the working day and, although the daylight was yet to fade, the park gates themselves would soon be locked up. She assumed he had walked down the left hand side of the museum which led out onto the wide open lawn at the back which led on again to a number of wider fields and paths and playing fields which spread across towards Brentford. Indeed the park was sprawling and contained a large children's playground, a boating lake, a fishing lake, as well as a number of hidden ruins within its wooded grounds. She wondered where he could be heading but her confusion over this was only secondary to her need to actually lay eyes on him again. She figured that if she couldn't see him soon she would walk the length of the western wall that followed the road down towards the Chiswick roundabout, there was a gate halfway down near the old school where she could exit and double back up towards the station and home.

The disappointment was setting in as she curved her way towards the tree line at the end of the lawn into the second field without laying eyes on him. She was beginning to feel foolish and the boldness was slipping back as she began to withdraw within herself again.

"Get outta my way, bitch!"

She jolted back in fright. The figure had burst through the trees from a narrow path that weaved through to an old boating shed. There were a number of different paths that conjoined here and even from her youth she remembered it was a regular place for gangs to congregate as it was easy to starburst in all directions and make for a good escape from anyone chasing.

It was a black youth, no more than fifteen, skinny with his trousers riding low on his backside and a blue puffy body-warmer over a thin jogging top, the hood of which he was trying to pull up over his head as he nursed a bloody nose. He pushed passed her and began running across the lawn to the path on the other side towards the boating lake. She watched him go, suddenly unsure of her own safety.

There was rustling in the bushes and running steps she recognised as someone heading along the same path as the youth that had just passed her, and voices too, had they been there all along? She thought so. How had she not picked up on them before, for they were loud enough, shouting even? She stepped aside expectant of someone bursting onto her path. The youth that now confronted her was similarly dressed to the first, only this one's face was fully visible and this one didn't speak. He was in a worse shape than the other one: his arm hung loose looking as though it had been broken, and a wide gash was pouring blood from his face. He didn't need to speak, the look on his face said all that needed to be said. He tore at her face viciously with his eyes before bolting up the path and then across the lawn in the direction of the first. Had they not been preoccupied with whatever gang warfare they were embattled in she hasten to think what would have befallen her alone and unprotected.

Her thoughts then returned to him. She wasn't even sure whether he had come this way, probably hadn't, hopefully hadn't. Her thoughts were rocked by a loud bang. A firework, a banger – at the right time of year you could have been mistaken for thinking so, but she knew better. It was a gunshot, and back here muffled by the traffic noise and lost in the direction of open space few else would hear it – but she had, and suddenly all thoughts of *her* man vanished and she quick stepped it back up the path, not now worrying about looking foolish as she ran back for the safety of the road.

7

Shit flies, that's what he called them, only these weren't the small green buzzing kind that hovered around faeces, these were deep black (or dark muddy brown) mostly Somalian looking with elongated chins and protruding foreheads on wiry thin bodies, a couple were maybe Ugandan or Nigerian, at least one was Afro-Caribbean, occasionally there were some fringe Asian's in the group but they weren't present now.

Oh how the demographic had changed. In years gone by this would have been his gang, only back then there would have been no paki's, although a token nigger or two would have been acceptable so long as they showed their worth in muscle, but otherwise the gang would have been all white British and as hard as nails, none of these pussy threats and squabbling over an ounce of weed that he'd heard them boasting about as they bellowed the taunts at each other across the street with their limped swagger and lose fingered hand gestures and a language that was lost on all but todays street youth and feral brat.

This particular gang had unfortunately fallen into the habit of loitering around the park of late. There were plenty of hideaway points for them to do their business with little chance of the law being able to chase them down. He knew they were up to no good, peddling their drugs to passers-by, mostly kids who didn't know better, and a handful of older ones who'd passed their sell by date on harder stuff than what was on offer but would settle for what they could get their hands on.

There would be one of the gang initially, then two, then a third and before you knew it you'd be surrounded by them. They outnumbered the police who seldom dared to patrol the park and its many pathways, cowardly sticking mostly to the safety of their vehicles unless specifically called by members of the public to deal with an incident; they knew there was a problem with these guys, but like the model citizens of the area they too were intimidated, not to mention under resourced and their hands tied with red tape.

He heard the whistles as he stepped from the lawn towards the trees, up to this point enjoying his short walk through the park on his way home. He knew she was behind him but he hadn't turned to find out how far her nerve held up this time, he would have turned soon to find out; he didn't want her following him all the way home and would either slow to let her approach or duck off the path to lose her depending on how timidly she reacted.

She was no one to him, just a familiar face in the crowd. He'd bumped her once for a purse she probably thought she'd dropped – Miss Abigail Henderson her credit card had named her – a gym membership card, a Blockbusters membership card, little in the way of store cards or cash. She worked as a physiotherapist at St Mary's in Paddington, not that he'd gotten that from her purse, that was from the staff ID pass she once left attached to the waist of her trousers, which he was sure was for his benefit for the physios he'd seen in the NHS always wore a uniform and she clearly got changed at work. He wasn't dumb, nor blind, he knew she had the hots for him, and really she wasn't all that unattractive, baggage laden quite probably, but he could see that once upon a time she would have been more than tempting. Most men by now would have found her actions disturbing, slightly stalker-ish and promptly labelled as a 'bunny boiler', but he was reluctant to be so judgemental, being all too aware of the histories in people's lives that alter their behaviour and make them fearful; in the end it didn't necessarily make you a bad person but sometimes simply lonely and beside yourself.

He hoped, as he walked along the narrow grey concrete path through the trees, that she was well back, and that her courage had already left her.

As he broke from the trees into the clearing of the next field the gang surrounded him in typical shit fly formation. Only one had spotted him at first, the Afro-Caribbean who probably wasn't yet old enough to start college. He sauntered over kicking his legs wide as he stepped like his trousers would slip from his arse and fall to his ankles if he didn't adopt the strut. By the time he'd drawn close enough to give his scowl of disapproval of the crisp suited figure intruding on his turf the others of the gang had taken note. Two more crossed the dry bed of grass licking their lips for what they clearly saw as an easy target. One other slowly dared to leave the pack, trailing behind the other two as he left the remaining four to observe in the distance; maybe the ones at the back are holding the gear, he thought.

"What do you think you're doing here, man?" It was unmistakably aggressively toned and said with an upwards nod and a kiss of the teeth.

He didn't respond but instead looked over his opponents shoulder to count how many were intent on joining the party.

The first boy half looked over his own shoulder also, more sensing rather than seeing his friends approach. On his own he probably wouldn't be so bold but the back up of his companions bolstered his ego and gave him the stupidity real courage could do without.

"Wallet," he said with an outstretched hand.

It was a dumb robbery and he was tempted to slap the hand before him rather than place anything of value into it, but then he didn't want to soil his own palm with the dirt of the nigger before him.

He hadn't always been racist, at least he hadn't thought of himself as so, but he was growing increasing impatient of the growing numbers of foreigners who seemed to be taking over. Gone were the days when you knew where you stood with the gangs, and you had a code, and standards, and a reputation, but these little oiyks were nothing, just jumped up little wannabees who didn't have a clue, they'd never have survived on the streets with the gangs of old, they'd have been hunted down and sent packing to whatever little corner of the world they'd sailed in on.

He thought about just turning and heading back the way he came; he was fit enough so had a good chance of out running them, though the smooth soles of his black leather shoes probably weren't the best for the job and he could picture himself sliding for second base with the next batter hot on his tail.

"I said give me ya wallet!" He'd been joined by the other two now, one of whom was rearranging his baseball cap so that it pulled down more over his face thinking it made it harder for him to be identified. Idiot!

He smirked, he couldn't help himself, and if they'd known who he was they'd understand. Even without this knowledge it didn't take a genius to recognise that, although a lone white male in a business suit in a secluded area, he was broad around the neck, shoulders, arms and chest, had thick brute fingers with scars across the backs of the knuckles, his hair was cropped and a thin long line ran from his temple through his hair to the back of his ear, and his nose was crooked from having been broken on more than one occasion. For his age he was in good shape and none of life's scars had decimated his good looks, and any good judge of character would have told you at a glance that he was a fighter, and his stubborn silent stance said he was up for the fight.

"Dumbass, you deaf?"

"Smack the bitch up, man," said the one with his hat pulled down.

"Look at him, he thinks he's hard, man," said the third, who if he'd read the signs properly should have backed away already.

The first boy, the one closest to him took a step closer so that he was almost head to head and poked with his finger at the solid shoulder before him. There was a moment of enlightenment as that finger realised that what it was poking was much firmer than it had hoped, but the moment was brief, cut short as it was grabbed and snapped like a short dry twig, then twisted and spun, the arm and body following so that they now backed onto the other two. He brought his arm down hard on the elbow so that the arm bent in the wrong direction, the break audible in the otherwise stillness of the park, he then followed through with his other hand to the face that was trying to turn back up to him from its lowered position.

A number of things then followed: the Afro-Caribbean boy fell to the ground barely conscious, had he been able to cry he would have done, bawling like a baby, but he'd save that till later when he was out of sight of his friends; there was a cacophony of astounded voices raised in defence as those that had held back suddenly sprinted forward; the two skinny Somalian's that had been directly behind the first guy had stepped forward so that they were now directly behind him, and that was when he realised his mistake.

He didn't know why he allowed himself to turn his back; it was one of the first rules of combat: never turn your back to your opponent. Yet here he was at the beginning of the fight leaving himself open. He felt the sharp point of the blade digging into the small of his back - they had the drop on him. Fortunately it was the one with the cap who thought he looked hard and not the other one; the other one would have stuck it in without thinking about it, at least this one could think and was unsure enough to hold back, not that that made him smart, for if any of them were smart they wouldn't have begun this little escapade in the first place.

He could feel the hesitation shaking through the blade and hoped that adrenalin in the boy didn't slip into a forward thrust. The other one had circled round now and looked sure to throw a punch into his stomach but pulled it back at the last as the fourth boy with his grey hood up reached the foray brandishing a gun.

So this was the leader of the group, the real one with the balls. It made sense: he'd allowed three to go rob the single white guy while he held back to ensure his runners with the drugs stayed clear before heading for the action himself.

The gun was levelled at his head, not too close that he couldn't manoeuvre and not so far that it was out of reach. He felt the knife relax against his back enough for him to make his move. He reached out with his left hand and grabbed the outstretched right hand holding the gun, clamping the boys trigger finger in his palm before yanking swiftly down so that his wrist snapped and the gun was released into his own hand. At the same time he twisted his body away from the knife and swung his right hand back behind him to brush the blade away to scoop his forearm back up around to the swivelling figure at his rear and up into a choke hold around his neck pulling him back towards him until he dropped the knife.

He stepped away from the group as the rest arrived behind him. He kept them all in his sights as he settled the gun in his left hand and raised it, withdrawing himself from the centre of the activity and pulling his captive back with him in the choke hold, his heels scraping grooves in the grass as he made as much distance as he could.

How long had that taken? Seconds? He wasn't sure, but the one on the ground was now stirring and beginning to howl in pain. He recounted. Seven, eight including the one sprawled out splatted on the ground. He could see the knife now, it was a six inch black handled kitchen knife, it lay in the grass between him and them, and for the moment he didn't think the others would be bold enough to make a dash for it. Their leader was injured, that was good, he was also silent but he doubted he would remain so for long.

He needed to maintain control. He released his grip on the choke hold, the hands trying to pull his arm back for air thankful but not for long as he spun his victim round and smashed his fist into his face so that he fell swatted to the ground. Six.

He raised the gun up and the six who had half jerked forward now jerked back again. The one he'd just floored did the only sensible thing under the circumstances, seeing that the gun was held away from him he bolted into the trees, half scrambling across the grass like a chimpanzee as he went, the other one down also thought he'd had enough and followed suit bounding into the trees. Screw this! They'd rather face the consequences of the gang later than take another beating now.

He had been certain that the gun was a fake, not a toy (he knew the difference) but a non-starter, a decommissioned piece with its firing pin missing. He hadn't looked closely enough at it to tell its make or calibre, it wasn't the pressing thing to know right now. What he did want to know was how far this little group were prepared to go and would he be forced to reduce their number further before they all thought it wise to disperse. He wasn't expecting to be capable of firing as he waved it threateningly at the group like a can of fly spray held out at arm's length in front of him, but something in their leaders eyes told him it wasn't as harmless a piece as he'd initially thought. He stepped forward levelling it at the head of the boy nursing his broken wrist, for that's what they all were, just boys.

"My park. Got that?" He spoke for the first time. "Say it!"

The boy gritted his teeth reluctantly and then kissed them as if to say *you haven't got the balls*.

He lowered the gun and the boy grinned. Then he fired. The shot hit the grass near the boy's feet and his grin vanished immediately, his dark complexion now ghostly pale as his bottom lip trembled. The others backed off a couple of steps.

"You lot keep moving!" he encouraged, allowing them the freedom of flight.

The shot had been loud and had surprised even him when it had gone off but he was adamant of not showing any expression of weakness on his face. He stepped forward to the boy who was sure to feel a warm trickle down his baggy pants soon enough if he hadn't already done so. He could see the others sprinting for the far gate, flying far from the stench of crap they'd created, crossing the field with the occasional curious back running steps to see the fate of their friend. Surely this would mark the end of their gang as it had been, he hoped so. What little trust there was between them had been left out in the storm to be blown away.

"Say it!"

"It's your park," it was muttered through nerves but clear enough. "It's your park, ok!"

"You see me ever you'd better run." He then tucked the barrel of the gun into the front waistband of his black trousers and patted the butt. "I'll hang onto this if you don't mind."

The boy stood with his grey hood still up, his eyes welling up, a dark patch spreading across his crotch, waiting for permission to leave as though he were stood before the school headmaster for a bawling out over some heinous prank that he'd been caught out for.

Seconds passed and then the nod was given and the boy sprinted after his friends without daring to look back. If there was to be any retaliation it would be half-hearted and hesitant.

He stood alone in the field and looked around. The gang, the shit flies, had indeed dispersed. A few figures were stood lingering over in the distance behind him looking but probably not able to make out the details of what had just happened, and most likely too scared to find out. Two dogs ran about their feet as they moved off aware that the attention was now on them.

He shook his head amazed that he had escaped unscathed. It had been close and he had been lucky. He wasn't the man he once was, and for the most part he had left that life behind, had tried to at least. Now he was feeling too old for the fight.

8

'What fates impose, that men must needs abide; It boots not to resist both wind and tide.' King Edward's words from Shakespeare had almost become a mantra as he often recalled them whenever he came across resistance.

Going against the grain was something Jack tried never to do. He'd learnt over the years that cranking the wheel that doesn't want to turn does nothing but blister the palms of your hands and put an ache in your shoulders; a little oil to loosen was always worth a try, failing that try turning it the other way, if it moves then happy days.

He applied this to everything in life whether it be the opening of a jar of spaghetti sauce or to the weightier life changing decisions that crossed his palm on a more than frequent occasion than they would your average joe. The rule of thumb was that if you met with resistance then it wasn't meant to be, change tack, try another route, play a different game, but basically don't sweat it if you don't have to. He figured that resistance to something, any sort of obstacle that played a scratch in the record, was a sure fire sign of nature that things weren't meant to be, that your path was destined to be different and that to keep banging the same drum despite the racket it was making was like smacking your head (or preferably someone else's) against a brick wall in an attempt to get them to the other side without hurting them. Call it a spiritual warning beacon if you like (not that he believed in spiritual mumbo jumbo), but to him it was almost a mantra, one that made sense and not worth arguing with - nature wasn't a debater, it either moved or it didn't - if there's a fork in the road take the one with the sign pointing to your destination, only a complete douschbag would take the road that was labelled *'er, not sure if this is the way but try it anyway and see what happens'*.

It always played out true. He couldn't recount the number of times he had turned from a pre-made decision based on the right door not wanting to open and then hunting around and finding an easier route in, or a planned route having a squeaky floorboard or door with a creaky hinge, or a road with unforeseen construction work, or the wrong weather; always a new and easier approach would present itself, so long as he didn't stick to trying to force the jar lid the wrong way as he'd originally planned. It was that reluctant cock when yanking the hammer on the gun when using the butt to whip would have the same lethal effect and attract less attention. That's telling you something whether you want to hear it or not, and if you listen, then happy days. If you don't listen, well then you're just making life hard for yourself and you're a sucker for the consequences.

Cock the hammer, crack the thunder, and flash the lightning that would scuttle the rats in the drains below and shudder the worms from the dead long buried in the earth. That was Jack's way and he stuck to it no matter what.

So when he was presented with five black youths sprinting towards the park gate he was about to enter he naturally paused. He took a moment to take them in. All five were wearing hoods and were cowardly trying to hide their faces as they slowed towards the gate and attempted, and failed, at a casual yet speedy quick step. The young lads had clearly been up to no good and were now keen to flee the area without being identified. The one in the lead pulled the gate from the inside and slipped out through the narrow gap he had created. The others followed suit, each one keeping their eyes low and avoiding the stare of the stranger at the gate who now stepped back to allow them to exit. They got a few paces onto the pavement and began walking against the oncoming traffic, and then as though a starting pistol had been fired the four burst into a panicked sprint, once more drawing more attention to themselves than he was sure they realised.

A sixth youth was now cutting a path across the grass on his own, a murky figure storming out of the fading light as a mist began to lift from the shallows of the open space. His hood was down and he was cradling his right arm in his left hand. The boy was thin and wiry with a pointed chin and reminded Jack of one of those typical alien pictures that were bandied about, and a flash of Richard Dreyfus at the end of Close Encounters of the Third Kind sprang to mind. Only this alien was deeply dark in colour and was cursing loudly. Jack could see as he got closer that there was a well of tears being held back beneath an angry rant announcing that someone so fractious would be dangerous to cross. Not that he was afraid, but the inconvenience of having to deal with it was enough of a deterrent - that and the fact that maybe this was a sign to use another gate or even to leave his business for a more opportune time. Despite his employers insistence of the job being urgent he had judged it differently and so wasn't in too much of a hurry.

"Bitch! I'm gonna shank his ass, man! Gonna ter 'im a new arsehole! Pow pow pow! Gonna shoot 'im up. Hunt 'im down an' put more holes in 'im than a cheese grater. You watch, I'm gonna..."

The rant was an unrelentless attack on the wind which caught and brought the words to the gate before the cussing figure arrived. Jack had already stood back and was turning to follow the road north along the brick wall line of the park up to the main crossroads further up. He had parked the Prius in the layby behind him but he could go back for that later. The boy was angry, murderous venom spat from his lips, something Jack was all too familiar with.

"Yeah you turn and walk away you honky bitch..." a four lettered tirade followed but Jack let it flow with the wind above his head.

The youth bounded through a wide gap he'd made in the gate, having brazenly flung it open with his one good hand. "Yeah you keep walking you chicken shit; you an' your mumma aughta lose some pounds!" It was a nonsense jibe and Jack knew it, he was in no way big enough to attract such a comment and his *mumma*, bless her soul, was far from view, most probably restlessly drifting through the abyss of Hades waiting for her son's last breath, but something struck a chord in him deep down at the mention of the absent figure in his life causing him to pull up a step short.

mamma said keep the town clean...toe the line...toe the line.

Jack turned and looked to the young angry youth, whom, he had no doubt, had a history of violence and brokenness in his life, and maybe even mental illness. He knew the boy would be looking back at him as he wandered off in the other direction just itching to take out his hate fuelled pummelling on someone, anyone. As he turned he did indeed catch eyes with the boy and the boy opened his mouth to speak, but then hesitated and closed it again, his blink was also hesitant as he back stepped. He had probably decided he had taken enough of a beating for one day, but most probably, Jack thought, he had recognised in his own eyes the coldness and fearless determination of a killer more intent on murder than any four lettered abuse could convey.

As Jack's eyes bore into him the youth turned and ran in the direction of his friends.

***

That night Mohamed Abdi sat at home in his bedroom not caring that the latest of his mother's ex-boyfriends was downstairs trying to force his way into the communal entrance of the block, insistent that she terminate the child she was carrying or he'd terminate it for her, all the while she was on the phone trying to arrange for protection, not from the police but instead from the guy two streets away that supplied her regularly with skunk and occasionally crack or brown.

If his dad had stuck around this would never have happened, but he hadn't, he'd gone off to the mosque one Friday and never returned, it was only later in the day that they realised that he'd cleared out his wardrobe as well as their bank account. Mohamed didn't know where he was, nor did he care, he was the head of the household now, he was the man who ran things around here, and on any other night he'd be down at the communal door ready to bust some teeth in defence of what was his – but not tonight. Tonight Mohamed Abdi's mind was elsewhere mindlessly planning his revenge.

He knew where to find the son of a bitch, that old tosser that had snapped the wrist he'd spent the last few hours nursing as he waited in A&E for the x-rays to tell him what he already knew and for the cast to be put on. He wasn't afraid of the repercussions, they all knew he'd had enough scrapes with the law to be on first name terms with most of the officers on the borough, and they all knew he'd gotten away with far more than he'd been convicted of or even caught for.

There was a cloud of red mist that had descended on him with the fall of night, one that clouded his ears and blinkered his eyes as he kept replaying *My park! Say it!* over and over in his head. The fog was thick and had set in with a lingering cold and violent chill.

10

At the same time Mohammed Abdi sat stewing in his room, Trudi Smith sat staring at a ruggedly handsome older man sat at a busy bar looking glum and staring down into a half pint glass of lager.

Trudi, who had wandered into the pub glammed up but with nowhere to go and no one in particular to go there with, was a regular and well known to most other lonely regulars who drifted in after work and stayed to the early hours getting steamed, and hoping to leave steamy. She, like most others, had her group of friends whom she met up with but wasn't exclusive to as she mingled through the tightly squeezed bodies sheltering their pint glasses from the jolts of through traffic whist relishing in the gentle strokes of loosely covered flesh as it brushed passed. Mostly they were students getting tanked up before hitting the nightclub, a few like her were older by a couple of years and abandoned to the working life but desperately trying to hold onto youthful days and not give into the pressures of going steady and settling down; she couldn't think of anything worse than spending nights at home in front of Coronation Street while some grunt she called a boyfriend hacked at his nails on the other end of the sofa.

In this sort of bar few people stood out, and when they did they generally weren't attractive enough to approach. This guy though had reserved good looks: cheek bones that protruded from the strain of training in the gym drawing back to the slightly protruding jaw line with its constant stubble that grew in an attempt to hide the thin white gash that slid at an angle beneath his left cheek and stopping well short of his Adams Apple; his eyebrows were full with fingertips stretching out to meet in the middle as they overshadowed the depths of his wildly spirited yet mysterious dark brown eyes, eyes he tried to hide as he let the slink of his black fringe flop over them so that he could spy from beneath; he was muscular and athletic, not so much that he bulged but just enough so that his clothes hung well and his stature stood straight enough so that should you take him for a push over in an argument you may pause for thought at his average height and build. Yes he was good looking, but at the same time ordinarily so, easily blending into a crowd unless you just happened to catch his eye, or he caught yours. And she caught it as she sized him up in the mirror opposite, his head tilting back slowly to spy her creeping up on him from behind.

His head dropped once more as his eyes filtered into the glass before him, apparently disinterested.

"Why you looking so sad?" she bellowed from over his right shoulder as she carved herself some elbow space between him and the group of lads stood propping up the bar beside him. "Anything a girl can do to help?" Her voice was raised above the music but her tone was intimate enough not to draw obvious attention from the lads next to her, at this she was well practised.

His response came with a dry laugh, "Well, now there's a question!"

"I didn't mean it like that," she chuckled.

"I know," he replied warmly knowing full well she had.

"Seriously, anything I can do to help? I've been watching you from over there for the last half hour and you haven't touched a drop."

"Things on my mind I guess," he said without looking up from the half pint glass that still bubbled slightly at the line where the froth had long dispersed, "but sure, friendly company would help." He half smiled feeling sorry for himself. His mind was troublesome, a heavy burden was weighing him down, a recent dilemma not only of a future event that needed to be dealt with but also a past one, or a collection of past ones, which were only now beginning to play on his conscience and come back to haunt him. "You ever watch Back to the Future?"

Trudi half yelled an affirmative reply above the laughing group of loutish lads sidling in and out jostling for position against the bar next to them. She had hoped his first comment would have included an offer of a drink but it would seem she would have to work for it this time as he genuinely seemed to want to talk.

He raised his voice uncomfortably, grating against his demeanour. "Did you see the third one, the western?"

Again she responded positively.

"You know the scene where Doc Brown is stood against the bar all night with the glass of whiskey in his hand but not having touched a drop? That's how I feel about this glass, that if I drink it it'll overwhelm me and I'll pass out flat on the floor just like Doc Brown."

"Things can't be that bad, surely?" she said with a chuckle designed to boost his cheer.

He shrugged his shoulders, his body arched over the glass.

"Trudi," she offered her name and her hand.

He took it and shook it firmly. "Jon Rivers, most people call me Jack."

"Jack it is."

She had no room for pity but pity him she did. She felt drawn to him. Maybe it was his looks or his demeanour, most likely both; he was a bad boy, dangerous, it was written all over him; she found it attractive. She found an inner desire to help him, no man this cute looking should be sitting at a busy bar alone drowning in nothing but his own thoughts.

And so the seduction continued, the next hour followed a deep heart wrenching story of hardship and betrayal and misfortune, it was a sob story - the content didn't matter, splintered with just the right smattering of laughter and carefully placed eye contact, a casual walk ensued, her friends now abandoned, or had they abandoned her, either way they walked together to her car, they kissed gently, coy excuses made as she tried to coax him out of his shell, drawing him closer, teasing him out, falling for his bashful charm before inviting him back for coffee.

That was his game, how many times had he played it? Making sweet love, taking all he could get, squeezing all he could from her till there was nothing else to give.

Only this wasn't the same was it? Trudi Smith laid ear to a story that at first seemed too fantastical to be true. Some had heard the story before, the true story that is, but he rarely told it except for when his conscience demanded it to keep him in check. At times like this when he felt fractious he told it, but these times were growing too frequent now as he began to doubt himself more and more, knowing that eventually he was likely to get caught out. Damn, he'd even told her his real name.

Trudi knew deep down that it was a move, that he'd thrown out his line and baited her, and then slowly reeled her in. It was probably his long practised play, but she had no idea how deep it went.

This was his play: different cities, different countries, never the same place twice, never recognisable, always forgettable, there one minute, gone the next. He had her and she bled, not realising the deranged truth until its hands were suffocating her and his blade was gutting her while she writhed about on the bed with him still erect within her, his hand stifling her screams as Trudi Smith played out her last one night stand at the hands of a psychopath.

And when he was done he cleaned up, disinfecting all the infected areas, sanitising himself from the crime scene, the body, the flat, the car, disappearing before anyone noticed, like he was never there. Except for the dead girl that would be found later, long after he'd gone. No one hearing her dying orgasmic screams but him; no one hearing his cruel insane laugh but her - but she didn't matter.

11

That night he slept in the back street bed and breakfast that he'd found in sleezeyhotelsrus.com. He paid cash; in a place like this you paid no other way. There was no TV in the room, nor a kettle or soap, and breakfast was likely to be the basics of a cup of coffee and a slice of toast, or if he was lucky they might push the boat out and place a bowl of cornflakes (stores own, not Kelloggs) on the table. There was no CCTV watching him as he checked in, and all the more importantly there were no questions asked.

He had got back to his room by 1am, no one was there to greet him as he entered the extended makeshift hotel which in essence was an enlarged family home with a number of rooms carved up in a botched fashion to maximise the occupancy with no mind to comfort. Local whores used the place if their clients insisted on a bed, they'd charge double for it to cover the low cost of the room and then make more as the punter got comfortable and begged for more time with her as she opened her legs on the already soiled sheets. Dealers also used the venue but they were rare, mostly it was ex-cons placed there by the council who were picking up their tab as they gave the B&B as their bail address.

He was tired. It had been a long day, only short a few hours of being up a complete 24 hours cycle since he'd set off for his early morning jog around Portland, less than a day since getting the call; one day and one life diminished, still it could have been worse. He was well practised at the clean-up so it hadn't taken long.

Trudi didn't live alone; she had a flatmate who by chance was away on business for a couple of days - what luck! It meant he could take his time and sanitise the scene properly, sanitise her too and place enough misdirected evidence to keep the police circling the wrong fields of enquiry. He was good at that, making things look like something they weren't; how many accidental deaths had been anything but? Not that this one could possibly be made to look accidental - this was murder, cold, calculated and brutal, and it looked nothing less.

By the time he climbed into his single bed he was exhausted, his eyes closing rapidly and that heavy weight of not just his head but his mind also sinking into the too flat (not that he noticed) pillow and into the darkness of the void and dreams and nightmares.

He wanted his mummy afterwards, when the police were interviewing him and the psychiatrists were probing him and the counsellors were assessing him, and for days after, but he didn't understand why she wouldn't come to him, naively assuming they wouldn't let her; he didn't think that she was the one who didn't want to see him.

He played the song in his head that she often sang to him, it was a silly song and he guessed that was why she jokingly sang it to him, he imagining her voice ringing lovingly in his ears as he rocked back and forth... tic tac toe that's the way to go...

'Why'd you do it son?' *asked the psychiatrist but it was his father's voice.*

My mamma told me

'But she didn't tell you, did she?' *spoke another face, this one a judge, his mouth drooling over an aging wrinkling chin, his voice a despondent frustration of authority.*

When they're broke, Don't take the cake…

'The only thing broke is you!' *spat a policeman, but with his father's voice; he remembered this one, he was the one who had sat with him in his room while they decided what to do with him, no one quite knowing whether he needed to be arrested or sectioned, and what do they do about the blood? Do they wash it off?*

…and they all rode round on the little boy's trike.

'You're one screwed up kid!' *said the psychiatrist again as he sat in the grey cell alone with him. Only he wasn't alone was he, there had been a guard at the door. The guard's not there this time, maybe because I've been good. I didn't charge at the doctor this time and try to stab him with his pen insisting that I see mummy.*

Maybe she'll buy you a glass of wine.

But she won't because she's dead. They're all dead. You killed them all. You're a monster! You feel nothing!

'It's not true! I do feel!' *he shouted, but they weren't listening.*

'I am sorry! I do feel! I want my mummy!'

They were all before him now in the calming pale blue room decorated with his pastel crayon drawings of happy families and houses and cars on a sunny day. This was the room where he grew up, a special facility, a hospital, not that he knew it then, a secure wing where he had constant care and schooling in his formative years before he became aware of the outside world and grew eager to touch it, before they misguidedly moved him to the young offenders prison. Everyone he seemed to know, or had known in authority over him was in the room, crammed in as the walls seemed to expand and swell: policemen, doctors, judges and solicitors, nurses and guards, and of course his father stood naked with blood dripping with blank staring eyes. All were before him except the one he wanted.

'I want my mummy! Where's my mummy? I want mummy! Mummy? Mummy! Mummy!'

His shouts got louder and louder but no one seemed to hear as the figure started moving in closer to him, his father's hand out reaching for him. He tried to move away but found he couldn't, he was frozen in position as he screamed out: 'MUUMMMEEEEE!'

Jack was lying on his back, his head sunk deep in the warmth of the pillow which was slightly damp from the perspiration bleeding through his hairline. There was a daemon perched on his chest, he couldn't see it but he felt it, its weight bearing down on him immobilising the carcass that was his body and trapping his mind inside with no means of escape. He could hear the words trying to force their way out from his sealed lips as the oppressive force pinned him down into the mattress. The words were clear in his mind but they were muffled behind a swollen tongue and pursed lips in a voice that the cold air around him would never claim. His eyes too were sealed yet seeing the haunting figures reaching out for him still with arms that couldn't quite reach and connect with him as he spasmodically twisted his body to avoid their embrace, his adult body doing no such thing as he lay motionless, his eyeballs alone rapidly shuffling upon the impulses of his dreaming mind.

His cry for his long lost mother was of no help to him, she nor anyone else were likely to come running to his aid, and even in his dream he knew all breath and energy was wasted on crying such, and so he cried out the only thing he had left: *"Oh God, help me!"*

The daemon fled, though not far he felt, as he opened his eyes to the dark of the strange room and allowed a stifled breath to escape his lips. He swallowed hard and lifted his head slightly before dropping again on acceptance that it was a dream, just another dream.

He was used to these dreams, these nightmares. He remembered more and more of them these days as he woke. Often he dreamt of his childhood home and the old bureau his father kept by the cupboard under the stairs where he once got trapped in the expanse of dark within with nothing but a pile of old receipts and dirty laundry for company. He hadn't been locked in there long before his father had heard his cries above the sounds of the football results being read over the radio in the living room. Sometimes he dreamt of more gruesome events, and occasionally the police were there eager to catch up with him, but mostly his dreams merged into one senseless montage. He had suffered from them for as long as he could remember.

Sleep paralysis, that's what the doctors at the institution had called it, although the paralysis wasn't the whole of it; the sleepwalking, or somnambulism, to give it the term he often heard them use as they hooked him up to monitors at night with cables and tape netting him in a sheet of their own, was what frightened them all the most. These parasomnia dreams often overcame him at night in the form of demons controlling his mind, stealing his actions like a possession, parading him like a puppet, a child puppet manipulating his every sleeping action since childhood.

He blamed the demons, the doctors did too, at least the part of it they understood. It was a sleeping disorder, a chemical imbalance, a part of his unconscious mind either paralysing or mobilising his body. At times when he was paralysed it was terrifying for him, but the times when he was mobilised it was terrifying for everyone else, for he would wander, and his intent was often dubious at best.

Little had they realised his murderous intent was awakening to his conscious mind as he spurted into puberty.

Who knew the sins of his father that had left him cursed? He often wondered whether his father deserved his fate and whether deep down he knew some deep dark secret that as a boy he'd seen something hidden from the rest of the family. Surely it was better than the alternative that had been proposed by the African nurse, Grace, who attended him nightly with his meds, dark as the night beyond the window he couldn't open and wider than the door she locked behind her. She was the superstitious kind, deeply religious and enslaved to the forthright teachings of her African tribal pastor who clearly she'd confided in and been told that the boy was possessed of the devil, or *'da dev eel'* as she pronounced it in her thick West African accent. To Nurse Grace he was an evil little boy who had been guilty of worshiping the dark destroyer and bringing upon himself such evil spirits that he welcomed with open arms.

Nurse Grace's days in the medical profession were numbered, not that Jack ever knew what had happened to her, she just stopped coming to force his medication upon him and for that he was glad. No one told him that she had been arrested and was being investigated for child cruelty following the reported abuse of a number of 'demon possessed' children that attended her church.

There was a guy at borstal, as it was called back then, a prison guard who thought along the same lines as Grace and kept her mantle fresh in Jack's mind, fuelling his imagined fears. This particular screw thought that Jack was just an unfortunate lad who had been randomly selected by a drifting entity, or spirit, (he never actually used the word demon, but Jack knew what he meant) an abhorrence seeking a victim to prey on to do its bidding and had found a young fresh mind to pervert in Jack.

He tried to close his eyes again but had a sense of someone just outside the door hiding in an oppressive cloud waiting to rush in and strike once he let his guard down again and closed his eyes. He snapped them open quick time but the room was empty, the door closed.

He tried to keep his eyes open but a heavy weight was pulling the blinds closed. He could feel something akin to electricity firing off the synapses as he drifted back off to sleep. Then a jolt. A sense of someone outside the door just as he began to sink slightly beneath the cover, the thick duvet feeling like it was rising or being lifted or pulled away, the feeling intensified by the certain impression of someone there now pulling at the cover as bodily movement once more slipped into a frozen shell of helplessness and a foreboding at not being able to prevent the inevitable happening, and not being able to call out for help; the panic setting in and getting worse as he fought to wake from it.

He snapped his eyes open once more and felt the cloud jerk back away from him. The room was still empty but still he felt the electric tingling on his skin. Yet still his eyelids lowered once more.

There was a feeling of someone holding the cover, or pulling it, shifting it from his body as the tingling of electricity radiated around his body. He even felt as if something heavy was resting on him, like a small person had climbed gently on top of the cover.

His eyes snapped open immediately but once more the room was empty.

Was he still awake? He wasn't sure as he allowed his eyes to drift dreamily. Was someone holding his arm? No.

He opened an eye then closed it again.

Something was gripping his right leg. The sparks of electrical tension were bouncing off different parts of his body as they danced the air around him pushing him back till he finally succumbed to the sensation of falling back through the bed into the abyss of forgetful sleep.

He rode the boat wrestling the waves, the paddles of his eyelids splashing the waters of wakefulness a few more times until he finally gave in to the deep onslaught of forgetful sleep.

When he awoke in the morning he was only vaguely aware of the nightmares that had occurred in the thin crest of time as he entered the dream-state between the abrupt disturbance of wakefulness and just dropping off to sleep, the point of still being in control but not quite as you're not yet asleep. He acknowledged it had been a fearful night and was thankful there was a locked door to keep him in. He looked towards the chair he'd propped there and the bag filled with his work tools he had weighed it down with. The memory of Trudi (whatever her name had been) was far from his mind as the thought of who he called out to for help in his darkest hour these days plagued his mind and, not for the first time of late, he considered his own mortality.

12

He took a deep long drag, the butt burnt down till it was at the cusp of burning his finger and thumb, tasting its tip end with his tongue accidentally as he drew as much of the nicotine that he could burn into his lungs, he tossed it before exhaling, letting it spin to the floor to roll to the gutter, ignored by all but the wind. He breathed out the exhaust fume, walking through it as though pushing passed the curtain into the haze of a harem, exotic girls lounged on cushions, their tantalising flesh sparsely covered in lace, covering most but not all of temptingly pert breasts as their eyes teased from beyond the veil.

The mist of the mirage dissipated as the late autumn fog hung in the crisp air of an early London morning. He put his hands in his pockets and stepped off the pavement into the road, aware of an oncoming car, its exhaust fumes only slightly greater than what he'd spewed out; it would miss him, by miles, yet he quickened his step anyway to a half-trot half-skip, his wrists tucked beneath the seams of his coat as his hands clung to keys and loose change and a half filled pack of cigarettes with a lighter filling the void, all clutched tightly in his trouser pockets as they tried to jive to the rhythm of his feet tapping the tarmac with the steady rising rumble of wheels drumming the road towards them.

He was most ways across, only a few steps of grey tarmac separated him from the lighter shade of paved pathway ahead and yet one more obstacle rolled steadily towards him: a skinny white cyclist, a young man, maybe late teens or early twenties wearing a dirty yellow t-shirt with a small green indistinguishable logo on one side and a flapped over tear on the other. Hanging just above his lobes and deep in the indent of his ears were earphones attached to a white cable dangling down to an mp3 player or a mobile phone (it was hard to distinguish between them these days) which he operated with both hands as he steered with the gyrating momentum of his legs and the weight of his body.

He paused to let the cyclist pass, the youth barely looking up at him but unstereotypically acknowledging him with a murmured "thanks" that was little more than a grunt but much more gratitude than had been expected.

"You're welcome," he replied chirpily with an uncharacteristic smirk.

As the cyclist rode passed confident of his own safety he skip-trotted the last couple of steps joyfully, suavely catching the breeze beneath his soles as he lifted above the curb and onto the pavement. The contents of his pockets bobbed with him but he kept them tidily steady within the clutches of his clenched fists.

He would usually carry around a pack of sweets of some description in his pocket (usually mints) the packets wrapping fading and crimpling as it rubbed on the ever mobile lining of the trouser and the swollen thigh beyond, clanging occasionally with the loose shrapnel of muted bronze, gold and silver as the heads and tails kissed in the dark. He rarely ate the mints, they were there in case he needed them, to freshen his breath should the waft of dryness become too unpleasant to stand, or the morning coffee be too lively, or the last suppers unhappy returns still linger once the brisk air had stolen the gas from his mouth. He had no desire to be off putting to any such favourable lady should he dare to encounter (even Abigail Henderson would be treated to the honour of minty breath if she ever drew the courage to get close enough) nor to be memorable for any distinctiveness other than the familiarity of sweetness attributable to anything other than an easily discarded pack of cheap mints occasionally fumbled in a lazily hung hand. They also covered up for when he was unable, for whatever reason, to brush his teeth, as it were today, he being short on supplies. Today he had to suffice with the mints freshening his breath following the bitter lure of nebulous caffeine accompanied by the habitual draw of one of his few remaining cigarettes.

He stepped onto the pavement across from the Broadway Shopping Centre, it was a fair walk from where he lived and not the closest parade of shops. Acton High Street was closer by far but he didn't blend too easily there in his customary suit and it was always a bad idea to shop on his own doorstep. No, Ealing was better for a number of reasons. For a start the area was affluent enough to not batter an eyelid at someone doing menial shopping in a suit, and secondly there was a greater selection to choose from, not that he was snobbish about his purchases, but he did like to spend his time browsing the selections and passing his time window shopping.

Despite his clean cut image and roguish good looks his health was actually in decline, not that you'd immediately be able to tell at a glance. He still held his figure well but the cigarettes and rough living were catching up on him and he had developed a nasty cough of late which initially hadn't concerned him too much until splotches of blood began appearing in his spittle, that coupled with the regular loose bowel movements and the constant dull ache beneath his ribs gave him a fair idea that what was wrong was serious enough to need treatment, not that he had any inkling of seeking any. He knew he couldn't keep on living the life he'd been leading for much longer, and knew that maybe a few nights in a hospital bed would do him good, but there was a stubborn side to him that wanted to be left alone, that wanted to lay in the clearing at the end of the path and go out alone the same way he came in, abandoned to the elements.

He looked into the first shop window he came to, a small independent men's clothes shop with a pair of mannequins in the window, one wearing a pair of loose fitting combat jeans and a sweater, the other a suit, their hands posed lifelessly as their bloodless achromatic faces stared out at the foot and vehicle traffic passing by outside the glass, traffic that was reflected as he stood staring at himself and comparing his suit to the one on the mannequin.

His suit wasn't as sharp as it had once been. At a glance he was still snappily dressed but a closer inspection identified a multitude of sins and unveiled a truth hidden behind the mask of a dying man. His muscular frame bulked out the suit so that it clung handsomely, appearing a tailored fit though the edges of the flaps of the blazer were curling and stained with weathered age. The white shirt looked crisp and ironed but if you were too close you could smell the faint odour of unwashed and regularly worn cotton, and the dirt on the collar where it had begun to creep over the edge from the scum that had rubbed off from his neck, something which then drew your attention to an overgrown patch of stubble beneath his chin that he often missed when shaving, as he had done this morning. The trousers were creased but not obviously, he had tried hard to flatten out the lines and had carefully scraped the speckles of mud from the ends which he had picked up in the park yesterday. The shoes were probably the biggest giveaway, they were worn at the heel and the sole and the black of the leather was fading to weary grey. In the reflection he also noted that he hadn't done himself justice with his hair either this morning and was as a whole appearing abhorrently scruffy.

Using the window as a mirror he licked the palm of his hand and attempted to flatten down the side of his hair where he'd slept on his side, not just from last night, a matted crimpled parting from consistent pinning down in a regular sleeping pattern now moulded his head, so much so that he couldn't manage or style that side of his hair but was forced to let it grow in its slightly disjointed style lopsided. He could gel it of course but that seemed like so much hassle in the mornings, besides he couldn't bare the slime on his hands and it would mean he'd have yet another thing to clean off. To the uninitiated his hair style could pass as just that, a style, yet to him, for whom appearance mattered a great deal, it just wasn't good enough.

The momentary glance, for in truth that was all it was, in the shop window told him all he needed to know, all he already knew, a confirmation that he needed to go shopping and stock up on some much needed supplies. First on his list were toiletries: deodorant and toothpaste were the essentials, shampoo and soap were running low but he could bide his time for those; as for clothes: a new suit and shoes were essential; he didn't want to return home without having something fresh to be presentable in.

The old girl in the tweed coat and tea cosy hat may have looked prim and proper but Jim and Dewayne knew better.

"She's still got the tights in the basket and the perfume in her left hand," informed Jim over the radio, his Australian accent was slightly muffled behind the bunged up nose that was plaguing him and affecting his fitness of late.

"Yeah, roger that. I can't see her from where I am at the moment," came the reply from Dewayne on the shop floor.

Both men were contract uniformed security guards who had been fortunate enough to have been assigned to the same store together for the past six months during which time they had formed an effective working balance and won the appreciation of the store's management, as well as the respect of the local police. They took it in turns to pace the shop floor whilst the other scanned the CCTV from the security room in the basement.

The old lady in question was a regular. She wasn't your typical shoplifter: items were never concealed but always paid for. She was gentle and polite and as doddery as you'd expect from a frail woman of her years - but looks were often deceiving. This old lady was calculating as she took her time on a regular basis scanning all the items that had been marked down with 'reduced' stickers, most of which, due to their sudden reduction in price, didn't have a special bar code on identifying the product code. Both the shop floor sales staff and the two guards had long believed she was swapping the price tickets before reaching the till but no one as yet had managed to catch her in the act. Jim had even gone across to a few of the other stores in the shopping centre with a photo of her he had printed out and confirmed that at least two other stores had her on their watch list but had yet to catch her out.

"She's moving back to the shampoo aisle," Jim relayed with a sniffle.

"Ok, if you can see 'er clearly I'll hover by da door," replied Dewayne in his thick Jamaican accent.

"Yep, no worries mate," Jim's Australian twang bounced back across the airwaves. Jim wiped his nose with the sleeve of his shirt not daring to take his eyes off the cameras to look for a tissue. His head was a bit cloudy and he would later use this as an excuse for being slow on the uptake.

The old lady stopped by the men's shampoo and gave a devious glance to her side. This was it. Jim was sure he'd have her this time clear on camera; they'd wait for her to pay and then grab her as she left the store. He wasn't worried about how mean they would look for picking on an old lady; they often got a barrage of grief from the do-gooding public who thought it was their duty and their right to interfere, but he knew how much of a pain in the arse this old lady was and he had made it his mission to catch her out.

He could see her hand reach into the basket she was carrying and her finger beginning to pick at the sticker of the tights that were sat there - but then something else caught his eye.

For a moment he wasn't sure that he'd seen it clearly but the old woman's hesitation confirmed that she too had glimpsed it as she pulled her hand out from the basket and started moving out of the aisle. It was the coughing that had given it away, clearly unintentional and for him drastically inconvenient timing as he would otherwise have gone unnoticed.

"Change of plan mate," Jim called excitedly into the radio, "IC1 male, smart black suit, just slipped a bottle of shampoo into the left pocket of his trousers. Looks a big fella. Wait outside the store an' I'll let you know when he leaves an' I'll come join you."

"What about the old woman?"

"She can wait." Nothing more needed to be said and so the radio fell silent. They both knew the drill: Jim would watch on camera ensuring all the evidence was captured till the suspect was passed the last point of payment and heading for the exit and then he would race up the stairs and out onto the shop floor close to the entrance using a door only they had access to and would get to Dewayne just as he was making the stop just with enough time should anything kick off, which occasionally it did, not that they were afraid of a little roll around; they were both fairly big and agile guys and well into their sports, and in truth a shoplifter resisting arrest made the job all the more exciting, so long as they came out on top.

Jim watched the man in the suit with the keen focus of an eagle soaring above the land waiting to swoop down on its prey. He no longer sat in his seat but had kicked the chair back and was assuming the starting block position ready to sprint out the door which he'd already propped open with a fire extinguisher (a big health and safety no no he knew, but needs must). He twiddled the focus knob to get a closer look at the guys face and decided that he had the potential to be a handful. He pulled out the zoom just in time to see a twin pack of soap disappear into the inside of his blazer. Amazing! Had he not seen it on camera he would never have registered it from the guy's body language. Jim knew the typical signs to look out for in a shoplifter, they usually gave themselves away with a furtive look of shifty eyes and a nervous shake and a reluctant hesitation, followed by the fumbling of trying to conceal the items – but this guy had none of that, this guy was slick, and ordinarily he would never have paid him a blind bit of notice; had it not been for that unlucky cough he would still be watching granny.

Dewayne had stood outside to the right of the door so that he was out of sight of the suspect when he walked out. The last thing he wanted was for the shoplifter to suddenly see security and then go back inside to pay. He had to make sure that once he was out he had no excuse for not paying for the concealed items.

He could feel the morning chill in the air as he stood in his white shirt with his radio held high so that he didn't miss a transmission lost to the passing crowds, a few of whom seemed to acknowledge what he was doing and stood at a distance observing, waiting for the action to take place as their curiosity was spiked as to who was about to be caught. The chill of the air reminded him that he had a full bladder and he hoped this wouldn't be drawn out too long, he didn't function well when nature called; he just hoped this guy didn't want to put up a struggle.

Dewayne rubbed at his shaved head as he psyched himself up. He was supposed to wear a hat, they both were, but they rarely did as they felt it got in the way, when the boss was around they'd don it but otherwise the store management themselves didn't seem to care so long as they were reducing the stock loss, which undoubtedly they were. 'A big fella', Jim had said, and he wondered how big 'big' was.

"He's passing the tills and heading for the door!" came the cry over the radio and Dewayne could tell from the urgency in Jim's voice that he was already racing from the security room.

PC Mark Lawrence was a long serving officer, too long in the tooth to try anything new and too heavy in girth to chase anything not immediately within his grasp. It had been a while since he'd had to run the bleep fitness test and was sure that if he was made to do it now he'd fail miserably. He'd spent the last five years sat behind a desk doing an admin job that should have been done by a lesser paid member of police staff and now he, like so many other officers, had been forced back out onto the street to show a visible presence and make some arrests. It wasn't what he had planned for his remaining two years in the job, but then things rarely panned out the way they were expected.

PC Lawrence was a jovial character who genuinely got on well with the shoppers and shopkeepers alike in the Broadway Shopping Centre. He rarely had to put himself out as usually the store staff or security had detained someone and then called the police, so usually all he had to do was turn up and arrest them. Working the shopping centre had its privileges too: he had plenty of young ladies to chat to and plenty of coffee stops to hide in, and when he got bored of walking around he could go and sit in the centre's main CCTV room and just watch everything from there. In this fashion, he hoped, his last two years as a police officer would be pretty uneventful.

He had no real direction of travel this morning as he window shopped like tumble weed blown through the hallways of the shopping centre, bouncing wherever the wind took him. He turned one corner and was about to side step a businessman walking towards him when he noticed the white shirt of a security guard quick stepping behind the gentleman. He looked passed the man in the suit who was politely trying to step aside out of the officer's way and saw that it was Dewayne and that he was motioning for the man in the suit to be stopped.

PC Lawrence wasted no time in placing out a hand and obliging.

It wasn't to be his day. His cough was worse than ever and he could feel a cold sweat forming on his brow. He had the money to pay for the items and was now wishing he had done just that, the folded notes lifted from the crazy black lady on the tube yesterday cushioning the inside of his blazer.

He'd glimpsed the black guard hiding to the right of the door as he'd walked out and had casually walked to his left to avoid him, figuring he could run if he needed to. It was nothing but bad luck that the police officer just happened to turn the corner at that precise moment, and just in case there was any doubt he felt the black guard swiftly grab his arm followed by the out of breath pacing of a second guard bounding out of the store behind him. He had nowhere to go and they, no doubt, had him banged to rights on camera.

"He's got shampoo in his...trouser pocket...and soap here in his jacket," huffed Jim, pointing for the officer's benefit.

"Well, is that true?" asked PC Lawrence of the smartly dressed suspect before him. He got a raised eyebrow in response, one that said *'I guess so; I'm not in a position to argue the case'*. There was something in the look that was familiar, something deep down in PC Lawrence's mind triggered recognition, it would come to him much later on when he would dwell on how the mighty had fallen, and he would tell his tale back at the station to excuse the day's events, a tale a younger and less experienced officer would not have been able to link together, and then later in days to come he would be forced to recollect it all again, only then the investigation would be more in-depth and more serious.

PC Lawrence sensed a need for caution, he couldn't place it, something in that raised eyebrow and the deep down recognition of a face he'd once encountered long ago. He drew his hands down to his kit belt and unclipped his handcuffs.

"I'm going to handcuff you, sir, just as a precaution so that you don't run off, then these gentlemen will lead us down to the security office and we can deal with the matter there rather than embarrass you up here in front of all the other shoppers. Does that sound reasonable enough?"

It did. It sounded perfectly reasonable and he nodded his assent with his outstretched hands allowing himself to be handcuffed and then led back in towards the store.

As he was led back through the store entrance a number of things span through his mind, least of all the route he was being taken as he was ushered through a discreet door behind a curtain near the store entrance which led to a cold empty staircase leading into a dimly lit basement.

He'd been down this route before, in another life, another store, another set of handcuffs, the escorts back then of a firmer hand, and very rarely was he the one on the receiving end. He was almost beginning to feel comfortable with the scenario as he played along for old times' sake, allowing himself to ride the wave of nostalgia as he drifted into the beach of familiarity.

They reached the security office at the bottom of the stairs with its door propped open with the red fire extinguisher. As they entered with Jim leading, followed by their prisoner, Dewayne holding back by the door to allow the police officer to enter before lifting the heavy extinguisher away from the door so that it could be shut leaving that the prisoner nowhere to go.

It was a small room that consisted of a small desk to the rear wall with two plastic bucket chairs pushed in beneath it and to the side of which stood a tall four drawer metal filing cabinet, a two foot space separated the table from the console and its bank of six monitors that lined the wall opposite and Jim had to push the wheeled office chair aside so that they could all fit into the tight space as Dewayne closed the door to the right of the console sealing them all in.

"Now," began the officer as he fell into a casual well practiced patter, "my name is PC Mark Lawrence and I work out of Ealing police station, now at this stage you're not under arrest but I'm going to ask these gentlemen to explain to me what's gone on and then you'll get your say. Does that sound fair enough?"

The was a calm nod of approval and so Jim took up his commentary as he reached across to the top of the filing cabinet for a tissue and quickly blew his nose.

"I saw this gent on camera place a number of items into his pockets and then make his way out of the store without paying. I'd informed my colleague here," he gestured to Dewayne who was at the default position of guarding the door for no other reason than he had nowhere else to go, "via the radio of what was taking place and he went outside to stop him and that's when you arrived. Obviously the whole thing is recorded on camera and we're both prepared to make statements to that effect."

The broad Australian wiped his nose again having said all he felt necessary for the moment. As the tissue brushed his nose he picked up a hint of body odour in the room he hadn't noticed before and realised it must have been fairly strong to break through his blocked nose. Surely it wasn't the officer that smelt so bad. He started to look the shoplifter up and down, inspecting him a little more closely and feeling a sudden pang of guilt knowing what the items were that he'd taken.

"What's he got?" asked the officer.

Jim indicated the two pockets that he'd seen the items concealed in and the police officer took the liberty of relieving him of the shampoo and soap and placing them on the table.

"Anything else?" this time the officer's question was posed to the suspect.

He got a resigned shake of the head in response.

"So you've heard what the security guard has had to say," jumped in PC Lawrence quickly, aware that it was still early in the day and if he could get this one dealt with quickly he could get back out on the beat after lunch, "and based on what I've heard and seen I'm arresting you on suspicion of theft by shoplifting, and I must caution you that you do not have to say anything but anything you do say may be written down and used as evidence, do you understand?"

The suspect began to cough heavily, holding his manacled hands to his flushed face as he tried to nod his acceptance of the situation.

"Do you have anything else on you that you shouldn't have?" asked the officer, he meant initially any other stolen items but quickly clarified that he also meant something else, "Nothing sharp, no drugs or anything like that?"

The suspect shook his head. He was a silent type but appeared harmless enough and had so far seemed compliant, so much so that PC Lawrence was happy to put off searching him until the last minute.

"What's your name?"

"Lee Fletcher."

It was the first time anyone in the room had heard him utter a sound and an unexpected shock filled the room as though someone had sworn in church. PC Lawrence felt the uncomfortable air in the room but dismissed it as being simply an unusual scenario of a businessman stealing soap. He hadn't taken the time to peer over the dishevelled suit and assumed the smell of body odour was typical of the enclosed room (as so many of them did tend to be fresh with the lingering pits of the long term camera operators who also sat privately letting rip on their squeaky seats). Instead he had been focusing on the rugged jaw and the piercing eyes that stood head to head with him in a non-threatening manner. He jotted down the name in his little red pocket book.

"Date of birth?"

"June 6th 1967."

"Home address?"

"71 Lammas Park Gardens, Ealing W5."

The police officer wrote it all down carefully, a note of recognition at the details given as well as the refined but brash local working class accent.

"Have I dealt with you before?" the officer asked curiously.

"If you have I don't remember you," Lee replied honestly enough.

The officer squinted his eyes trying to force to the forefront of his mind some deep buried secret but it wouldn't catch onto the line he dangled there.

"Do you admit to taking the items without paying?"

Lee nodded with a shrug of the shoulders and a resigned raise of his eyebrow and then waited for what he'd already realised, but that had yet to dawn on the officer.

PC Lawrence made some final notes in his pocket book and then indicated for Jim to pull out a chair for the suspect, he had after all been compliant so far and was unlikely at this stage to put up any sort of struggle, besides he was still cuffed.

As Jim pulled out the chair Dewayne whispered in his ear. Jim considered what was said for a moment and then nodded and Dewayne stepped out of the room; the call of nature had finally gotten the better of him.

"Xray Bravo from…" PC Lawrence stopped in mid flow as he looked down at his police airwave radio that he'd begun to speak into. The usual green light at the top was now red indicating that he was out of reception range and he shook his head in annoyance.

"Your radios don't work down here mate, you'll have to go up top," Jim offered helpfully knowing that the officer wanted to do a quick name check. If Lee Fletcher checked out ok he was likely to get just an £80 on the spot penalty fine, but if his past was at all chequered then they'd more than likely have to wait for a van to take him back to Ealing or even Acton police station to be booked in.

"Can I get it at the top of the stairs?"

"Yeah, just go back up the way we came in."

Jim stepped away from Lee as he settled into the chair that was pulled out for him. He moved across to the console as the police officer crossed the room towards the door and turned the camera to the curtain that hid the door at the top of the stairs. He was scanning the monitors for the old lady; he hadn't forgotten about her and would love to bring her in now whilst there was a police officer on hand.

"Will you be ok with him for a minute?" he heard the officer ask. Jim looked over his shoulder at Lee Fletcher who had once again started coughing and gave a reassuring nod before scouring the screens again.

As he slipped the cuffs off he couldn't believe how easy they had made it for him. He had thought that he would have to over-power all three somehow and was playing out scenario after scenario in his head so that he could evade his current dilemma. His coughing had been genuine, however he had used it to his advantage as he twisted his hands to undo one of the cufflinks on his shirt. He had three devices hidden about his person, all of which served the same purpose: one was a black plastic bracelet in the vein of a friendship band which when pulled apart its link connection formed a vertical ridge purposely shaped with one thing in mind; the other two items were his cufflinks, black onyx circles with a silver lion insignia in the middle, the silver slip bar of each also shaped with a vertical ridge the exact shape and size to fit the slot of a standard pair of police issue handcuffs. If PC Lawrence had searched him properly he would have found much more: the ghost holder for instance, a small sidearm holster designed to hold a small firearm, yet to the innocent uninitiated eyes of the world it was a large mobile phone clipped to the hip, usually this was empty, in fact he rarely wore it these days, except what else was he to do with the gun he'd acquired yesterday? Leaving it at home didn't seem an option and now he was regretting that he'd come by it at all - the last thing he wanted to do was to have to use it.

He began to cough again, this time uncontrollably. It got the big Australian's attention and he turned around concerned and put a hand on his shoulder in a gesture of kindness, a gesture that was quickly abused as the ratchet of the handcuffs tightened on his wrist as his suspect swiftly twisted round and thrust him against the filing cabinet and slipped the other end of the cuffs through the locked metal handle of one of the middle drawers. With lightning speed he ripped the guard's radio from his belt and tossed it to the other end of the room and then grabbed the keys clipped to his belt. He could see the police officer speaking into the radio on the shop floor having just poked his head out from the curtain to get a clearer signal. That was good, he was out of the way.

There was another exit, he'd seen it scroll across the flickering image of the screens, and it should be easy to find if luck was on his side.

He thought about erasing the footage of him in the store but on closer examination of the system he realised he didn't know how to operate it, back in the old days you just ripped out the tape and took it with you, but with this set up there were too many buttons and it all looked too confusing. He didn't know where the toilets were but he guessed the Jamaican guard would be back in a minute. He had no time to hang about. He fled the room and locked the door behind him dulling out the protests of the guard left handcuffed behind him.

Logic told him the store rooms were the opposite way they'd come in and so he walked casually, nodding to a couple of female sales staff with a smile as though he were some store manager or sales rep they'd not met before. They accepted his gesture without question as he turned the corridor into a caged area, little knowing that as he did so Dewayne had stepped out of the washroom behind him and without looking in his direction had started to make his way back towards the security room.

As he reached the end of the stockroom he found that luck was indeed on his side as the shutter grill was open for a delivery truck being unloaded onto the raised concrete bay, the staff there too busy to pay him any attention as they manoeuvred pallets and cages within the back of the truck. He jumped down from the bay and casually walked towards the goods delivery entrance, confident that it would be the last place they would look for him. The shampoo and soap bulging in his pockets once more as he disappeared from view.

13

Coffee - he only drank the good stuff, or tried to anyway. What he held in his hand was anything but. He hadn't expected anything grand from the kiosk outside Acton Town tube station but something that tasted better than slightly stirred sludge swept in from the nearest drain with a little added sugar was surely high on the expectation list of most, or had society fallen so ill that they merely accepted and paid for in pain whatever was presented to them these days without just argument? He sipped at it anyway, if only to wake his senses and clear his vision, his mind swimming cloudily through a mist of murky unpleasant images that left a taste more bitter than that in the Styrofoam cup that warmed his hands from the morning's autumn chill.

He walked back towards his car from the direction of the station. He had already been to check on his target but he had left already, the place being empty, the result of Jack having slept in too late, much longer than he'd expected, his energies burned up and his mind weary of the nights activities. He was getting sloppy; he scolded himself for it, but at the same time wondered whether that was all he was berating himself over.

As he walked back to the car passed the station he noted the rush hour flow of pedestrians had dwindled to a slow trickle of hunting ants rather than the frantic march of the colony into the nest only an hour earlier. Not that this had much effect on the road traffic; it seemed that on the roads in some places in London rush hour lasted all day and some roads queued for an eternity as they waited for the poorly timed lights at the end of the street to change and stay green long enough for them to clear the yellow box to join the queue for the next set that had already turned red. Of course clearing the yellow box was always an impossibility and so the system failed and the backlog tailed back along the Gunnersbury Lane all the way back to the tube station and the junction where he now stood watching as numerous motorists made the last minute decision to take a detour down Bollo Lane in search of an alternative route to wherever their destination lay.

The car was parked at a meter along Bollo Lane itself, a busy road which ran adjacent to the tube station with commercial properties on one side and a notorious maze of high rise council estates on the other; it was the sort of estate you only ventured into if you had to or were familiar with the residents and their way of things, for anyone else it was a dangerous place. Jack knew it of old and knew of many of its long standing self-appointed sheriffs and guardians, protection racketeers and drug lords, gun runners and pimps. He doubted many of the old gangs still held control, respect yes, control unlikely - times were changing, things didn't work the way they used to.

He'd parked quite a way down near to the car service shop which seemed busy with cars up on ramps and a collection of bored customers sitting loitering in the waiting room for the mechanics to finish the necessary repairs, MOT's and services.

As he walked he paid little attention to all this; he saw it all and naturally his mind stored the information but he wasn't consciously observing it all. Later he would wish he had. Instead his mind flashed images of Trudi and of the bloodlust that had overcome him and how, no matter how he had tried to hold back and contain himself, he couldn't resist putting himself in that situation where he would be tempted to act in a way that was growing more and more uncomfortable in the waking hours of sobriety, when that crazied flood of adrenalin and evil temptation had diminished.

After all these years was he finally growing the conscience that had been absent as a child and that he had pined so much for after his mother's death? He hoped so, but at the same time feared to give in to it for he knew what followed: guilt. And he had plenty to be guilty about.

His mind flashed back to the girl in the back of the car yesterday and how he had held himself back, caring for once about what would become of her if he killed her father over a simple road rage incident. He had done much worse without thought, sometimes not knowing who or why, sometimes just acting because he'd been paid to, or simply just told to. She had reminded him of a job he'd undertaken a couple of years ago and as he played it in his mind he noted his own lack of sensation in the memory.

She slept. The witching hour had passed and the intermittent flashes of light streaking the ceiling through the curtains had slowed to the odd casual peek-a-boo of the graveyard traffic as the late night reveller or shift worker made their way home along the still and silent back roads of suburbia. The angels gentle chime could just be heard above the rustling of the trees as the wind tinkled on the hanging metal bars some five doors down the street, a black and white moggy being the only creature aware of the irregular tune as it huddled beneath the bumper of its owners car, staring in wait for the ginger tom to appear from across the rear garden of the house opposite, crossing its territory from the street beyond as had become its unfortunate habit in recent nights; tonight the moggy was ready and lying in wait to pounce, but no one knew, and no one else cared as the night hid the malicious and devious thoughts of the loveable family pet.

She slept. Her feet tucked toastily against the furry animal cover of the hot water bottle that by now had lost most of its heat and had been relegated from the chest hugging position to the about to be kicked unknowingly from the bed position. The faint orange glow from the night light was the only thing that lit the playhouse and the dolls smothering the chair beneath the times table chart that clung to the wall with its large colourful numbers that shone through wakeful eyes in shades of grey splattered with a hint of tangerine.

She slept, despite the groans and repetitive creaks of the mattress of her parents room next door, the raised covers barely covering the naked throes of passion as nails dug deep into hairy shoulders and buttocks thrust forward in the dark, getting faster and harder as he neared his point of satisfaction which for her wouldn't be enough but it would do.

She slept as downstairs the black Labrador gently padded along the hallway carpet from the kitchen having woken from the chill of the open door and the creaking it made as it slowly angled inwards. It stood staring at the family car parked in the driveway and the street outside, waiting for movement, preparing to raise its voice of concern and intrusion. It sniffed but the incoming wind distracted the scent, its hesitation, its confusion, costing the vital seconds before realising too late...*pssieuw.* The dog fell with a slight whimper and a thud. Then stillness.

She slept. In the master bedroom he rolled over as she reached for a tissue, his head sinking into the pillow having expelled and exhausted himself. A creak of a floorboard and his eyes shot open wide awake. She froze as she fumbled at the tissue box on the bedside table. They waited. Nothing. It was nothing, she would have called out or come running in if she were awake. A false alarm; they'd not been caught, but still they both thought they ought to start blocking the bedroom door. She retrieved the tissue and began to wipe herself, he closed his eyes selfishly ready to leave them shut as she would snuggle towards him in a moment or two.

pssieuw... pssieuw...

She slept. The slight smell of burning as the smoke from the barrel wafted through the master bedroom didn't travel much beyond the landing. The spark of amber that strobed the room only enough for the ginger tom to glance up as it entered the street from the garden opposite, distracting it from its own fate awaiting it below with wide eager eyes. The blood that soiled the sheets flowed slowly onto the pillows as the two sleeping figures lay side by side, one with open eyes of shock and bewilderment, the other closed, asleep if it weren't for the hole in his forehead oozing, expelling more of the life-force than he'd intended to release that night.

She slept, and slept on. She was safe, until the waking horror of the morning would destroy all her waking hours and sleepless nights, shredding her thoughts and emotions into a lifetime of destruction and therapy till eventually she would be numb from it, and as a girl who never grew up she would wish he had been merciful and had taken her with her parents. But he wasn't interested in her, and part of him knew the terrorising life it would leave behind if he let her be, and in the darkness he smiled, then silently left.

He was cruel, purposely so. He didn't know where the tendency came from and until recently didn't care. Most of his kills were just jobs that had to be done, but others, like Trudi, were done just for the pure pleasure of it. Only now it was becoming a guilty pleasure and even the thought of this latest job left a bitter taste in his mouth. The shuddered at thought of killing someone who in many respects was probably his oldest and most committed friend, the one who had set him off on his wild adventure through life, and had it not been for him he would have no doubt spent his life incarcerated. Doing this job was leaving a knot in his stomach to the point he felt it might erupt in a hernia, painfully doubling him up as its dull blade pierced through his flesh.

Was there a hidden morality to life hiding in plain sight that he was only just beginning to realise? He knew of course the moral standard: the law, the justice system that carried its weighty hammer blow across men like him, the logical position of society of having a system of right and wrong, and not to mention the philosophical disputation between good and evil, the side of which he would, by society's standards be placed in the latter category. All this he knew in his head and had witnessed to through the years but for as long as he could remember had never felt; an actual real live conscience seemed to have been vacant from his mental makeup, though he knew this not to have always been true.

As a child he had acted as any normal child, had attended school and interacted as any other normal boy, had formed friendships and bonded with his parents in the normal way with loving hugs and kisses no different from any other child. He knew it because it had been in his file, those parts of it that had been read to him by the psychologists in an attempt to draw out the child that appeared to have died with his father. There were testimonies from teachers and neighbours, from his mother (shortly before she had taken her own life) and other distant family, of whom none were brave enough to maintain any close relationship with him during his incarceration.

So it had been there once, which led on to the other area of moral standard that he had never paid any attention to: religion. He had brushed with the various religious orders in the course of the work he'd undertaken and was aware of the factions and in fighting between them and, as with most secularists and agnostics, knew of the main differences and basic beliefs transferred through modern media, but to have dwelt upon them personally, it had never crossed his mind until now.

Walking back to his car along Bollo Lane his mind was filled with the images of Trudi (he tried to think of her surname but it escaped him, had he known it? Yes he must have done, but dredge it from the sink of his mind he couldn't) and the girl (again he didn't know her name, would have done at some point in the research of carrying out the hit on her parents, but it was a long lost body weighed down there with Trudi whatshername). He knew what had become of Trudi, but of the girl? He'd never stopped to question what scarred and twisted fate had become of her after he'd left her home, knowing full well she would be the one to find her parent's bloodied corpses in the morning as she climbed into their bed for a cuddle, or in the dead of night running into her parents room seeking the comfort from a nightmare of her own. He remembered relishing in the fact that he had corrupted her innocence beyond belief, and that, he was beginning to understand now, made him evil.

He likened his soul to that akin to Dorian Gray's, trapped in the portrait of his hidden unconscious mind awakening now each new morning to something fresh and new away from the horrors of his soul. Though where Dorian Gray had his portrait in which to hide his sin, Jack had only his dreams. And in his dreams he walked the damned blood lust of the murderous Nosferatu, and with the sickening desperation of Victor Frankenstein trying to secretly undo the monster he'd created, the monster himself unaware of the hideousness he'd become, yet like Gray his charm was endearing, despite the horrors of danger written in his eyes.

If ever there were a god, how could he accept a sinner like he?

He knew some religions professed to. The Christian church he had heard claimed to have a god who welcomed all no matter what they had done, if they turned to him and away from their wrong doing. He sniggered at this as he walked, not because he thought it was amusing but because he thought of himself as no ordinary sinner and in closeness to Satan rather than God. Maybe Satan had appointed him as the embodiment of Death himself - it would surely explain a lot! Niggling away at his thoughts, chipping away at the wall between his conscious and unconscious mind was this growing conscience that clashed with the dark hooded figure carrying his scythe of many designs, and it was this conscience that asked in a weak and trembling voice: *What about me? Can I be saved? How do I stop?*

He reached the car and placed the rank cup of coffee on the roof whilst he fished in his pockets for the keys. He didn't need the keys of course, the car was unlocked and clean of prints should it be discovered in his absence, but he went through the pretence routine anyway as his gloved hand slipped inside his trouser pocket to retrieve the small bunch of harmless everyday keys, one being a master for the ignition but was useless on the door itself.

There were other things in his pockets used for different things: in one he had a pen and a long piece of tightly woven extra strong string neatly coiled; in another, the inner pocket of his jacket, was a rolled up newspaper, in the other a small multi-tool which if you knew what you were looking at contained some rather specific set pieces. Each innocent item wasn't all it seemed. They were items he always carried, for they could be used and improvised as something much more sinister if the imagination allowed itself to play its course.

He dropped the keys as they left his pocket and they fell to the floor with a jangling clink. It looked accidental but things with Jack were rarely accidental. He bent to pick them up, studying the footfall around him to see who slowed and who swerved round him, checking the reflections in both the glass and the bodywork of the Prius and the number plates of the cars parked in the meters both in front and behind. It was a slow and measured action which looked perfectly normal but to say he was paranoid of being followed would be an understatement, in his line of work how could he not be? Besides this latest job made him uneasy and, although he saw no obvious signs, he felt that haunting glare of someone watching him.

He grasped at the bunch of keys and felt for the black fob of the car key, not the one that turned the ignition on the Prius, this one wouldn't start it (some cars it would but not the Prius), this black fob was of the flip out variety, its small silver button poised to snap out the key, or in this case a small inch and a half blade that could do enough damage if held in the right hands - and they were.

He looked around as he stood and reached for the coffee cup to allow him to stand straight and broaden his view across the street without making it obvious. He saw no one. The footfall was still light. No one sat in cars trying not to be seen. There was no one of note - but then he had no view of the flats rising up above, but if someone were watching from there then it was unlikely they were watching him with intent of who he was, more likely someone just patrolling his turf, for no one had known he would park here but him.

He opened the car door and swung himself in, closed the door then locked it from the inside and inserted the key into the ignition but before he turned it something caught in the corner of his eye. Lying on the floor in the foot well of the passenger seat was a photograph.

He didn't bend to pick it up immediately. He knew who had put it there, or thought he did at any rate. He checked the mirrors without moving his head, his dark eyes flitting like desperate flies trapped inside a window, dancing desperately to find the way out yet failing to see the opened window in plain view before them.

He couldn't see her. *She* was nowhere in sight.

There was no one hiding behind the wooded bark of the few remaining oak trees that had yet to fall to the councillors axe, nor was there anyone attempting to use the lined lampposts as cover, not that their dirty grey metal bodies were wide enough for any other than a small child.

He knew she was available at the moment, he'd read the results of her latest job in today's newspaper that was slid coiled up inside his jacket pocket. A British family shot dead on holiday - suspected robbery gone wrong, or they stumbled upon a drug bust, the police would later figure out the bodies were professionally hit (double tapped in the head most probably) and they would start looking into the family's affairs back home to try and find a motive. A cyclist was found dead near the scene and it was suspected that he'd stumbled across the shooting and tried to intervene, or got caught in the crossfire. The bodies had been found by a rambler near the French town of Saint-Laurent-de-Céris alongside dozens of spent cartridges that were scattered around the scene, although no firearms were recovered. He recognised it as *her* job immediately; *she* loved the dramatics but often left things a little slap dash, besides that he had been offered the job first but had turned it down and knew she'd be next on the pecking order, just like the plane job in the States; he was glad he didn't get that one, it was complicated and at high altitude too, and it involved taking on a team; he didn't do teams, never had done and never would, he preferred to work alone where all he had to rely on were his wits.

The plane job was one of Derek's jobs. Jack used to get most of his work from Derek at one point until things went sour.   Derek Wahabi was a filthy rich Arab, suave and sophisticated and extremely manipulative; who would have thought a wealthy powerful guy like him would turn out to be a suicide bomber, not Jack at any rate. He didn't believe it for a moment, he knew what staged killings looked like, he had planned and acted out enough of them. There was definitely something hooky about Wahabi's death and he suspected she may have had something to do with it.

Not long after the bombing in the States she had showed up at the bar in Chiswick and he thought she was there for him, knew she was; there was no other reason for her being there. He'd fluffed his last job for Wahabi, not that Wahabi had lived to know of it, but Wahabi wasn't a sole contractor and his associates may have found out.

He bolted out of the back door of the pub when he saw her but strangely she let him go as though she were toying with him, tormenting him even. It didn't occur to him at the time, despite their mutual attraction to each other, that she had let him go because of her feelings for him. His mind didn't think that way. They were paid to kill people so there had to be emotional detachment.

Ever since then he'd been looking over his shoulder expecting to see her, or another paid to finish off the loose end that he'd become after that last Wahabi job, but so far they'd left him alone, not that it eased his mind as to why she'd let him go as he'd never taken her for the sentimental type.

He hated her and loved her at the same time. For years they had circled each other on the circuit playing cat and mouse, often competing for the same work (and often passing on work knowing the other would get it), never speaking and never meeting socially, but both aware of the other with a genuine nod of appreciation and respect. She was a girl with deep psychological problems, as he was himself, but he saw her as problematic rather than crazy, interesting rather than overtly complex, despite her almost masculine looks carved out of bitterness and self-loathing she was desirable rather than grotesque.

Cat and mouse for the work they may have been but the tension between them left them like starving wolves around a carcass, slobbering and growling and gnashing their teeth as their eyes never stepped aside wanting their bellies filled but also sensing the odour of the opposite sex lured to the smell of death as they ferociously tore at the flesh with a snarling grin, all the while desiring each other in their heated aggressive game of foreplay (but never intercourse - not yet, but maybe one day). He shook off the idea, knowing full well that the day either of them gave into that animal attraction (or was it more than that even?) - he shook that off too, either way if it ever happened it would most likely be the day he or she, or both died, when they were at their most vulnerable and with their guards down.

He looked again. And again.

He couldn't see her but he felt her watching, felt someone watching, or was that just the paranoia.

If she'd wanted him dead she would have done it by now. And why leave a photo? No, this was something else. His mind was now reasoning that all was not as it seemed, that this job was maybe a set up in itself.

He bent to pick up the photo, a swift movement so not to be caught out by any unsuspecting movement outside of the car. He sat behind the steering wheel, his thin leather gloves gripping hold of the wheel with a nervous tightness he'd never felt before. In his lap sat the photo staring up at him. He only glimpsed at it as he'd placed it there on his thighs, but the slightest of glimpses was enough. Enough to tell him someone knew who he was – who he really was! He recognised the picture from of old but hadn't seen it himself for many many years. It was a family photo (a black and white paper photocopy of one), a happy family photo, one from his childhood, and there was he himself, a five year old boy stood in the middle outside the family home smiling and holding hands with his parents as though life couldn't get any better.

THE KILLING

PART TWO

C. P. CLARKE

But I have one want which I have never yet been able to satisfy, and the absence of the object of which I now feel as a most severe evil, I have no friend, Margaret: when I am glowing with the enthusiasm of success, there will be none to participate my joy; if I am assailed by disappointment, no one will endeavour to sustain me in dejection. I shall commit my thoughts to paper, it is true; but that is a poor medium for the communication of feeling. I desire the company of a man who could sympathize with me, whose eyes would reply to mine. You may deem me romantic, my dear sister, but I bitterly feel the want of a friend. I have no one near me, gentle yet courageous, possessed of a cultivated as well as of a capacious mind, whose tastes are like my own, to approve or amend my plans. How would such a friend repair the faults of your poor brother! I am too ardent in execution and too impatient of difficulties.

Mary Shelly
Frankenstein; or The Modern Prometheus

For all of them, deep darkness is their morning; they make friends with the terrors of darkness.
Job 23:17

'The dead travel fast.'
Bram Stoker - Dracula's Guest

"Do you believe in an afterlife?"
Jack Walters

C. P. CLARKE

1

Jack's grandmother died a few years later, his father's mother. |She had died of a heart attack. He thought probably that her heart had broken the day he had killed his father and that it had never recovered. He was the favourite of her grandchildren, not that he knew it, but ever since then she had been frightened to be near any of them, and so slowly the family was torn apart, with few keeping contact with her, and all disowning him. Even his own sister hadn't tried to make contact with him, but that he understood more, and as he grew older and more inquisitive in his understanding of things he would be informed of her comatose state, awake yet not; a young zombie being force fed in an institution not unlike his own. For he had killed many that day, starting with his father, then his mother, his grandmother, and his sister whom he'd imprisoned in a mental cell far worse than any sentence he was forced to serve; locked away until finally one day she could take it no more - it would be years later that he would discover the truth that she too had followed her mother's lead and ended her own ordeal.

So there the body count began. Not that he knew it was a beginning as he hid amongst the metal trash cans of nearby houses scuttling from one house to the next, keeping low, a young fourteen year old fearful of his new found freedom.

He knew where he was heading; he just had to get there unseen.

2

Everyone has a song in their head, so he guessed anyway, a song or a tune: for some it might be classical, Mozart's Eine Kleine Nachtmusik, or something from a musical like Fiddler On The Roof with Topol dreamily echoing 'If I were a rich man', or maybe it was that annoying kids theme tune from the programme you were watching before you left the house in the morning - Postman Pat following you down the driveway reluctant to leave your shoulder, or the last track listened to on the radio as you got out of the car - a tune you've no right singing aloud in public like 'It's Raining Men' or 'YMCA' or something equally uncool, or a distasteful popular hit that would embarrass the tweenies let alone the teenagers; and it would be a track that wouldn't fade into the business of the day but would burst forth in a whistle or a hum as those around caught the tune to infect like a plague passed from one to another along the corridors of power as you shrink into guilty embarrassment as the seven office dwarves sing *'hi ho hi ho it's off to work we go'* across the office floor until someone comments on what the tune is and where it came from, and then slowly the echo fades. Some tunes though seemed acceptable, nostalgic even: The A-Team theme tune or the *dum dum dum, dum da dum, dum da dum* of Star Wars, or the *mah na mah na* of the Muppets; but no matter what the tune none seemed as concerning as the unseasonal rendition of a Christmas carol as the sun burst forth in late June or early July.

They be the lingering tunes that echo through the day nagging away at the subconscious mind to blurt out whenever the unsuspecting are not really focusing on anything in particular - and this one was his: *'The Toy Town Salute'*. It was a silly childish song; the words didn't make sense, not to him anyway. It echoed in his head continuously, always had done ever since he could remember. It was a song his mother had sung to him but he didn't recall that memory in his waking hours, instead he simply presumed he'd heard it playing over and over when he was young, before times – before he could remember, and it had stuck deep in his subconscious buried in the depths and locked away with the things *'my mamma told me, If I toed the line'* before the world caved in and *'they're all broke'* and the world got so messed up.

He was in there somewhere, that little boy, locked away waiting for the fun to materialise and *'maybe she'll buy you that glass of wine, flat cap, snap chat'*, the song his silent key to the tomb of rubble he'd piled on down there. Not that he would acknowledge it to anyone. The shrinks had tried, oh how they had tried! He'd sat there sometimes singing, or rather mumbling the words, sometimes humming, always the same song. They knew it was the key, but he would never unlock it, not for them, not for anyone.

Tic tac toe that's the way to go
Mamma said stick ya fingers to ya head
Flat cap snap chat

Mamma said keep the town clean

Rockin' horse soldier boy
Toys in line
Toe the line
Flat cap snap chap

My mamma told me take care of teddy
And when you're ready
Keep going steady
Take charge, toe the line
Maybe she'll buy you a glass of wine

Who sang that damn song anyway? It was a question he always asked himself but never attempted to answer. He could find out easy enough; probably it had been covered a couple of times and he'd heard a number of different versions over the years, but in truth he had no desire to know its origins, nor his own. He let the record play through his head as he worked his way through the corridor feeling inside his jacket for the small black pouch that lined the left breast pocket.

He wasn't quite sure how the kid had managed to sneak in the picks and he hadn't asked; some things you knew not to enquire about. Besides, everyone knew the kid could acquire stuff; he was connected, and in a big way, and he spent his time working the ward, visiting the cells, getting to know the talent, and generally recruiting for when he got out; he was one smart, organised, and dangerous cookie, but most importantly for Jack, his new friend knew a lot about doors and locks and how to open them.

It was only a small set of picks, which at first Jack had struggled to master. They wouldn't work on the cell doors for the locks were too big for the delicate flat angled metals that were easily concealed in his room, but on the office doors, the ones with the Yale locks, if he got an opportunity to slip along there undetected then maybe he would have a chance.

His offer of escape didn't come for free. A fourteen year old lad with a brutal sense of disconnection to emotion would be useful to the right person on the outside, and the young new boss of the ward was keen to recruit him for when he himself got out, not that he planned to escape like Jack, his term was shorter: at sixteen he was on remand for manslaughter, a charge which had been reduced from murder and for which he would eventually be acquitted on a technicality. For Jack though, there was no such forecast ahead; he'd been sentenced and locked away for as long as he could remember and only recently had the psychiatrists deemed him fit to be free from the psychiatric ward to mix with other inmates as he showed increasing signs of coming out of his shell and a desire to conform to a life of normality. Puberty was to blame for this change they said, he wasn't sure himself, he knew his internal desires and they weren't as wholesome as he allowed those responsible for his care to believe.

He was happy to learn the trade from his new friend, one who would employ him on the outside as a relentless heavy hand in his gang, a gang connected to bigger things where people took note of the emerging talent and where both boys would have a promising future in years to come, at least that's what his ambitious friend promised.

Tic tac toe that's the way to go
Mamma said stick ya fingers to ya head

Flat cap snap chat

When they're all broke
Don't take the cake
And they all rode round on the little boy's trike
Take charge
Flat cap snap chap

The feeler pic and tension wrench were secreted up his right sleeve, securely held in place by two fingers of his loosely clenched fist which allowed his other fingers free to open doors and grasp at things as if his palm were empty. A further set of picks were available in their slim black pouch inside his thin grey jacket should he need them but he hoped what he had in his hand would be enough. He'd been on his best behaviour of late, always calm and polite, he did his school work as taught, his routine being different from those who were there for the short term. Very few of the inmates at the young offenders institute were as young as him, those that were (and he had only seen a few in his time) were special cases like himself, although none held the gravitas of violence that lined the pages of his file.

Some of the guards showed him leniency due to his misfortune and the fact that what they saw before them now was simply a sad little boy who was condemned for something that had happened when he knew no better. He still had nightmares where he would wander about in his sleep with eyes scarily wide, and for this reason he reasoned they would never let him out unsupervised, but during the waking hours he was a polite and increasingly communicative young teenager. No, the fault wasn't his, per se, but some deep route switch in his subconscious where the wiring was crossed causing him to malfunction when he closed his eyes at night. So he let them believe, for he knew there was more to it than that, and when he got out he'd ensure he locked himself up at night as a precaution and revel in his freedom when he was awake.

Tic tac toe that's the way to go
Mamma said stick ya fingers to ya head
Flat cap snap chat

My mamma told me if I toed the line
The toys would toe the line
And they all rode round on the little boy's trike
So Take charge
Flat cap snap chap

The guards now let him move through the corridors on errands, as he did now, taking books to the library wearing his own clothes of jeans and t-shirt but insisting that he wear the thin grey uniform jacket with its one front pocket sown on the front left side. They were supposed to watch him the whole time but they often didn't, relying instead on the clumpy poor quality cameras that lined the corridors (it would be a few years before the technology was good enough to give a perfect picture that could be zoomed in on). It was a gamble, he knew, but he hoped he could cover what he was doing with his body and get into the room quickly. He fumbled with the low lying lock, slipping the feeler pic in as his new friend had taught him and feeling along the barrel, the tension wrench tipped at the edge waiting to twist the barrel round with every pin that fell.

He worked the pic up and down, struggling, panicking, and knowing he had little time. His hand began to ache with the forcefulness and then he remembered what he'd been told: slowly and gently, don't force it, work it gently. He relaxed, took a deep breath and tried again. This time it clicked and the tension wrench began to move round. He pulled down on the door handle and it opened. He quickly pulled the picks from the lock and stepped inside the room.

Tic tac toe (snap your fingers on the go)
That's the way to go (snap your fingers to your head)
Mamma said (one two three)
Who'd ya wanna be
When ya stick ya fingers to ya head
Flat cap snap chat

The room was just a store cupboard but it had a window to the outside. Once upon a time it had been used as an office but he figured its close proximity to the inmates was deemed too risky and the guards had probably turned it down for a break area in favour of the larger room they now occupied on the ground floor below. Still it was a long drop down from here, but looking at the grassy path that he could just glimpse beneath the window he was willing to take the risk of falling awkwardly. No one was likely to be watching this side of the complex, security was fairly lax anyway as the risk of a bunch of mainly low risk juveniles locked up for misdemeanours attempting to break out was hardly thought realistic, but then they hadn't counted on Jack and his co-conspirator hatching a plan together to get him out.

Jack owed him alright. His new friend had given him instructions on where to go on the outside to lay low, people who would look out for him and take him under his wing; he'd be part of the gang, a gang his new friend had aspirations of taking over once he'd earned his badge of honour inside.

The unbarred window opened easily. He dropped. Amazingly he landed well though it still hurt like hell, the rush of wind as he dropped from the first floor scaring him half to death. He scrambled to the big metal bins and used them as cover and then waited patiently for an opportunity to slip towards the car park. The security would change dramatically once he'd gone and new procedures would be adopted, and no doubt heads would roll and staff would be replaced, but that was none of his concern. For now he was free, and once out he had no intention of returning.

He checked his exit routes and then reset the needle to the start of the record in his head.

Tic tac toe snap your fingers on the go…

3

"So, that scallywag sent you here did he," said the statuesque brute who sat behind the desk he'd been yanked before by the scruff of his collar, his feet had barely touched the ground as he'd been hitched from the floor beneath as his feet skimmed the carpet of the closed pub. The guy who had thrown him into the office was bigger than the one sat behind the desk by a long way, but the one before him held a gravitas that weighed a far greater authority than the oaf that served as Lurch, besides Jack was still young and had a long way to grow so to him everyone was imposing in stature.

"I'll handle this," came again the gruff West London accent of the older man from behind the desk as a means of dismissal. He was in his forties at a guess, with thinning brown hair parted at the middle, and wore a short sleeved white shirt with a small collar that met beneath his chin where the top button was fastened. The shirt showed off his muscles, which weren't huge but toned enough to let you know that he was tough enough to throw his weight around. He winked at the other guy who was still holding his left shoulder in a vice-like grip. Suddenly the grip was let go and without another word he left the room. Jack turned to watch him go before the door shut behind him, noting that he wasn't heading back downstairs to the bar but was probably loitering along the corridor awaiting his master's call (this was a ploy he'd witnessed as standard practice by the guards at the young offenders institution whenever one of them entered the cells on their own, they always had their mate waiting outside somewhere in case something kicked off. If they came alone with no one outside, then you had something to worry about.).

He had found the pub quite easily and had managed to ride the buses to the right part of town without any trouble, jumping the backs of four or five red double-deckers before finally being thrown off by one of the conductors, but then he just waited for the next one to come along and tried his luck again; he was getting quite good at swapping seats and making himself unseen by the time he arrived at his destination.

He hadn't expected the pub to be closed when he arrived. He knew little of pubs and the hours they kept. Brentford's The King's Head Public House had been easy to spot from the bus for it had a building unique to most others he was used to seeing. He was a familiar with the looks of a few from the TV series like Minder or Only Fool and Horses that often played in the communal rooms back in the slammer, but he never had cause to take note of how they looked on the outside: wide, grandfatherly like gestures reaching out and beckoning in with a regal smile with its white-washed cheeks, royal red curtained eyelids and black mouth and eyebrows with its name emblazoned in gold and its crest of a crown hitched on a sturdy board from its brow. He pushed the door and found it wouldn't budge. He had no idea what time pubs opened so just stood there rapping his knuckles on the black wooden door until the burly and sour faced rogue had hauled him in and berated him for making such a racket.

There was a black Staffordshire bull terrier, a mere pup by the size of him, just inside the door that growled and barked furiously as he entered but fell silent with a kick from the clod with the short back and sides hardman haircut and portly belly that showed he rarely ventured far and had given up lifting heavy weights in favour of liquid ones that dulled his senses. Once he told his story of how he came to be there on the doorstep, he was cast upon with a lingering cautious look until he produced the lock picks, and that was when he was hauled upstairs.

Dave Foley was the name of the guy sat behind the desk, the guy who now eyed him suspiciously up and down with the command of an army general deciding what to do with the deserter flung before him stood sheepishly in his disheveled uniform in an uncomfortable an ill at ease stance that had given up on his superior's chain of command, yet at the same time knowing his very fate hung in the balance of his next few words.

The desk itself was oak he guessed, not that he could see it clearly under all the clutter, nor was he an expert in wood, but it looked grand enough for the name; he'd seen plenty of office desks in his time as each therapist or judge, or potential guardian that presided over his life had a desk of some sort, and this he judged to be oak, a heavily varnished and stained thick set wood not unlike the man who sat behind it, and he no different than the rest.

"So, what were you in for?" Foley asked with a deep sigh that expelled a fume of cigarette smoke in his direction.

"I'd rather not say." Jack may have been isolated from society but he was no simpleton, he knew his story wasn't for the eager telling.

Dave Foley looked at him curiously. "Fair enough, no doubt I'll find out in time. Got any skills?"

Jack thought for a moment of all the things he'd been taught by his tutors and of all not one had stood out as a natural skill other than his love of all things and yet nothing in particular. He was about to say as much when it dawned on him that these weren't the skills to which was being referred. "I can pick a lock," he said quickly motioning down to the loaned picks he'd presented when he entered the pub and which he'd been swiftly relieved of.

"I've no doubt you can young man, but I'll bet you can only do what my protégé inside showed you, am I right?"

Jack nodded slowly, embarrassed, lowering his head to the darkly varnished floorboards beneath his feet.

"I can mimic," he said sharply flicking his head up, his eyes alive knowing he truly did have a valuable skill.

"Mimic? Go on, how so?"

"I can copy behavioural patterns and voices."

"How does that serve me?"

Jack knew it was important that he gave the right answer but for the moment he wasn't sure what it was, only that he'd found it valuable to himself, but how? His eyes lowered once more but only briefly before he returned Foley with his same domineering linger, aloof through half closed eyelids, a slight snarl in his lip.

"I can read people," said Jack in the same gravelly

tone as Foley had spoken to him moments ago, higher pitched but bang on the money so far as attitude was concerned. "I can tell what people want to do, read their minds so to think, not literally of course, but I can see it in their eyes. I can play for what I want by saying what they want to hear; it got me some fair slack on the inside, that's how I got to roam, that's how I got the picks, that's how I got out."

Dave Foley sat back in his chair and narrowed his eyes; he was interested, not yet caught but definitely nibbling the bait waiting to be hooked. Reel me in, his eyes said, reel me in.

Jack continued, "That fat bastard you've got out there," he nodded towards the doorway, "is waiting for your command. You'll either call him in and tell 'im to show me the door, in which case he'll take me downstairs and give me a hiding and tell me never to grace the hallowed turf of...however big your domain is, before throwing me out the door, or you'll call 'im in and tell 'im I'm hired. Either way you don't care a monkeys about me unless I can make you some money or serve a purpose."

Jack fell silent, raised his head fully and opened his eyes wide making it clear he was coming out of character but straightening up to his normal stance which he had dropped in order to roll his shoulders forward like Foley's.

Foley squinted through the cigarette smoke as he took a long hard drag, blew it out slowly as though he were thinking hard and then flicked the butt across the table so that it landed in front of Jack's feet.

"Put that out boy!" he growled.

Jack didn't hesitate, his right foot quickly stamping forward before the end could scorch the wooden floorboards. It was a test, he knew – obedience.

Dave Foley smirked through the haze and barked out loud for his henchman to enter. Moments later he did, the door swung open and stayed open behind him ready to haul the kid out.

"What's your name boy?" muttered Foley.

"Jonathan Jack Rivers. I prefer Jack, sir." He hesitantly added the last bit on the end, somehow it seemed appropriate.

"Rick, take Jack here downstairs and get him something to eat, and make a call and get him a bed for the night."

Rick stepped aside the door to allow Jack to turn towards it of his own accord, not the preferred response he had hoped for Jack was sure; Rick he supposed was the type that would have reveled in beating the boy, if only a little; he'd seen plenty of his type pass back and forth through the cells.

"Aren't you forgetting something?" bellowed Foley from behind him.

Jack turned in time to catch what had been flung at him from the desk: the lock picks. He was in, so this was the beginning of his new life.

4

In those early days at the bedsit his night time wanderings and nightmares had strangely fled leaving him with months of peaceful slumber to the point that he began to wonder whether he had misplaced reality for a dream and vice-versa, or whether it was all a lie that the doctors had concocted to keep him drugged up, their way of explaining his demons perhaps. He had ditched the medication many moons ago, way before his escape, and had found that they made little difference on his sleeping condition but did leave him more alert and freer to think clearly, occasionally he would be forced to take them in the run up to the regular testing when they would check his bloods and urine; he knew they had to find what they expected to find and so he was pleased not to let them down. He wondered whether it was the change in culture that allowed him to sleep so soundly, or the sudden freedom he'd attained, but for now the old demons had fled him, or so he thought - they would be back, but that would come later.

The bedsit was about a five minute walk from the pub and he shared it with three others. He'd never learnt the basics of living on his own and was glad to find that his new cell mates were very accommodating of his age and inexperience and quick to give him slack and moral encouragement where his skills were lacking. Very quickly he had learnt the basics of washing clothes and dishes and cooking and cleaning house. He didn't mind these chores as they kept him occupied and he took each experience as a learning curve and relished every moment for fear that he might one day be caught and sent back, a very real possibility as his face had been plastered over the national papers, both The Mirror and The Sun had his face on their inner pages, The Sun on page four just after a bare breasted picture of Jilly Johnson, The Mirror had him on page three where the model was more discreetly attired and only allowed thankfully for a smaller picture of himself. The same picture was used for both papers, as was the news item that played on ITV and BBC1; it had been rare that his picture was ever taken, he guessed there had never been much need for it and certainly there were no family photos that would show his likeness now.

He was news for a couple of days, a week at most, Foley ensuring he was housebound until the heat died down, and then bigger things were happening far away in South America that seemed to haunt the headlines: the Argentinian's were invading some island off their coast and for some reason we were going to war with them, he didn't understand it fully but it was a blessing in more ways than one. Once his cell mates had decided which side of the page was to be pinned to the wall, his face or Jilly's (Jilly's won which led onto a debate as to which model was the prettier Jilly Johnson or Linda Lusardi, resulting finally an in 'agree to disagree' on each other's taste in women), a decision he was thankful for, they then all seemed to get excited about the impending war. There was an advantage to be had at going to war in the sense that people were distracted and worried about the future which meant they were vulnerable to being taken advantage of; something the gang was quick to act on.

Jack had feared that the article would reveal all about himself and that he would quickly be forced out of his new home, but he was pleased to see that there had been discretion in what the authorities had released, probably they feared that if it was widely known what he had done it may have a more psychological effect on him and cause further panic in the public than necessary; after all, his behaviour inside of late had been none but exemplary. So he was soon forgotten in the public eye and after a while released from the confines to engage with the gang.

Tom Frost, known to all as Frosty, was in his mid-twenties. He had the main bedroom at the front of the house on Windmill Lane, which was a stone's throw from the library with the public swimming baths set behind it, further down passed the baths was the Griffin Stadium with a network of pubs cornering each end of the pitch, pubs that were fingers twitching to the reflexes of Dave Foley's wrist as he flexed it from his base of operations at The King's Head. There were other gangs out there, and the relationship between them was genial, but Foley's boys ran far and wide and kept control of the manor from the river at Brentford up through into Chiswick and Ealing. Greenford and Northolt had their own barbaric Goliaths that they didn't dare rumble with, and on the other side of the river sat a class more sophisticated and out of their league save for the odd skirmish and raiding party when business was slow, which it wasn't.

Frosty ran the house, he was the boss here and what he said was gospel, unless word from the Head contradicted him. He was a wiry fellow with drainpipe trousers and short sleeve shirts, always with the top button done up. There was a constant cry of 'One Step Beyond' or 'Mirror in the Bathroom' echoing from his room as the Two Tone 12's and 45's echoed in playful competition with the one The Who album Rooney often put on the record player in the living room to purposely wind him up. Frosty upon first appearance looked harmless enough but close up there was a devious smile betraying him that told you he was slippery and well-connected and, although not a big brawler, knew how to handle a knife and was quick to slip it out and carve himself a piece of flesh to teach anyone a lesson about keeping shtum around him.

Rooney, was Jon Joe Mulrooney, he too was in his mid-twenties but was in many ways the opposite to Frosty. He was an Irishman with a thick Dublin accent he was proud of. He was wide in appearance and rosy cheeked, mainly from the many pints he sunk in The Globe where he spent most of his days and evenings when not running errands. The Globe was across from the old **Performance Cars** dealership sat behind the 91 bus stop that perched on the edge of the busy A4 on the way in towards the Chiswick roundabout, hiding in the shadow of the M4 flyover that thundered above clipping the edge off Brentford away from the main town. The Globe was his focal point for work as well as pleasure; there he checked the books, kept an eye on the patrons, and talked, but his greatest talent was listening. Rooney was good at talking to people and drawing out a mountain of information without them realising it. He could play drunk, and actually be drunk, but still retain what he'd been told and feed anything useful back to Foley the next day when he'd sobered up.

The third man in the bedsit was Matt Bradley, a thin and mostly quiet love struck nineteen year old. He tended to be moody depending on his latest altercation with his girlfriend of eight months, a blonde named Karen who was all tits and no brains and had a history of using the boys to get what she wanted as she knew they'd do almost anything for her to get into her knickers, in this she was smart but not in who she chose to toy with as she skirted around the fringes of the gang trying to find favour; she would pay for it one day and sooner than she thought. For the most part Matt was pleasant enough and Jack and he struck up a brief friendship as Matt acted big brother in showing him around the patch and helped point out those he would do good to steer clear of. The thing Jack appreciated most from Matt was that he never once tried to ask anything about him; he was happy to talk if Jack wanted to, but he made no effort to intrude (which all the others did at some point, though all respected his need for privacy - they'd all done time at one point or another, some boasted about it, others preferred to keep it to themselves; each man had his own journey and his own story to tell or not to tell). Matt had picked up early on that Jack's sentence had been long enough to keep him uneducated in the ways of the world and so had taken it upon himself to subtly, and without the others realising, educate him in all things socially acceptable.

Jack and Matt spent a fair amount of time in each other's company in the early days as Frosty put Jack to work helping Matt copy the VHS recordings of E.T. they'd somehow got in before it's UK release date at the cinema. The videos were selling at a high price and were proving water in a dry desert as they sat in day after day linking two VHS players together and copying tape after tape. In the end they were so familiar with the script they had begun re-enacting scenes in the living room with the volume down on the massive TV that bulged out from under the enclave beneath the front bay windows that faced out onto the street outside, as they waited they would often score the girls that passed by to and from Brentford Girls School not too far down the road; Matt gave him tips on which ones to avoid, which ones were likely to be high maintenance, which ones were too loud, which ones he had already tried it with and which ones in their school uniforms were no longer virgins. Jack took it all in and cast his eye over a couple that he quite fancied (they being of a similar age to himself he thought this okay) but took with a pinch of salt Matt's opinion and value on women; he was after all dating high maintenance Karen, and though professing to be madly in love with her clearly still had his eye on dipping his wick with any legal or illegally aged girl that graced his doorstep.

In a short time Jack was aloud out and no one seemed to recognise him from the story that broke not that long ago of an escaped prisoner from borstal, a prison system that would later that year be abolished and replaced by a supposedly better system, though he never found out whether the changes were for the better as he never returned, but he often wondered whether his own plight had contributed to the changes.

Matt showed him the area, the social area and the business area so far as the gang was concerned. Having no school to go to he was used initially as a runner for anyone who needed messages passing along, a job that in years to come would be used as the drug runner selling on the street corners to the kids coming out of school, and holding the stash so that the big boys didn't get caught. Running was Matt's job too, but with Jack now on the scene he was given a little more responsibility and tasks of a little more sensitivity were given to him. Matt's judgement was doubted though within the gang, mainly over Karen as she was clearly making a fool of him, and yet he failed to see it. Jack had tried to warn him but it had not gone down well as Matt took offence to being given relationship advice from someone younger and clearly inexperienced. Harsh words were past which seemed to push him more into Karen's arms than he had been before.

As the weeks went by Jack proved his worth and both Frosty and Rooney reported well of him to Foley as he already began to push his talents towards saying the right things so people heard what they thought they wanted to hear, allowing the Brentford Boys to ply their trade a little easier and gaining Jack a good deal of respect with the hierarchy at The King's Head.

5

In the dream he was in an old house where hidden in the furniture were trinkets and catches that when discovered and twisted in the right way opened up tiny secret chests of mechanical design, a hidden drawer here, a trove of worthless treasure beneath a floorboard trap there. Whoever had designed such intricacies was a genius of queer imagination.

One such catch opened up a secret room where he found hanging inside a collection of old children's clothes, and on the window sill, which was an old style open concrete frame as within a battlement with no glass and strangely visible from the outside, although no one had apparently ever spotted it, was a pile of paper receipts for things bought from various shops dating back forty years but looking crisp and fresh and not at all worn or weathered by age.

On a ledge sat an old record player with a big horn speaker arching out over a freshly printed copy of The Toy Town Salute that had just been released, a song he knew to be climbing the singles charts as a reworked version of an old track that his mum used to sing to him, the sound echoed off the walls amidst a looming droning hum that seemed to come from the walls themselves.

A fridge sat against the far wall, its white casing illuminating the dimly lit basement room. Was he in the basement now? He didn't recall descending any stairs but the room had a dungeon-esque atmosphere to it. He opened the fridge with little real curiosity to the flood of colour of frozen congealed blood that hung like stalactites from the metal grilled shelf where a severed head sat accusingly staring out.

He rushed from the room back the way he came only to find himself re-entering the room a moment later but an age had passed within the dream.

The clothes were no longer there, nor the receipts, but the fridge was, and this time blood was seeping from its seals.

As he returned to the room, conscious of unknown shadowy figures at his side directing his steps, he had the sense of being followed by pale round faced and squidgy bodied monsters, their limestone figures blending with the walls as they shuffled through the labyrinth as the room opened up through a doorway into a secret low passage of an underground cavern, the monsters trying to catch up to him to turn him into copies of themselves, wanting him to conform to the ways of their world and not to stand apart with the dark hordes that relished in the blood of death and destruction.

The song followed as he rushed blindly forward away from grasping arms.

He straightened up as the cavern widened out so that he passed an indoor basketball court which morphed into an outdoor sports field resembling the yard of a prison, it led out onto a dull grey street where there had been an accident of some sort. The police had cordoned off the road and it looked like someone had been run over. A female officer was crying and being led away and rumours were circulating amongst the sniggering hooded shadows of ghosts that she had run over the child that lay bloodied on the tarmac. Just then two rival football teams who had been playing on the field behind stepped out from the cavern entrance which was now the gaping mouth of a monstrous house, an institute he recognised as the home of his late childhood.

The two teams marched passed him armed with bats, maces, and axes and took up a lined position along the front wall of the garden facing the street. They began to grumble against each other so he stepped forward and stood between them to keep them from fighting for fear the child was dead and their brawling be seen insensitive to the grieving family stood frightened and tearful by the roadside watching.

Suddenly the opposing armies, the voices of dissent, disappeared, as did the shadowy ghosts, and the chameleon monsters morphed back into the walls.

The street was empty and he was on his own with the blood of the street scene before him. No child lay in the street and no family or police stood guard. Only a rising echo reached his ears as he stood alone staring at the blood on the pavement and now on his own hands, an echo of 'The Toy Town Salute' ringing in his ears.

It was a familiar dream, although elements of it were new, not that he would remember when he woke – he never did, just a blurred sense of remembrance clouding his thinking as he stirred from his slumber, as he did now with the dull echo of the song shattering his thoughts and sending the images of the dream to the hidden recess of his mind.

None of it made sense even within the bizarre realities of the dream state, just like his life that was in itself a nightmare. He supposed that if he broke it down maybe he would be able to attribute elements of it to his crimes and his fears: the police echoing his caution of being caught, the football teams maybe being part of the dysfunctional household he now lived in, the monsters of conformity to what was expected of him, the room and the accident echoing the destruction he'd caused and the people he had harmed both past and present, and the years in which he'd been entombed.

Maybe one day it would make sense, he doubted it, but for now the whole dream served a purpose, setting a signal that it was high time he needed to take measures to safeguard himself at night as the evidence of his roaming was evidenced by the mud on his shoes and the blood on his hands, telling him the demons were back and he'd been wandering murderously in the dark.

6

The bitch downstairs was barking; whoever had entered she didn't take a liking to by the sound of it. A yelp later and it was clear the feeling was mutual.

"See Dave, I told you I didn't do it," laughed the weighty youth stood before Dave Foley with a domineering presence of his own almost on a par with that of the crime boss sat behind the desk.

Footsteps could be heard creaking up the stairs as the big boss accompanied the youth with proud laughter. "Told ya I'd sort ya out, didn't I son, eh!" bellowed Foley with a slight wheezy rasp as the door cracked open slowly unnoticed. "Got a good brief there," then in a half mocking whisper said, "you can be as guilty as sin an' that bastard will find a technicality somewhere to get you off. Keep 'im in your pocket at all times." He handed over a small business card with the solicitor's phone number on and the youth slipped it into the back pocket of his jeans.

The door opened a fraction more and Foley's eyes rose up to see Jack, whom he had sent for via a hearty yell to Rick next door in the other room. The youth turned also, looking over his shoulder to see what had got his boss' attention.

The youth smiled, not a wane half gesture but a delightful and genuine pleasure of a greeting of a long lost brother returned from overseas.

"Well look what the cat dragged in," he beamed striking his hands into his trouser pockets with excitable raised shoulders and keeping his fists clenched in the

hidden, if not uncomfortable, depths of the darkness of
the blue jeans he was keen to change out of now that he
was home. He hoped that he was succeeding in
disguising his complete satisfaction at seeing his friend,
it wouldn't do good for the old snake to know how fond
he'd become of this unfortunate character during his
brief flight at borstal, having used him initially to gain
intelligence on the workings and layout of the place and
then pitying him on his already served lifetime
sentence, to then surprisingly finding that he was a
likeable kid. Yes, he had seen potential in Jack and
could justify aiding in his escape, which Foley no doubt
would berate him for later and in private for taking such
a risk on account of the establishment (one he thought
he'd forgive knowing that he would see in Jack what he
also saw as a usable asset – he and Foley thought much
alike in such matters), but it was more than just the
potential that had prompted the plan to free him. He
could see that Jack had little hope of fleeing the system
that he had been placed in as a mental health patient
convicted of such a crime, even if they did let him out
he would never escape the legacy of what he had done
and would be forever accountable to the state for it. It
was the short friendship they had struck whilst whittling
away the hours with the other boys that had convinced
him to help get Jack out of there and return his freedom.

When confined to such enclosures with little else to
do one tends to either make friends quickly or enemies
that send you fleeing into further isolation. Jack had
chosen the latter by purposely isolating himself, not that
he had enemies; he was different, disconnected, yet
amenable to all, friendly with the screws as well as the
violent cliques that had formed, even the wimpy nonces

got a nod. No one knew how to take him. He seemed kind enough but had a detachment of emotion that pricked at the senses telling you to be wary. As the two spent time together, Jack seemingly fully aware that he was being used for information yet still providing what was needed anyway without request or demand of payment, he grew attached to his unquestioning and unconditional companionship.

Jack it would seem was the only person in that rabbit hutch that didn't seem to have an agenda; most inmates sought friends and allies first, life could be a bitch on the inside without them (or you'd be used as one), then skills; there was a training ground to be had on the inside, *The College of Cons*, that was where you learnt your trade before you sought the next thing on the agenda, that was if you didn't already have it on the outside like he had: a network! Unless you decided the correctional facility was truly reforming your character and converting you into a model citizen then you needed to develop a network, find an associate, a buddy, someone with whom you could ply your trade upon release, someone would vouch for you on the outside.

Getting into one area of crime systematically and automatically was a road of many tangents, but ultimately they all led to the same place just on a different route through town, often circular winding through the streets of London on a bus marked 'Slammer' that allowed you off from time to time to dabble in the chase with *the filth* in blue, the bacon simmering as they got hot under the bonnet of their white Rovers with their blue dalek lights flashing away playing tail to the slow moving bus. One skill always led to another which in turn led onto another contact. The smart ones knew that the easiest way to get caught was to not adapt, or not be part of a gang that looked after its own; if you stuck to the same old routine and laid the same cards down each time then you were forever on a losing streak.

He'd learnt from his old man (way back before he'd taken that fatal hatchet blow) that you learnt all you could and you used all you could, honing all number of necessary and expanding skills needed to be utilised in the carrying out of any and every task undertaken in the now chosen (or rather slipped into) profession.

His father had been a bastard, tough as nails, a bully who had made as many enemies as he had friends, and in truth he despised him and denied him to most, but he had taught his son some valuable lessons about how to get ahead and beat the rest, literally if need be. He barely remembered the old man now, nor the fact that those things that seemed so natural an instinct to him now were taught when he was but a babe in arms, before his father had limped away from the ambush at the stadium when payback came a knocking over a sour deal over..., well who knew what it was over, and who cared in the end? The deal had gone bad and blood was spilt. He'd bashed some heads on the way out and managed to walk away with a deep slice to his midsection, and not the sort of wound you just walked into casualty with, trying to explain away a gash like that was likely to raise eyebrows, and besides, *the rosser's* were bound to be on the search for the wounded following the skirmish, so it was always best practice to keep clear of the hospitals. The wound was deep and gaping by the time the gang called in their own doctor who treated it best he could and told him to lay low, which he did, for a little too long as it turned out as the tear in his gut tore open and got infected so that when they sent for him to resurface, thinking it was safe to be seen, he was already dead having died a painful and lonely death as the poisoned blood fed rapidly through his system.

He vowed to be smarter than that. He refused to make the same mistakes as his father.

Jack smiled back at him now and nodded a pleasing greeting as he entered and stood to the side of his older friend in the middle of the room. The two boys, for they were barely men old enough to work with their pimply faces and rarely scraped cheeks straddling the ides of mid-teens, were being sized up by Foley as he sat casually smoking behind his desk with the curtains closed behind him.

"I told you I could follow instructions," said Jack seeking the approval of his friend, knowing his role to help promote the judgement of this lad that had gambled on helping him escape.

"Yeah, I knew you wouldn't let me down. They bin treatin' you alright?"

Jack nodded, "Been making myself useful like you said."

"So he has," chipped in Foley.

"You got balls Jack, I'll give you that!" he laughed taking one hand out of his pocket and slapping the younger boy on the back.

"Now you're back you can have Matt's room," broke in Foley, he wasn't keen on shows of affection of any kind and didn't have a taste for it especially in his office. His eyes drifted up slowly to take in the reaction, which came slow as the words caught in the think fume of fog that dragged them back through the air as they escaped his mouth, the smoke cushioning their impact before the mind caught up to make sense of them.

"Why? What's happened to Matt?"

Foley looked across at Jack and was amazed to see that the boy didn't even flinch, barely even blinked at the mention of it, indeed showed no emotion at all. He knew why Jack had been inside, of course he did, not that he let on to Jack that he knew; there was no way he would take on a runaway kid wanted with a warrant out for his arrest without checking him out, no matter how skilled an asset, of which he thought the boy held back on and thought he had more to give; something else was hiding in there he could use and he thought he knew what it was but had yet to tease it out of him, but he was confident it would come in time with the right prompting and opportunity.

"Matt's dead," Jack said bluntly without caring or even thinking to care as to whether there had been any deep friendship between the dead youth and any in the room.

A mop of hair flapped in the middle of the room like a collie dog stepping out of a river and shaking itself off as the head spun to Jack and then back to Foley with incredulous questioning.

Foley nodded his head slowly, he knew that they were friends, not deep friends, acquaintances really, but they knew each other well enough. "He took a swan dive one night off Clayponds."

Clayponds referred to the three blocks of flats at Clayponds Gardens on the South Ealing Road, it was where Karen lived.

"What? Why? No don't tell me, it had something to do with that blonde slag Karen, right?"

Foley took a deep hearty breath then let it out with the words, "Young love! He *thought* he was in love. He caught her screwing around and couldn't understand how she could do it to him, *thought* she loved him."

"It's not worth throwing yourself off a bloody building for though, is it?" There was anger in his voice, not so much at the loss of his friend Matt but more at the stupidity of the act itself. Why anyone would want to kill themselves was beyond him, and over something so trivial as a girl like her! Suddenly his joy at being back, at gracing the table of his benefactor, at being beside a friend, all seemed meaningless and trite. He closed his mind off and gave himself over to the whim and command of Foley.

The dust settled in silence, even if the smoky haze didn't. The mood had changed but neither boy knew how to change it. Foley cared little for Matt and so had detached himself from the emotion of any sort of friendship, although it was never pleasant having to lose a member of the family. Matt Bradley was a useful runner but showed little potential in progressing any further, his talents were limited if at all worthless, and his judgement doubtful. In truth Foley already had his eye on him as a liability and would have happily cut him loose if he'd sought a less painful way out, so long as it didn't betray the fold that had looked after him for so long. Many had gone their own way in the past, some even going straight; those that did so with all good intentions were given his blessing – others received something else altogether.

Foley broke the silence with instruction, his way of saying 'enough for now, get out of my office', "Jack will take you back to the bedsit, I want you to get up to speed on what's been happening while you've been gone so get the low down from Frosty.

"Rick," he bellowed, and they heard the hefty man next door scramble to his feet and step into the corridor ready to escort them out of the building.

7

That night there was a celebration to be had. The King's Head was packed out and the drinks were free for many of the regulars as Foley propped up the bar in respect of their returned captive, like a released prisoner of war. Wads of folded notes were on show: ragged green ones and blue fivers, but mostly crisp tens and twenties, and the richest of all weren't shy in flashing a roll of fifties as bootleg merchandise was hoked and deals were made and backroom cards were dealt. Flashing the cash was a real crowd pleaser and fanny tingle; there was nothing like having a few sobs in the pocket to get the juices flowing.

"So Rick, when you next doing a frog run?" bellowed the liquid loose tongue of the youth across the bar, merry from his release and the party being thrown in his honour.

"Yeah, in a couple of weeks lad," came the gruff but unusually cheery voice of the bar manager, "what yus after?"

"Bring us back some faggs if you can fit 'em in the back of the van with the booze." He ended it with a nod and a wink. They all knew Rick ran the gauntlet over to France once a month for Foley to stock up on the cheap stuff to resell to the Paki off-licence down the street.

"I tell you what, when I'm king of this manor," he continued aside a little too loosely to those around him, lowering his voice but not enough to have escaped the attention of Rick's keen ears, as cauliflower bruised as they were, "I'm gonna be so filthy rich that this place is gonna be open bar to you lot every night." Frost and Rooney raised their glasses and glugged heavily. "And you my little man! I'm not leaving you out!" He pulled Jack close into the circle and encouraged him to drink up, not caring that he was so underage that it was unlikely he had ever been drunk before in his life. Jack drank hesitantly but happily enough.

"Yep, you'll all be my crew, except you Micky, you're a bloody spastic!" The comment was yelled across to another group circled near the other end of the bar, his glass held high and then dropped low to the bar for a refill. "Only kidding Micky, you're a top fella, you can polish my shoes any day." The four of them broke about laughing, not caring about the reaction of anyone else in the pub, that was until he had his collar tugged from behind.

None of them had seen Dave Foley step out of the back room, he'd come out just in time to have heard all he needed to hear and reached out to the drunken youth with more speed than any of the younger group would have given him credit for.

"That's enough," whispered Foley into his ear so that only those close could hear what was said. "Don't disrespect my hospitality or others in the bar. This is my gaff and my outfit. Watch your mouth or you'll outstay your welcome. Got it?"

"Yes boss, sorry boss." There was a sudden sobering embarrassment among the four housemates that stood at the bar. Suddenly they were the boys being jeered at by the old time hero's and giants that had established themselves over the decades alongside

Foley, and they were firmly put in their place as still wet behind the ears jumped up little upstarts.

Rick refilled his glass as Foley sunk back into the depths of the backroom. "Don't worry about him, lad. It's still your party and he's well proud. Just don't be a gobshite and the drinks'll still flow."

"Cheers Rick, you're a gent!"

Despite his age he had gained a great deal of respect amongst those in the pub, he'd held his own and manned up and showed real leadership potential, sure he was a hot head, and sure his temper often got the better of him, but compared to most of the losers in the pub he was a born gangster, a quality not lost on Frosty and Rooney who, despite being almost ten years his senior, were happy to bow to his authority and take his leading in most matters.

As for the other pub regulars, most were in their twenties or thirties, but dotted amongst them were the aging godfathers who pushed into their forties and fifties, with maybe a couple even pushing sixty. Some of these old timers were lifetime gang runners or long-time associates either through business or through family. Most of the gang had proper full time jobs: Eric, a sloth of a man, obese and pock marked, worked in the council's housing benefit office; Derek (also known as Three Fingered Del, having been born with only the thumb and forefinger of his left hand - not that that was the story banded about among the boys, the legend had become more colourful and bloody with each telling) he ran the petrol station on the Great West Road opposite Gillette Corner which served as a handy gateway and staging post on the way in and out of Brentford; Rob Letchworth who swanned in and out amongst the crew cheerfully, and with the complete trust and confidence of all, was a police sergeant based on the borough who often worked out of Brentford police station where he could keep his ear to the ground for a heads up for the boys - in loud fits of bolshiness he would bellow how he despised his own kind as much as the rest of them. To say that the regular patrons of the pub were well used and well in the pocket of Foley would be an understatement.

Along with the regulars there were the ladies, wives and girlfriends mostly, not that most of them cared to grace the men's celebrations, and those that did stayed fleetingly. The younger girls that stayed were those who longed for the danger and risk that was attractive in the bad boys and which would ultimately in many cases end with abuse both physical and emotional, as was the nature of the men they chased. Such was the case with Foley's wife: she had taken a battering five years previously and had fled bleeding and bruised leaving her job, her home, and her friends all behind as she skipped town and moved north as far away from the clutches of her husband as she could get. No one knew what the argument was over, no one dared ask.

The pub bounced along way beyond closing time, the doors being locked and the lights being dimmed and the hardened old timers still propping the bar like they had no homes to go to. The numbers dwindled and the crowd became less raucous as the luckier of the men paired off to get lucky hoping their other halves wouldn't find out and that the young girl they screwed wouldn't be a pest about it afterwards. A few of the guys drove home tanked up, but most of those who stayed to whittle away the hours in Foley's presence were his inner circle, his enclave of bandits, they were the ones most likely to saunter home having stayed long enough to sober to the effects of the earlier drink.

Way before all this, before the last pints were pulled Jack and his new best buddy were already tucked up on the floor of the bedsit having staggered home, having both emptied their stomachs by the roadside (Jack within the pub itself to the amusement of all but Rick who relished little the job of cleaning up after the youngster - Foley had ordered them home at that point under the escort of Frosty and Rooney, who themselves both returned to the pub afterwards).

So roughly they slept arm in arm on the floor the way Rooney had jokingly placed them. Brothers in arms they slept in peace, and no dreams befell Jack that night.

8

It had been the 2 Tone age of Ska. Madness was big and collars were small and Fred Perry polo shirts and La Coste and Sergio Tacchini shell suits were all the rage. The Jam and The Human League were also big on the chart scene often ringing out from the Steve Wright in the Afternoon show on Radio 1, along with Culture Club, Yazoo, and Dexys Midnight Runners with 'Come on Eileen'. It was a diverse music scene where reggae bobbed along nicely alongside heavy metal in the charts, rubbing shoulders with some new electronic sounds and tacky Eurovision pop, Musical Youth and Eddie Grant sharing top ten slots with the likes of Iron Maiden, Kraftwork, and Bucks Fizz. It was the year the dandy highwayman bowed out, as Adam, the man with the distinctive white stripe across his nose (more pirate than street robber), decided to ditch 'the Ants' in search of a solo career.

It was the year when Dynasty, Fame, Knight Rider, Hill Street Blues and Magnum, P.I. were all big on TV, and Wogan still had his chat show on BBC 1, and The Young Ones and Shine on Harvey Moon would birth a new generation of comic actors playing alongside Only Fools and Horses. The year when British television would take a new turn with the launch of a fourth channel, the aptly named Channel 4, with Countdown leading its programme list and with The Tube seeing a new outlet for music in an attempt to rival Top of the Pops.

It was the year that saw the birth too of action stars like Arnold Schwarzenegger with Conan, and Sylvester Stallone with his Rocky sequels firing out all punches with First Blood having been drawn; Star Trek took the lead in sci-fi with the first of many sequels, with Poltergeist popularising horror, while the likes of Porky's and Tootsie reigned in the laughs along with stand up's like Eddie Murphy and Richard Pryor.

The top toy of the year went to Glo Worms, the plush pajamaed worms that lit up and played a soothing lullaby when squeezed. The Cabbage Patch dolls were also selling well, along with a certain Masters of the Universe action hero figure that left boys of all ages triumphantly raising their hands in the air pretending to brandish a sword and screaming 'By the power of Grayskull!' as they mimicked the mighty He Man in-between watching the brown plasticine figure of Morph on Take Hart and the 'here's one I made earlier' pursuits on Blue Peter - all the while chewing on the goodies tucked away in the paper bag bought from the local paper shop on the corner with their selection of well stocked sweet jars behind the counter and the Double Dip and Dip Dab sherbet packets temptingly in reach alongside the Fizz Whiz popping candy as you handed over your pennies and half pennies.

All in all it was a good time for cheap knocks offs of all brands and of all guises as boxes shipped in and shipped out, their contents distributed in the market places and the put-up stalls on the High Street where the lookouts learnt to whistle high and loud at the first sighting of PC Plod that would prompt a case of grab and run, merchandise of clothing and bootleg cassettes (next year it would be CD's) thrust under arm as you sprinted for it. It was an easy time to steer around the police as they were still in fear of another uprising from the Brixton riots of the year before and the continued IRA threat against the city. As for the punters, well let's just say the tension and attention was still focused on the Falkland Crisis and other big events, enough to make a cry about when you wanted to drift a conversation this way or that to make a bob or two in distraction. Around the world Carlos the Jackal was terrorising France, Israel had invaded Lebanon, Laker Airways had folded, the US had gone into recession, the Ocean Ranger oil rig sank in the Atlantic, and the gates of Gibraltar were opened; to add to all that laughably Michael Fagan had decided to pay the Queen a visit by letting himself into the palace, and oh yeah Italy won the World Cup. Oh yes, there was plenty of distraction. Plenty of misdirection. Plenty to get people talking about on the market stalls to deflect from what was anything but genuine whilst the punter was sussed out for a robbery or a con or just simply swayed easily enough to purchase more of the hooky crap they had on offer.

Who cared that the Dip Dabs were out of date, or that the Madness cassette cover was a photocopy, or that Sergio Tacchini was spelt wrong on the shell suit, or that the tape recorder didn't work properly, or that the Poltergeist had gotten into the VHS so that it didn't play properly. If the customer was foolish enough to buy their knock off junk then that was their look out, and it made for easy money for *the boys* thank you very much - luvly jubbly!

Rooney was pissed as usual and didn't have a clue what they were doing as the four of them strolled out of the snooker hall next to the fly pit cinema in West Ealing. It was just as well, had he been sober he'd never have consented to what their ringleader was planning.

They'd debated about which club to visit first and had landed on the Northfields club heads up. He was glad for it for a number of reasons, chiefly among them because the car wouldn't have been there had they gone to West Ealing first as it hadn't been parked there when they arrived.

"Where'd you park the car?" he murmured to Frosty.

"Just down there by the church," Frosty replied pointing along the poorly lit street with the car key.

"Go get this fat paddy in and start the car."

Tom Frost looked back at the sixteen year old with a snarl. He didn't like it when this upstart tried ordering him about, but he had the sense in him to see the lay of things. The boy was going places and everyone knew it. Even Foley was giving him space to flourish as he carved out more chunks of responsibility, letting the youth take command of a garrison, soon on his way to being a general. The kid was smart, at times impulsive, but mostly dangerous. Tom Frost had seen him at work and wasn't intending to argue the toss no matter how much he disliked the order. He grabbed Rooney by the arm and led him staggering into the darkness like a blundering Laurel and Hardy routine trying desperately to keep to the path.

"What we doing?" asked Jack of his friend who had casually slid over to the edge of the main road in front of the cinema and was checking the flow of traffic. At this time of night there wasn't much but there would be soon, the cinema would be kicking out in fifteen minutes so they'd have to be quick with whatever they were about to do.

"Ever nicked a car?" came the reply as he walked back into the shadows.

Jack looked around at the cars parked about and spied the only one he thought his friend might take a fancy to. It was a black Ford Escort Mark III XR3i with all the trimmings. Someone had spent a lot of money on it and it looked mint.

Jack shook his head. He was a little afraid of what they were about to do but didn't show it. So far he hadn't backed down from anything he'd been lured into and found that the more he did the more they gave him to do and the more respect he gained.

"You game?"

Jack took a breath and swallowed deeply before nodding his head. He wanted to ask what they should do if they were caught, or if the owner suddenly appeared, or if an alarm sounded, but he didn't, he kept his mouth shut and trusted his friend to take the lead.

They both sauntered over to the car. A merry shout rang out further up the road followed briefly by a car door slamming, a second later it was followed by the sound of the Cortina's engine springing into life.

"Keep an eye," came the order as the two boys circled the Escort.

Jack did as he was told, watching the street with a keen nervousness while the driver's door was played with from the roadside. He heard a click and then the door opened and closed again as a head bobbed beneath the steering wheel. There was no alarm sounding. That was good. Although he couldn't understand why the owner would spend so much on the car and not install an alarm, unless it had been disabled already, and if it had been then he was better than he thought.

The window of the passenger side was wound down and the command to get in was given. He wasted no time in yanking open the door and jumping onto the leather seat within and pulling the door to behind him. The engine started up, it purred wonderfully, then growled as the accelerator pedal was depressed lovingly. Both boys laughed at the sound as the stereo blew into life with Survivor's 'Eye of the Tiger' blaring out through the open window.

The headlights came on giving the signal to Frosty to get going.

The car was parked in tightly so it took a few moments to edge backwards and forward until it was at a place where he could swerve it out into the road. He turned the wheel hard and hammered on the pedal just as a hand reached through the open passenger window and grabbed Jack by the collar.

The car swung out into the road but at too sharp an angle so that it pointed too far across the street in a position that meant he would have to reverse again to get the car underway. Meanwhile the vice-like grip tightened on Jack with no sign of letting go.

Jack calmly and silently tried to hit out at the arm feeling the bulging muscles of an unseen brute who was shouting something Jack couldn't make out under the blaring music but could understand the meaning clear enough. He half turned his body in his seat to try and pull away but couldn't - then the hand released suddenly, the result of a carpenter hammering down on a stubborn nail embedded in a plank of wood on the floor below, the weapon-less hand rising and falling with unrelenting speed and power. Jack turned to the driver's seat to see it was empty and the door was open. He turned back and looked out the open window to see the face that owned the bloody fist. The fist had stopped moving and posed threateningly towards the open doorway of the snooker club where a couple of familiar faced patrons stood aghast.

"Got a problem?" came the voice from outside of the car.

The two figures turned and went back inside. They weren't going to be a problem. They knew better.

Within seconds he was back in the car and reversing it, almost running over the dented and bleeding figure lying by the edge of the road. He thrust the gear stick into first and screeched forward into the street ahead where Frosty sat parked in the middle of the road staring back through the red tail lights at the thrashing that had just been handed out, knowing full well he wouldn't be needed. The job was done and they were off.

Rooney lay sprawled across the back seat blissfully unaware as his head grew heavy to the gentle rumbling of rubber on tarmac.

9

He stood staring at the old cinema, boarded up and abandoned yet still magnificent in its stature and grandiosity as it overlooked Northfields tube station opposite on the Northfields Avenue. The magnificent 1930's building had once been the Northfields Odeon (before that the Avenue Theatre) with its original Spanish style décor, its wide stage before its enormous screen, and an upstairs balcony. The café come restaurant had closed down at the beginning of the '70's and the organ had been removed following flood damage the year after, since then the building had been in steady decline with the decorated tented ceiling material eventually needing to be replaced with a pleated plain red cloth due to years of dust, grime and tobacco smoke damage. It had become the Coronet in 1981 but closed in January of 1985 with its last showing being Arnold Schwarzenegger's aptly named 'The Terminator'. Since then it's exterior had gone into rapid decline at the abuse the avenue threw at it as kids sat on its unguarded steel runner lining the steps up to the main foyer now blocked from view, a foyer he once remembered housed one of the Bond cars as he'd gone into see the film - he couldn't remember now which car it was, just that it was yellow and tall, the film itself forgettable, but the nostalgia attached to the experience still lingered.

He had ambitions for this place but that would have to wait.

For the moment he'd been given charge of the snooker club down the hill to the right of the cinema as he looked at it. It was down a side street on the left, hidden away but not quietly unknown to the numerous patrons that frequented its eight green felt lined tables under a haze of cigarette smoke and chalk dust. It had two billiard tables in a small room upstairs as well as a bar down stairs housing two £100 fruit machines; the two slot machines made almost as much as the game play itself, especially on a Friday night when some men, fresh with their weeks earnings, were known to addictively sink it all within an hour's sitting before going home downcast to the family that relied so heavily on what should have been brought home. Occasionally the behemoths would pay out, but it was rare. One youth, a tall lad with floppy brown hair and heavily built (not fat, but a chubbiness not yet grown out of his youth), he could only be about fifteen for he often wore school uniform, the emblem of his black blazer telling he was from the all-boys catholic school, Gunnersbury, round the corner, of the house of Bourne according to the colour of his tie, the red stripe slinking to hide beneath his grey v-neck jumper, this boy was friendly enough but had an uncanny way with gambling - he always won. It seemed he was a natural at picking the win on almost anything and would stand for ages just watching someone feed in their hard earned cash, patiently waiting his turn, then stepping up onto the stool with his ten pence pieces in hand before emptying the machine within minutes. It got to the point where Vince, the silver haired, chain smoking, whiskey swigging old timer who managed the place, was ordered to turn off the machines when the kid walked in, sending him packing to The Hungry One, the fast food burger joint on the parade of shops round the corner where they had a couple of machines, not big payers but enough to cough out fifteen or twenty quid. The kid would prove to be useful to the gang one day he was sure, and so he'd ordered Vince to let him back into the club so long as he took it easy on the slot machines. It seemed the kid had sense enough to know he'd over filled his pockets as he humbly returned to the fold and focused his energy more on playing snooker and betting on it where he could.

He wanted guys like that where he could see them so that he knew where to find them when the time came for using them.

The club was doing well and was in capable hands. It turned a good profit and provided a secure meeting place for their esoteric gatherings late at night when they wanted to map out a job or organise a supply run or the likes. A couple of the regular car thieves, including the Coleman twins were known to slink in after doing a smash and grab of a stereo (which they'd hide under another car or in a nearby bin) or having parked a stolen set of wheels in a street nearby - the club was a comfort to such as these, a sanctuary where they could relax as the adrenalin wore off knowing that they were amongst friends. Much of the gang's new business was now operating from here with a younger team, almost a branch of its own away from The King's Head and the control of Dave Foley.

He looked across to the entrance to the car park behind the old cinema. Had it really been three years since he'd parked the Escort at the back there, he and Jack cleaning it off for prints before abandoning it in the darkness while Frosty babysat Rooney in the other car, waiting to drive them back to the Brentford bedsit? They'd driven into an empty site even back then, for although it had only been closed for less than a year its custom prior to that had dwindled significantly as it gave business to the triple screened ABC in Ealing Broadway. The car park had emptied quickly as they got there shortly after the cinema had spewed out the last of its viewers, it would fill up again with a handful of cars before the late night showing at eleven which gave them thirty minutes or so to vacate the area.

He remembered Jack, once they were done, stepping out of the car and doubling over to empty the contents of his stomach across the cracked aging tarmac. It hadn't been the alcohol nor the food of the evening but the adrenalin that had caused his stomach to churn. He was new to this and was still young and inexperienced, but he had balls. He hadn't complained or whined about what they'd done but had quietly gone along with the job, then puked his guts, wiped his mouth and said he was okay before getting into Frosty's old faithful Cortina.

They'd all laughed about it at the time, and afterwards, but no one laughed at Jack, and no one had laughed about it in Jack's presence since. He had a look in his eyes that made even the boldest man cautious, a disengagement, the type a pyromaniac has while watching the burn; you could picture him stood beneath the tail of a rocket waiting for the ignite of its engines before take-off, caring not that his face would be burnt off as he looked up the crap hole of the tube. Such a man you didn't get on the wrong side of. Such a man you kept close - and so he did.

Best buddies they had been these last three years, and mutual respect was gained between the two as they enlarged Foley's kingdom. Boys become men in a lawless world.

Jack had many peculiarities for a seventeen year old but he rarely commented on them, and never in mocking jest, being always careful to approach his studious companion in a serious one to one manner where his attention was not distracted and where there could be no misunderstanding between them. He was his friend and wanted Jack to know it; he didn't know why, just that they had a bond as though their lives were somehow entwined, and so he wanted Jack to know that he had his back when the time came and that he cared about his friend fitting in with the others.

One of the things he never questioned was Jack's calling out at night, or the fact that he had placed a lock on his bedroom door and moved the dresser in front of the door every night before going to sleep; he could hear the heavy shuffling of it and the thud as Jack put it into place, the others could hear it too but he'd advised them strongly never to mention it. Only he and Foley knew why Jack had been locked up in the first place and part of him was thankfully reassured by the locked door.

Jack had begun sleep walking about the house not long after he'd moved into Matt's old room. He found him once or twice stood alone with eyes eerily wide open yet vacant and unseeing as though his waking mind had completely disconnected from the signal being sent from the retinas. Not much scared him, but that had. He never mentioned it and neither did Jack, but Jack clearly knew he was having these episodes and was himself fearful of what he was capable of.

He hoped Jack would handle the pressure while he was gone; they were used to working a certain way and running as a unit; mainly he, Frosty, Jack and Rooney running command in that order. Ordinarily someone like Rooney would never reach a position of authority but by nature of the four of them sharing a house they ran together, and so the tubby paddy was given a role of responsibility. Frosty would now take charge in his absence, a position he would relish as he always saw himself as a don with his black trilby hat firmly positioned upon his scrawny head, a head that would draw in further with sunken cheeks and eye sockets in years to come as business moved away from cheap knock offs to hard gear, gear that Tom would get a taste for and a dependency that would be his undoing till he would one day pull his knife too slow, his reactions deadened, and he would be left to bleed out as a has been tough guy turned junkie lying pitifully alone in an alleyway.

But that was years from now. Tomorrow he would take charge under Foley, made up as lieutenant in his absence.

"Hey, you ok? You look miles away." It was Jack who had sauntered up behind him looking glum as he span round to greet him.

"I was just thinking of the time you threw up in the car park."

Jack laughed but it was half hearted. "Don't remind me."

"It was a shame Rick wrapped it round that tree, I'm guessing his gut got in the way of the steering wheel.

Fat sod! What a waste of a decent motor!" He chortled with the comment but noted he was still getting no reaction from his pal.

"I'm in court tomorrow for G.B.H., barring a miracle I'll do at least six months. I've got reason to be sad, what's your sorry excuse?"

Jack walked over to the low white stone steps that lined the wide entrance lobby of the cinema's foyer, now closed off from view with its glass doors hidden behind painted black chipboards pasted with various events and gigs of the illegal poster flyers as the entrance now served as a public notice board. Jack sat and looked up at him shrugging his shoulders struggling to find the words.

"You know this old place used to be buzzing." He'd learnt that Jack talked more if not put on the spot, that if you changed the subject to address something else then he would eventually spurt out whatever was on his mind. "I used to come here loads before they closed it down, before everyone was forced to go to the ABC. You didn't get a choice here, there was only one screen and it was massive, one of the biggest in the country I bet! There was a big stage in front of the screen but I never saw it used for anything." His head tilted up to inspect the once shining teeth of fluorescent lamps that lined the upper lip of the enormous sleeping mouth. There were plastic covered poster panels which once upon a time displayed the film posters but now were just empty white fillings to the sides, one on each wall beneath the overhang of the foyer steps where the lettering of the movie was displayed and replaced every Thursday night in time for the new showing on Friday.

As he stood with his heel swaying back and forth on

the lower of the four stone steps his mind flitted back to how as a boy he had frequented the Saturday morning club with a couple of mates from school. He couldn't remember the entrance fee because mostly his mum had paid, like with most things: swimming at the Brentford baths or catching the 65 bus over to Richmond (it had an outdoor pool and the indoor one had a diving board), or occasionally they would cross the river to go ice skating in the huge indoor rink - back in the days before they pulled it down for plush riverside housing; occasionally they would ride the 65 all the way to Chessington Zoo and hope to tag on the end of a group as they herded through the entrance. Of course if all else failed there were the shops, not for shopping, not legitimately anyhow; practising the art of sleight of hand was often done in one's or two's with the rest of the group hanging around outside ready to run - Hounslow was the usual hunting ground due to its steady line of big stores, but once in a while (when transport was available) they would make the long drive passed Wembley over to Brent Cross and run riot through the long halls of the massive complex. His mum would stump up the cash he needed just to get rid of him for a few hours, hoping it would keep him out of trouble with the gang, a tactic that was doomed to failure as the boys he'd become familiar with were of the same breed and all had picked up their ways from their fathers; it wasn't long before their rides home came in the back of flashing police cars instead of the red double decker.

Of course his mother was disappointed, not surprised by any means, but disappointed nonetheless.

Long gone were the days when they were innocent

boys, the short lived mischief they and their peers refused to abandon till much later on, but which in others of the main stream had disappeared with the grey shorts they were forced to wear in primary school; so while all the other kids their age, the boys at any rate, would be out in the street playing football or simply slamming it against a wall and waiting for the rebound, or jumping mud hills in Gunnersbury Park on their BMX's, or building wooden ramps on the pavement and hoping the small front wheel of the red Chopper didn't buckle as it awkwardly gained air beneath it as the rear of its rider left the long leather seat, hoping it would land straight and not too close to a parked car, while all these typical school boy activities played out in public a would-be gang of youths was forming and learning a different set of life skills.

He remembered the thick heavy red curtain that hung from the ceiling down to the bottom of the stage covering the screen, waiting in anticipation for its slow drawing back to reveal the black screen behind like a demon stalking a darkened room ready to flee at the flick of the light switch and the entrance of life; the projector turned on and the multi-coloured angels danced across its face till the gloom beyond was no more but a forgotten phantom, and then came the golden gong as the iconic Rank cymbal appeared on the screen and was struck and that thrill of excitement shivered through his body as he sat engrossed for the next two hours.

They usually sat at the front in the stalls on a Saturday, though often he had sat in the balcony for a main feature, especially if the place was packed. If he was with an adult he usually behaved himself, but when with the lads there was always the opportunity of launching popcorn, drinks, and all else they could think to hurl over the balcony to the audience sat below, daring each other and hoping not to get caught by the ushers and staff that sold the ice creams during the mid-film interval or between the opening short and the main feature.

He'd got to know the place quite well over the years as he and his mates worked out how to get in without paying by wedging the side and rear exit doors open and then hiding in a lower disused room in the basement (he used this often as his office, even as a pre-teen, organising his mob into various underhanded activities from his secret base). There were parts of the building that even the staff didn't know about and so he had dug in deep when opportunity presented itself and only allowed a select few into his inner circle.

By the time he'd grown older his thrill for the old cinema had been overshadowed by the draw of fitting into the gang and getting himself noticed at The King's Head. His first invite in front of Foley was nerve racking as he'd been called in for beating up on one of Foley's boys, a mistake he'd put his hands up to but in his defence explained forthrightly that the guy had deserved it as he'd been acting a dick. Foley obviously saw the potential in him, and knowing who his father had been forgave the indiscretion and allowed him to loiter in the shadow of a couple of his henchmen until he proved his worth.

He never forgot the old place though, frequenting it occasionally in the presence of a young bit of skirt he was hoping to impress, or just simply grope, in the darkness of the back seats of the balcony. It certainly wasn't the thrill of seeing the films themselves as most he'd already seen on moody copies prior to their UK release date. His heart was attached to it as part of his misspent youth clung on sentimentally to the now empty shell of the building.

He pulled his eyes away from the expanse of the black screen, allowing the red curtains to fall back into place as he drifted back to the sound of traffic on the road behind him and the rumble of a tube train passing by beneath the bridge. He clasped eyes now on Jack, his soulful friend who had sat on the third step with his back to the opening and placed the book he'd been carrying on the step below.

"What one you up to?" he said nodding down to the book.

Jack glanced down at the book with its thin book mark peeping out like the tongue of a snake from the bible sized doorstep which was only a bit thicker, according to Rooney, than what Father Canlon used from the pulpit at St. John's on a Saturday night and Sunday morning. Jack's book was furnished with a blank brown paper cover which he'd taped to it after getting fed up of people commenting on his reading material, he now found that people thought it was an actual bible he was reading and so they let him be with a confused respect for a faith he didn't seem to act out, he wasn't even a church goer like Rooney who religiously attended St John's at the weekends as he waited for his pint of Guinness to settle, being as the church was in the shadow of the flyover at the other end of the road from The Globe. Oh that road was a busy one for the likes of Jon Joe Mulrooney, what with the pub, the church, and the Conservative Club (the social men's club was another haunt of Foley's where the boys did their scheming) all on one short street, he got to commit his sins, drown his sorrows, and then plead for forgiveness in the confessional box afterwards.

Jack had tried reading the Bible itself, a couple of chapters at the beginning, Genesis and Exodus, not getting as far as Deuteronomy as Leviticus and Numbers bogged him down. He tried the Gospels and found its main character a conundrum, yet appealing in a tantalising sort of way, but as a book of history he found it unbelievable, and as a book of fiction he found it lacked logic and failed to answer many of the questions it raised in him. He accepted that had he read it more it may have drawn him to some superior conclusion that he had failed to see in having failed to read the link between the two halves of the book. He thought he had the general gist of it but found it too hard going to persist with. It wasn't until he got Rooney to lay out the basics of the book being about God and his relationship with his people that he began to realise that it was neither a wholly historical account nor a fantasy, but a spiritually inspired message of what God wanted to communicate to his people about who he was; in this he was still a little confused for Rooney said the events described were actual and not made up, and that God could speak to us through the words written within the book. This made little sense to Jack who eventually gave it up and parked it at the back of his mind with half an inclination to pick it up again at some point in the future. In the meantime he had been captured by the eloquent poetry of the bard and had pushed all thoughts of the religious from his mind so that the only deity he spoke of was the one that often rolled off his tongue in blasphemy.

"Troilus and Cressida," replied Jack.

"Eh?" He may as well have spoken another language for the words meant nothing to him. "That's a play is it? I've never heard of it. What's it about?"

"I don't know yet, I've only just started it." Then in explanation, "I only finished King Henry the Eighth last night."

There was a raised eyebrow in response, as though that made things any clearer.

Jack was an avid reader, often delving into the laborious escapism of a thick novel or a classic tale that gave his mind an outlet from the memories of his childhood and where he'd come from and what he'd done. It wasn't a conscious thing he was doing. He wasn't aware of the things his sleeping mind played on. He just knew that he enjoyed the pastime of reading and that it soothed him - the more complicated the story the better as it got his mind ticking over like a well serviced car on a winters morning sitting on a driveway waiting for the frost to thaw.

Cinema didn't hold the same fascination for Jack, even watching films on TV tended to bore him as his mind glossed over the flickering screen, and at times when he was actually captivated by it he had often felt his eyes welling up at the slightest emotional thing but had always fought it off and denied his eyes the pleasure of weeping, it was a weakness he wouldn't allow, a pit of emotion he wouldn't accept.

His first outing to the big screen had been to Ealing's ABC and he had been appalled at the long queue that formed along the side of the building. He had gone with Matt, double dating with Karen and a friend of hers, Tracey, with whom Matt was hoping to saddle him with - Jack hadn't been interested in her but had bagged her anyway, his first sexual experience outside of a prison cell proved to be a disappointment as he found he couldn't climax, in fact found the whole experience bored him - she bored him. He'd seen her a couple of times afterwards but only to placate Matt before he was finally let off the hook by Matt's suicide. In all sex was not as much an issue with him as it appeared to be with most teenage boys, something he put down to his condition: the testosterone redirected and channelled elsewhere to other lustful activities within his semi-conscious mind. The film had been Star Trek II – The Wrath of Khan, a big budget sequel to a film he hadn't seen but wasn't completely ignorant of; he had seen a number of the series from the '60's back at the bedsit and more on the communal TV before his escape. He'd been impressed with the special effects of the film but failed to engage with the characters, to him they were lacking narrative, the actors being faceless figures going through the motions where he couldn't climb into their minds to discover their thought process until the action played out on screen. This wasn't a criticism of the film itself but of the whole medium. With a book he not only got to live the action but also the motive behind it and the emotion that lingered as a consequence, very rarely had he seen the impact of this on screen and too short too was the investment in time to examine each character to see how they ticked; to him this was the attraction.

Surprisingly he cared little for crime novels despite many of the characters portrayed being tortured souls that he could relate to, although he had read plenty, along with horror which he often found disturbing yet temptingly attractive. His main staple though, the task he had set himself up for, was his ambition to plough through the complete works of William Shakespeare, and so this was the volume he was often seen carrying under his arm when not otherwise engaged in the business of *'the boys'*.

Jack often borrowed books from the library just a little walk down the hill on the Northfields Station side of the road, but his volume of Shakespeare's works was too big and laborious to get through in a loan time and he found reading just a single play was taxing enough as he often flitted back and forth from the *Dramatis Personae* as he struggled to recall which character was which in light of an absence of narrative. You could tell when he had been reading often for his west end accent that he'd adopted upon falling in with his chosen crowd would suddenly become afflicted with the vernacular devoid of his usual prose. He was after all a mimic of some talent, and so it seemed this was not restricted to the whims of personality that befell him but also transferred from the written word as he seemed able to create a character suitably proficient in life as in literature.

"So you gonna talk to me or not?"

Jack lifted his eyes up knowing that he wanted to talk and knowing that he had to do it now; there wouldn't be time later, what with the last meal of freedom for a while and the edge of crankiness that would overshadow them all tomorrow. He'd let the nonsense talk ramble on enough and couldn't avoid it any longer.

His voice cracked with a tremble of his bottom lip and a welling in his eyes as he held back what was for Jack an unnatural emotion, "I went to see my sister this morning," he said turning to the only friend he felt he could confide in.

10

It had been brooding for months, if not years, the feelings he had tried to suppress as his nightmares worsened and his mind played over what he imagined had happened to his family. He had tried hard to keep his mind occupied and distant to the facts of his own history but his life was something he couldn't escape. Jack was Jack. What had gone before was what made him the young man he was today. Even changing his name had done little to escape the reality of what lay lurking in his mind. Officially he was now Jack Walters, courtesy of forged documents provided by Dave Foley, documentation that hadn't come cheap and had taken Jack a full two years to pay back the money along with his keep; living under Foley's roof didn't come for free and nor did his protection, you paid your way or you were out and no messing.

Jack had proved his worth ten times over and made his money enough to keep Foley satisfied and off his back, plus a little extra he shrewdly squirreled away in case he ever had to flee the nest to go it alone.

The choice of name had been his own. Foley had made some suggestions but Jack wanted to stay close to his roots, wanting to have some link to the family he had lost, the family he had loved; and so Jonathan Jack Rivers had become Jack Walters. The name was far enough removed for no one to make a link and yet for him the surname was but a thought away, a play on words: River – Water – Walters. His dad had called him Jack, that was the name he answered to as a boy, that much he remembered before the cloud covered his memory and the lightning struck his senses.

It was his musing over his family, that longing for something missing in his life, something that not even the family embrace of the gang could offer him, a hole that just didn't seem to be filled that drove him with a heavy heart to overcome his pounding fear of guilt and shame of what he had done and start pondering whether there was anyone else out there, any other family members that cared. Of the wider family there was none he was sure, none that cared, none that wouldn't hesitate to call the police on the first siting of him; not that he knew how to find them anyhow. He knew, thanks to the taunting of the staff charged with his care and treatment who had abused him as a child, often provoking his feelings by chiding him with what she had become, what he had reduced her to, that she had been committed to a home for the mentally unstable, incapable of any rational thought. It was a place so familiar to the prison that he himself had called home that he pitied her for what he had done to her, for she served a greater sentence than he did; he at least was self-aware and conscious of movement and life around him, she on the other hand was but a dead star: beautiful to view in the night sky, still and motionless as the world span t its view, its long distant light giving the appearance of life as it numbered amongst those still sparkling, and yet its soul had faded years before. She was just one in a galaxy of fading lights that served no purpose in that treacle sea of insanity of the asylum, for if she had a purpose only she knew what it was as he pictured her eyes staring vacantly, trapped in a visual rewind and replay of an age long ago and a night she could never forget.

Lisa Rivers was all but dead and Jack prayed she was numb to the abuse he felt sure she faced in the hell he had placed her in.

He remembered the name of the institute where she'd been placed, it was in his file, the one he wasn't supposed to have access to but had managed on more than one occasion to sneak a peek at, reassuring his doctors with the words they wanted to hear as he convinced them it was alright to leave him alone in the room for just a moment whilst they had that quiet word outside, or answered that all important phone call, or rushed to the aid of a staff member who had hit the panic button as they struggled with another patient. Manor Hospital, in Epsom, Surrey, cared for both children and adults and was a place Lisa Rivers was destined to spend the rest of her life.

It had been an easy place to find and wasn't too far to drive. His palms had been sweating profusely as he pulled up in the car park and sat there staring at the old run down building that bore down on him with a grimace of hate ready to swallow him up should he step over the threshold. He was aware that should he be discovered this could be the end of the road for him, and for this reason he hadn't told a soul of his plans, knowing full well Foley would never let him take the risk of endangering a trusted asset and would prevent him from going anywhere near the place.

She had been on his mind so much recently as the strange emotional feelings of regret began awakening a developing conscience within him. She had been nine when she was committed, just months after her mother's death and with no other family willing to adopt her, three years older than her murderous younger brother whom she had doted on and played happily with, occasionally bickering with as any siblings of that age would. That made her twenty now. What did she look like? he wondered. It had been so long since he'd seen her, only glimpsing her in family photos taken in happier times. Was there a way he could make amends? Was there a way he could mend her suffering? Would she, could she, ever forgive him? He doubted it, but he wanted to, had to, say sorry for what he'd done to her, to them all. The guilt of it all was now burning inside of him daily, radiating in him as his own mind had begun a healing process he didn't understand.

As he gripped the steering wheel of the car legally he had no right to be behind the wheel of (but had documentation to state otherwise) he found himself crying through a mixture of fear and regret, anxiety and sorrow, tears running down his face, the first to trickle his cheek since he was a boy of six.

Knowing the dangers he'd been careful about entering the premises, following another visitor and slipping through the doors with them as though he were a part of their party. He had got quite far into the hallways peering into rooms and into communal rooms without much luck. There were patients that matched her age but didn't quite fit the image he had in his mind of her, nor could he be sure that he hadn't seen her already and simply not recognised her. There were no obvious signs stating 'Lisa Rivers is here', no medical charts that he could reach for to check easily.

There was a medical trolley loaded with medication that was doing the rounds and he was sure it would have a check list of names that went with it but the lone staff member, a female uniformed nurse, looked unrelenting in the charge of her duty and so he had retreated back towards the entrance, retracing his steps and thinking of a cover story as he went, knowing now he would have to ask questions and would be asked some in return.

In the end the information he needed had been much easier to attain than he had expected thanks to a rather chirpy and sympathetic nurse who was temporarily sat at the front desk whilst the usual receptionist took a short break. Upon mention of his sister's name the nurse had looked sad, and when told that he was a cousin that was sent to enquire of her well-being by her uncle she seemed slightly cheered that the family had finally relented their acrimony towards her, albeit too late, for it came to be that Lisa Rivers had passed on from the Manor Hospital to pastures new, having taken her own life a few years earlier.

Jack's faced drained at this news and his breath stopped short to the point where he wondered whether he would ever breathe again. Once he had grasped back his spinning head that weighed heavily from his shoulders as his knuckles bore into the frame of the receptionist window preventing him from toppling forward she took care to enlighten him with the news of her demise, a story she seemed to tell with a little too much delight as though enjoying the cruelty of it, whether in some respectful sense of imposing justice on the behalf of the departed patient so awfully abandoned by her distant family or because the insanity of the environment had rubbed off on the nurse and the glee of the tale and the pain it brought to others lit a crazy fire within her own soul, either way he couldn't tell. And either way he cared not for the nurse but for the short story she told, the story that pierced him deeper than any one of Tom Frost's blades ever could.

Lisa, his dear sister, told the nurse, had begun to act strangely a few years ago. She didn't seem to know the relevance of the year, or she purposely omitted it from her story (he suspected it wasn't the latter for surely that would have rung alarm bells as to his identity) but the date lit a fire in him immediately as the year 1982 unravelled in her tale.

Over a period of weeks and then months she had been acting very skittish and yet more alert than ever, with a growing paranoia and sleeplessness that was having an effect on her aggressiveness towards the staff. She was eventually found hanging in her room. No note was left. No family was left to inform. No next of kin called to claim her.

He added up the facts quickly in his mind as he stumbled out of the place holding back the tears and the bile that rose up from his stomach. She'd been scared of him coming after her, scared that he would come to finish her off. The story of his escape had gone largely unnoticed, but not by her. He'd scared her to death. Her blood too was on his hands.

As he reached the car he managed to hold back the vomit, and then the tears, and then much more on top as he forced the emotion back into its hiding cell, the cell that his six year old mind had created when it couldn't comprehend and so refused to accept responsibility for the consequences of what he'd done.

As he drove back to Brentford darkness overcame him. The music on the radio sounded not in his ears. The road before him was blind to his eyes. He somehow made it back home but with no recollection of the journey. He went through the motions of living, caring not for the people alongside him, nor for where he was going, nor for what he had to do. He had one friend he felt he owed it to to tell, but not because he felt a need to share his grief, but because he felt it was an end, a death to part of who he was.

He mourned her death as it tipped him over the edge into an eternal emotional abyss, his senses numbing and deadening to death itself.

Tic tac toe that's the way to go....

11

The Bees were playing at home in the Griffin Stadium but no one was really in the mood for it. The pubs were packed and the streets flowed under a sea of red and white of the team colours as shirts were worn proudly and scarves were held aloft. The police were out in force but that was never a deterrent to *'the boys'*, if anything it usually added a bit of excitement to the game, but not today. Usually it was a good day for business when the streets of Brentford turned into Oxford Street with the footfall as heavy and the doors of the pubs swinging open as often as those big overpriced central London stores. It wasn't all about dipping, there was plenty to be had in the back rooms and meets that needed to be done on a business day such as this, but even Dave Foley had no taste for it, to the point that he'd given the order for 'the boys' to go and enjoy the game - "hopefully the Bees'll win," he was heard to grumble, everyone knowing it was unlikely as they were still trailing behind again this season.

It was a day of mourning. One of their own had been banged up. Not only one of their own but one of the most respected, and they all felt it.

Jack cared little for the football so had declined the offer from Frosty to walk down with him to the stadium. Frosty was also a little fractious on account of yesterday's events and had left the house with not one but two of his favourite knives concealed about his person hoping for a scuffle in the stands. If he wasn't careful he'd end up being the next one behind bars and Foley would be none too pleased at that. Jack didn't relish the thought of two of his housemates being put inside at the same time, mainly because he wanted to steer clear of Foley's gaze and away from any role of responsibility, in fact his thoughts of the last two days had been of cashing in and moving on.

He was alone in the house, Rooney having tottered off to The Globe an hour earlier, he had no intention of going to the game either but would listen to it on the radio from the comfort of his regular spot in the pub.

To make things worse it had begun to rain. The last few days had been dry, not warm, but dry, with a slight chill that bit like a toothless hound on sleeveless arms; you grew accustomed to it until the wind changed direction and then you felt its breath as you tried to whistle it back, rubbing your arms, eyes darting for shelter.

Jack wondered how the courts would fair today, wondering whether the bitterness would spill over into vandalism. There were three in the area: the civil court along by the river, the Magistrates Court along the High Street towards Isleworth, and then there was Isleworth Crown Court. It was the Magistrates Court yesterday that had passed the twelve month sentence in the Scrubs. It could have been worse, at least it was GBH and not GBH with intent, but still even the brief had been surprised that he got a full year and not the expected six months. He'd serve his time and things would tick over without him ready for when he got out and no one but family would go and see him unless he called for them; those were the rules.

There was a knock at the door and so Jack

reluctantly rose from his chair, placing his book on the coffee table in front of him. He opened the door to a snidey looking character, short with beady eyes, thick eyebrows and gingery wedge sideburns. He wore a jumper with a green duffle coat over the top which had caught the spittle of Zeus. He had a dark complexion but Jack couldn't place his nationality, Middle Eastern? North African? He wasn't sure. Jack's steely gaze met him and the little man held it for longer than most before looking down. Jack took an instant disliking to him.

"You Jack?" came the gruff voice, no accent that he could discern, second generation he thought, maybe Greek. Jack didn't answer. "Greg Dolan. Got some mail for ya." Dolan produced a small bundle from under his coat. Jack recognised it: it was Lee's mail that had been dropped off for him at The King's Head. Lee would normally collect it himself on a Friday or Saturday but a small matter of a custodial sentence made it a little difficult for the time being. Jack snatched the mail out of Dolan's hands and went to close the door without saying a word but the little man had his hand raised to the door quickly with one foot stepping forward to brick it open should it get that far. Jack's eyes widened in anger at the man's audacity and lifted his chest and drew his arm back ready to unleash hell on the doorstep. Dolan saw it coming, not from Jack's body language which was half hidden by the door but by the look in his eyes, that unflinching desolate glare that was a prognostic of unrelenting death.

"Whoa! Hang on mate, Foley told me to tell ya..." Dolan stepped back out of harm's way seeing that he'd at least thwarted the imminent attack.

Jack's expression spoke clearly, speak or leave, but don't leave me hanging.

"I'm to move in." Dolan didn't like the reaction to that. "Not permanently, just a few days, till he sorts me out with other digs."

Jack didn't like it at all and had no qualms about letting his face show it. What was this all about? Foley, of course, it being his house, could let anyone stay here he wanted, and of course it was foolish to allow an empty room go to waste for a year while its occupant ate porridge, but it was too soon, and this guy was, well... wrong. For a start Greg Dolan he was clearly not, what his real name was he was unlikely to ever know; honest he clearly wasn't either, not that *'the boys'* were honest, but there was dishonest and there was dishonest, and this Greg Dolan was oozing dishonesty - he was a man you didn't trust with your wife, your daughter, or your cat. What the hell was Foley doing sending him here?

"Well, you gonna let me in or not?"

Jack stepped aside without saying a word. One way or another this lodging was going to be short term.

12

It had been a week since Greg Dolan, or whatever his real name was, had moved into the bedsit. He'd lasted only four days in total. Rooney had been taking bets as to who would finish him first, Jack or Frosty. Jack for his part had steered clear of him as much as possible, trusting his instant disliking for him as a poison that could erode the gang if left to fester. Frosty felt it too only he was more vocal and had on more than one occasion threatened the short Italian, for that was what he was, only showing the glimmer of his blade once as he pinned the stern nosed cheat to the wall and drew blood below his ear with a warning not to go snooping about the business of the house. He was a guest and if he wished to stay, and in one piece, then he had better keep his head down and remain unnoticeable.

It was another profitable year for the gang as they grew from strength to strength taking advantage of yet another year of uncertainty. The coal miner's strike was drawing to a close ending a period of national strikes that left a bitter taste in many of the working class. Brixton was erupting again as it burst into flames with a new set of riots which happily kept the police on edge elsewhere. Internationally there were also riots in South Africa, the Soviet Union had a new leader amidst President Regan's Strategic Defence Weapons talks, 9000 Mexican's were lost to an earthquake and a volcano in Columbia claimed 25000. Terrorism was high on the agenda thanks to a number of high profile hijacks as no mode of transport seemed safe going through the Middle East, TWA fell victim as did Egypt Air and an Italian Cruise liner, and there were some fatally bungled attempts at rescue which put the general tactics of the authorities in doubt. There was a huge buzz around the Live Aid concert that saw nearly every big name performing on both sides of the pond: Madonna, Phil Collins, Bruce Springsteen, Dire Straits, Duran Duran, David Bowie, the list was endless, and the gang bootlegged them all as they burnt copies onto both CD and cassette. In sport a seventeen year old Boris Becker won Wimbledon, Barry McGuigan was on top of his game in the boxing, and football was getting a bad rep as the Bradford Stadium fire claimed lives and hooliganism stole the headlines from too many big fixtures, both at home and abroad. Foley's boys acted as bookies for the money that was to be made on some of these bigger sporting events, the losers (of which they ensured there were many) were often referred back to the gangs loans department as the sharks moved in for the kill.

There was a bit of excitement over the Sinclair C5 but Foley wisely steered clear of the gadget exclaiming how no one was to embarrass the gang by being seen driving one along the streets of Brentford. Instead the copying business went into overdrive as VHS thrived and mass copies of Back to the Future, Rambo and another Rocky film were spooled out with the use of purpose made multi-player machines stolen from the warehouses. Not only were mainstream films doing good business but so were the pornos. Most were brought in from the West End where most of them were made with the prostitutes that littered the Soho clubs, but one or two were commissioned by Foley with the use of local talent as he branched out and increased the number of brothels that came under his control, ensuring that anyone advertising in the personal columns was contacted and informed of whose patch they were working on and therefore who they were working for. Muscle was available if needed, but most of the girls rarely needed convincing, they too saw the benefits of having the protection of the gang, and on more than one occasion a rough punter was shown the error of his ways.

Friday had come around again and business was getting back to normal, only this time Jack was taking his orders from Frosty. Frosty had sent him to The King's Head to fetch the mail. The mail was in fact addressed to a number of people, few, if any, actually existed at all. The majority of the mail was usually addressed to Lee Fletcher, the favoured alter-ego of their absent boss.

The way it came about was this: Frosty, after a heavy night out at The Queen Vic, the pub opposite The Green at the end of The High Street in Ealing, where usually on a Friday night they drew a big crowd from the live bands that performed there, had stumbled down the stairs of the bedsit gripping his hair in one hand in an attempt to hold his thumping head in place – the base beat was still echoing, bouncing off the walls of his skull like a rubber ball recharging its energy with every bounce, only the ball felt more like a heavy rock squelching the confines of his squidgy pin head, the lights firing laser beams at his eyes as he fumbled for support down the stairs, his mouth dry and bitter with a burning sensation reaching deep into the back of his throat telling him that he had thrown up at least once during the night, he didn't know where but hoped it had been in the toilet and not the bedroom. It wasn't until he'd reached the living room that he realised he was clutching a memento from the evening. "Collecting souvenirs now are we? Did she come back with you?" Rooney had asked with a smirk. And so Frosty had collapsed to the dogged sofa and allowed Fletch to snatch the handbag from him.

Inside the bag they had found very little of worth: a hair brush, a collection of used make-ups, a purse with a crumpled £5 note and 43 pence in loose change, and lastly a library card stuck back to back with a cashpoint card. The cashpoint card was in the name of 'L. Fletcher' but hadn't been signed on the back, the 'L' being for 'Louise' as denoted by the library card. The cash disappeared into his trouser pocket without a second thought and without protest from Frosty who had yet to wake enough to what was being taken from him. The bag got tossed to Rooney to discard but then an afterthought had recalled it as he dived back in for the cashpoint card which he took over to the dining table and placed next to a scrap of paper upon which he scribbled the name L. Fletcher three or four times, once satisfied with his chosen signature he scribbled it onto the back of the unsigned back strip of the card.

Later that day Frosty, being of little cheer but of mind not to argue, knowing to do so would be more bother than he could cope with, was ordered to contact 'Pilfering Phil'. Pilfering Phil was a postman that worked out of the Royal Mail sorting office in Ealing, a regular contact of Frosty's who had served well in a number of areas in the past. Having a man on the inside looking out for easy gear had helped Tom Frost stay in favour with Foley when his occasional indiscretions - the odd gambling debt or fracas which led to upset within the gang - had to be smoothed over. Fortunately Phil was, like most experienced postmen, a dab hand at recognising things that went through the postal system without having to open them first; he knew a passport or drivers licence by the envelope it was in and the bulge or flexibility as well as the senders address, a credit card would often be preceded by the pin number a few days earlier, cash (something that never made it back to Frosty) was extracted from a sealed envelope before being posted without leaving a trace of tampering, watches that were sent into Casio's repair branch were intercepted upon return to the customer, as well as a great many other things, for just about everything went through the Royal Mail in those days.

Frosty had got wind of Phil initially from Rooney who'd pricked his ears to the posty in the pub one lunchtime (posties being known for a tipple, especially after they'd shabbed their second delivery in favour of an early finish in time for pub opening - the art of 'shabbing' being to dispose of or delay delivery of mail, usually the lesser second delivery of the day). Frosty had urged Rooney not to pass on the info to Foley directly but to ensure that they kept control of the contact instead of Foley. They had agreed between themselves that anything useful was to be redirected as they chose a side, seeing the new power match in the early stages of beginning to play its first set, and Frosty was no fool, he could see which way it was likely to go eventually and knew he had to side with the winning team. He suspected Foley knew it too and for his own reasons was giving ground and letting his young challenger run with the upper hand; maybe he'd had enough and was bowing out gracefully, or maybe he was wanting the easy life and was looking forward to a villa on the Costa del Sol in that haven for ex-cons where they had their own excusive yet still powerful club and network, having left the business back at home to a trusted don to deal with all the hard work of holding everything together and making a profit, at the same time as avoiding the long arm of the law and any rival gangs; the only other option was that Foley was so arrogant to not be taking the challenge seriously enough, thinking he could swat down the young upstart at any time he liked. Frosty didn't think Foley was that naïve but liked to think that if he was Foley he'd look for the easy life; there was no point in working hard if you couldn't reap the benefits.

The new boss had different ambitions, he liked the power, he liked the brutality of it all; and he liked the flash of the cash and living the highlife from where he stood - it would be his downfall time and time again as his glamorous lifestyle would draw too much attention from the police as well as Inland Revenue. He'd do a few stretches on this account, and not just him either as he took a couple of his own team down with him (they wouldn't thank him for it, but then again they wouldn't dare speak him down in his presence either for fear of a battering); they'd still work for him afterwards and amazingly they'd stay loyal till the end, but for all the wrong reasons, for he rewarded such loyalty well as his friends reaped the benefits as the glitz of the underworld life was shared; you could often spot one of the gang's inner circle by the smug grins they wore as they swooned about in their latest straight off the forecourt BMW's wearing their tailored suits. Not that Frosty was in to all that, he still wore his trilby and his drainpipes and was happy sharing the bedsit.

Pilfering Phil, on direction from Frosty had sought out an address that could be used for the alias of Lee Fletcher. He chose a street that only went up to number 70, and then he created the address 71, ensuring that any mail sent to that address was 'killed off' as being a non-existent address. Of course no one ever missed this mail as not being delivered as it made its way from the delivery bay of a colleague to his own bay (he never stole from his own 'walk', that would be foolish, instead he would wait until his colleague had left on his delivery and then collect the undeliverable mail without being seen, and then once a week he would deliver the small bundle to the pub and be paid in kind monthly by Frost for his services). False documents had been quickly drawn up to bolster the identity of Lee Fletcher and within no time a bank account, drivers licence and various other proofs of identification were being used to scam and steal across London.

Of course Frost and Rooney's stupidity had drawn a summons of the quartet to the pub one day as the obvious pile of mail they had delivered there raised the question of what they were hiding. Coy confessions were made, but instead of the berating they were expecting they were given a nod of approval for using initiative, and so Foley himself gave the name Lee Fletcher the seal of approval.

Lee Fletcher wasn't the only name he ran by, there were other names and other addresses but for some reason Fletch was the one he used as his default, the one he usually used if he was stopped by any police officer that didn't already know him by name. Lee Fletcher was the name he adopted, maybe to shed the shadow of death that his father had left him with, maybe so he could just pretend and drift off into an imaginary life, or maybe he had a long term plan that hung on the obscurity of his own name and that of Lee Fletcher. Whatever the reason, many of the new members of his growing network grew to know him only as Fletch as his previous name was lost to obscurity.

Jack rapped on the door of the pub and was let in by Rick who grunted in his usual cheerless fashion. He was a mountain born on the side of a volcano, ugly as sin with bulging black moles dotting his face and hands, and when he blew fire erupted in pounds of flesh as streaks of lava flew from his shoulders into the villages below.

Rick had once been a boxing champion which was how he had found favour as Foley's chief henchman, not the kind of boxing that played out in a roped off ring with gloves and a mouth guard, no it was more the 'no holds barred - no rules apply' bare knuckle fights that drew big money in the deserted warehouses and side alleys of the underworld gamblers; the same cliental who bet on a dog fight expecting blood and gore would have watched Rick expecting the same, as a result the moles that lined his face were dotted like a child's sketch with haphazard scars in an untidy map of his face.

"If you've come for the mail the boss has it upstairs. He wants a word."

Rick was holding the aging terrier back by the collar,

being well used to the way if went for Jack and knowing that Jack would love an excuse to snap its neck if given half an opportunity. He clearly had no love for animals, something the dog had picked up on long ago.

Jack took in a deep breath as he pushed passed Rick and headed for the stairs. It wasn't often that he got an audience as a one to one with the boss; most of his instructions came down the chain of command to the bedsit. He wondered whether he should speak his mind about leaving, after all, he was all paid up and owed Foley nothing. If he explained the circumstances then maybe Foley would understand. His only hesitation was that he would be leaving them short and that the strong and effective team they had built up over the last couple of years would in all likeliness collapse under Frost's impetuous leadership. As he ascended the steps he quickly decided to hold his tongue unless an apt opportunity should arise.

He knocked on the door firmly and heard the strong raspy command to enter from behind the desk. He walked into the perpetual cloud of smoke that hung in the room, a Milky Way hovering above the god that had created it.

"Come in, sit down," Foley said gesturing to the leather armchair on Jack's side of the desk and tossing the mail so that he could reach it near the seat. Jack did as bade, resting back in the chair but not reaching for the mail in front of him, seeing that it would be a distraction from whatever Foley had to say. "I have a problem and I think you might be the man to solve it for me."

13

It was a test, Jack knew it was. Foley was pushing the boundaries with him trying to see how far he would go. He knew his history and knew, or at least was hoping, that Jack was capable of doing it again. It was no secret that Jack was a man with little emotion: he laughed little, cried never, and exacted violence on a command from his friend with a calm coldness that had left him monikered recently as 'The Terminator' by *the boys* who whispered it behind his back; he knew of it only because there was one bold enough and caring enough to tell him, not that he cared for the title either way, a nickname was a nickname and if he caused the sharks to paddle round the rock in the middle of the stream then so be it.

Foley saw in him something buried deep that he had tried to deny, a killer hidden deep within, seeking opportunity to be uncaged. Dave Foley had offered him a key, so long as he didn't stuff it up.

'Make it look like an accident if you can', that's what Foley had said, but when it came to it he wasn't sure he could. He didn't know how to. He had to show a body to prove what he had done, so there was no possibility of burying it and covering up the act, which he thought he could do quite easily as the target wouldn't be missed and the vicinity of the River Thames made it easy to sink a corpse, but Foley wanted evidence, not for his sake but for the sake of the business. His power had been weakening in some circles, both within the gang and without, but mostly outside of the territory, and he needed to send a signal to his challengers that he was a no messing boss still in command of his patch and prepared to take the necessary steps to protect what was his.

Jack suddenly had a reason to stay. There was something tempting in the offer placed before him. Foley for one would be indebted to him and it would levy a high regard of respect not only with Foley but within the gang. Also it elevated his position as a man with a particular skill set that was unequalled within their peer group. There were many in the gang who were capable of killing, and the gang regularly used violence to strike fear into the community to retain its position of power, some akin to the likes of Tom Frost were capable of lashing out and striking, mindlessly taking a life, not that Frosty had done so, not yet anyway, but Fletch had, was that not what he was on remand for when Jack had met him? But premeditated murder, a hit, a contract kill, he doubted any, even Foley, had the effrontery or confidence to carry it out without the panic of a trembling hand and the heart of piercing guilt and shadowing fear of capture that would follow in its wake.

'It's someone you know', Foley had said and then had fallen silent waiting for Jack to work out who Foley had in mind. Of course Jack knew, it had been obvious as soon as Foley had made his intentions known that he wanted Jack to kill someone. 'We can arrange for you to disappear for a while if need be', he had continued. Jack had shaken his head; he didn't want to be reliant on the help of anyone and would go it alone if he needed to. Foley had begun to explain why but Jack again had shaken his head, he didn't need to know.

There was a promise of payment and provision of which Jack had accepted, and then with a troubled mind he had left the pub.

Three days Foley had given him to think about it and to get back to him, one week to carry out the act. No doubt if he returned to Foley in three days with a negative answer there would be no fallout between the two but it would force Foley into seeking outside help which would further undermine the gang. Either way the hit would take place.

Jack didn't need three days to consider the hit. Had he been asked a week ago to carry out the same task his answer would have been very different, indeed he would have been disgusted by the thought, but living now in the wake of the knowledge of Lisa's death he was of a different mind-set. He may not have been an Arnold Schwarzenegger muscle bound figure in appearance but mentally he had made the robotic transfer to the cold hearted programming that befitted the character he'd been likened to.

No sooner had he left the pub than he had mentally mapped out a plan of action. He would tweak it a number of times as he made his way to the bedsit. It was a complicated matter and required much more planning than he was giving but he failed to recognise the need to slow down. He knew things could go wrong but felt an impetus pushing him forward as though fearful of changing his mind. If chance was on his side he would do it today, or at the very least he would scout out what he had in mind.

Jack had taken up jogging a couple of years ago and had made good use of the area as his well tread routes grew longer and longer. He found that he could run for miles without getting tired and barely broke a sweat as the muscles in his legs comfortably pounded the ground beneath his feet. He loved to run near water as he rarely broke a sprint, preferring a calm gentle saunter along the river, it being flat and less polluted and with an uncluttered scenery which allowed the mind to breathe. It was from this that he knew the river trails and their familiar sparsely populated settings.

As he approached the canal from the bridge just passed The Six Bells pub on The High Street, he could see the man he'd been sent to kill lurking, staring at something in the water between two barges. There would be no scouting out today, chance indeed seem to favour him. From here the barges were moored along the waterway all the way down to the Brentford stretch of the Thames, a variety of vessels of quaintly decorated colours and with endearing names printed to the bow or aft of the boats, or in some cases both; these were floating homes to a number of the local residents but to some they were just empty holiday indulgences as they sat there awaiting to chug down the river. Most of the barges rarely moved but occasionally you could glance down from the bridge as you crossed it on foot and see one edging out in an attempt to trundle down to the river. Atop of many of the narrow boats lay chairs and awnings of different types and one or two hung hanging baskets of flowers in an attempt to create a garden feel to their home. On a good day a boat owner or two could be seen moping or sweeping the deck or sitting in the sun reading or listening to the radio, but not today, today was a bad day. The rain had been falling steadily for the last couple of hours, as it had been most of the week but with a slight let up this morning hopes had risen and then been dashed as the skies opened once more. It was the opportunity he'd been waiting for and one not to be missed.

Jack descended the short flight of concrete steps that led down to the pavement next to the narrow boats, his shoulders hunched and his face buried back deep in the darkness of the green parker overcoat he wore. He walked passed the two nearest barges glancing in through the low lying windows that came up to his knees. The curtains of the first were closed but he could tell a light was on behind them but there were no signs of a waking head suddenly breaching the hatch. The second barge had clear lace nets across its windows permitting Jack an unobstructed view of ageing furniture and the nik-naks of its elderly owner lining a shelf above a paraffin heater; the lights were off and no one was at home. All was good.

The short figure of Greg Dolan stood by the aft of the black and red Lady Muck, one of the few rentals moored along this stretch. Lady Muck was owned by Caroline Devaney, a battle-axe of a woman who kept bar at The Lord Nelson which was a back street pub a two minute walk from The Globe. Caroline used the boat for summer trips into the countryside rarely and in the main hired it out to anyone trust worthy, mostly, as it turned out, to short lived bar staff seeking local digs along with the job, but only guys who she thought might turn a trick or to for the business: storage and covert river runs along the docks to the smashed up shells of old warehouses they utilised were generally required of a worthy member of bar staff. Joe Slops was the most recent occupant, Slops being his bestowed name upon his bitter tasting habit of downing the dregs in the slops bucket that collected beneath the spilt pumps of the bar. Joe Slops was today tending bar at The Lord Nelson, a fact that would keep him clear of any suspicion later on in the death of his recent lodger, Greg Dolan, who had been placed there temporarily by Caroline Devaney's cousin, Dave Foley. It was a convenient placement following his brief stay at the bedsit, one that may have lasted a tad longer had Frosty not drawn his blade to his throat forcing Dolan to seek refuge with cap in hand at Rick's feet.

Jack understood now why Dolan had been sent to stay at the bedsit; it was purely for his benefit so that he could observe the weasel and judge for himself before being given the proposition to deliver his head on a platter. He was probably a deserter from another gang, or claimed to be, and was either seeking refuge or trying to penetrate the Foley set-up to spy for information. Either way it mattered not; Foley had his reasons and Jack had his.

"Did you see that?" shouted Dolan a little louder than Jack had cared for. He had been trying to get his voice heard over the ground assault of the rain which at that moment pounded down heavier to Jack's delight. Dolan hadn't yet looked up to see who was approaching but spoke only at the sense of feet hitting the pathway to his right as his eyes stared into the dancing ripples of the murky infested waters. Jack closed the distance to ensure that the Italian's voice was lowered on his next call; it wouldn't do good for any witnesses to see what happened next.

"That was a bloody rat! A bloody biggun too!" exclaimed Dolan excitedly as though he'd never seen a river rat by the river before.

As Dolan turned to see who it was who approached Jack turned on his heels and checked the path and bridge behind him. No one was in view there. His heart was beating wildly like that of a deer fleeing with a lion hot on its heels. Nervous fear was on the verge of overtaking him when all of a sudden he subconsciously flicked the emotion switch off in his mind and with it any sense of conscience, seeing only black and white as his mind numbed and a hazy brooding cloud, much thicker than that which poured out the rain, rested over his eyes so that he only saw his target from a distracted distance yet taking in all the detail clearly. There was no conflict in him; he was cold, calculating, and precise.

A tune hummed in his ear, the words rising and repeating in his head but not enough to spill out of his mouth.

Dolan was about to say something as Jack turned on his shoulder, but he didn't get the chance. Jack grabbed the back of his head and rammed it into the corner of the barge with the force of a jackhammer. The head bounced back with a spurt of blood that was instantly splattered into droplets mingling with the rain. Jack pushed him forward so that he fell into the water but as he went Jack reached down and caught his leg and held it long enough so that it caught, with his help, in a loop of the bow line lay slack against the bollard. The line held his ankle above the concrete cliff that lined the barges, the leg audibly yanked hard out of place from the body as it plopped with a hidden splash between the two boats.

... mamma said keep the tow clean

Jack turned and walked back to the bridge. No one saw him. No one was there to see him. He stopped as he stepped up onto the main road and looked back down over the bridge. In the distance he could see the foot still attached to the bollard. There was no coming up for air.

There was no going back now. The job was done.

Flat cap snap chat.

14

"So I hear you've stepped up in the world?"

Nine months had gone by and Jack sat on the edge of the bed of the previously vacant bedroom. Nine months had changed them both. Jack had stuck around on the promise of a more specialised role; he'd been given two more jobs since he'd impressed big time with the prompt hit on Greg Dolan, both jobs having been contracted outside of the gang boosting Foley's reign and reputation among the rival turfs around London; the unspoken knowledge that a gang had a heavy hitter in its back pocket gave hesitation to anyone who wanted to take them on and gave a reassuring security to them all. As for the bulked up plinth that stood staring out of the window overlooking the back garden and the line of houses that stretched back all the way to the gates of Griffin Park, well he had grown in more ways than one. His time in Wormwood Scrubs seemed to have hardened him somewhat; he seemed more subdued than before as his heavy chest, solidly pumped, expanding the t-shirt he wore (he would need new clothes for the suits he used to wear were unlikely to squeeze round his new frame) rose with a sigh of strained thought - he was unhappy with the way things were that was obvious, he wanted to move on, or rather up.

"They let you out early; you kept your head down I take it." Jack was curious, his friend was more studious than ever, he had the mind-set of one who had decided not to return to a cell but was long scheming a future that was likely to lead him back there.

"Oh I don't know about that," he said turning with a wink and a smile. "I worked out and made some friends."

"I can see that," Jack chipped in eyeing his muscular body up and down.

"It's different in there than in youth detention," he remarked seriously, "they can be bastards in there."

Jack decided not to pry, whatever had happened was likely to have been humiliating. They all knew what went on inside, they all joked about it, but this was no joking matter. He had gone in little more than an arrogant youth with good looks and an attitude of authority that held no sway on the locked down wings of the secure prison, where the rules were set by long term inmates more vicious and violent than anything the streets of Brentford had to offer; he had come out a man, broken and scarred with the lessons beaten into him behind bars.

There was a new gravitas in the demeanour of both men; they were no longer boys, but hardened men, criminals that, in their own way, had crossed a threshold of no return and going back to a life of normality and boyish innocence was no longer an option.

There had always been a concern, a grating from the older more established members of the gang long time loyal to Foley, that they resented taking orders from one so young and arrogant, and some had questioned Foley's motives on this, but Jack, staring at his friend now, suspected that time would now come to pass and that even Foley himself may shudder at the fierce determination in those eyes.

There was a hierarchy within the gang that hid what

was really a collection of sophisticated animals trying to avoid conforming to the natural order of things in the concrete jungle of their environment.

There were the monkeys: most people fitted into this category as they stood or sat observing passively, hanging in their trees whilst the traffic of life passed by beneath them, ready to jump out of the way if the action got too close but quick to trail along with the crowd to be able to say that they were part of what was happening if it was good or to deny witnessing a thing if it was bad; they came in all shapes and sizes as the Spider and the Squirrel stood side by side the Tamarins and the Patas and the Colobus; in the pubs cried the Howlers, silenced often by the meaty Drills while the Chimps laughed and chatted and the Gibbons swung with liquid fluidity and the Orangutan slumbered drunkenly in a corner somewhere.

There were hyenas that raced to and fro taking advantage of those already downtrodden and snapping their jaws with a cruel bitter chuckle at the torn pieces of flesh left behind by the elephants and rhinos, the meaty heavyweight bulldozers of muscle who slowly stomped on command, the rhino's bashing in doors while the elephants bashed in heads. Between them all were the birds riding atop all who would dare have them, flitting from tree to tree chirping a high pitched tune and often crying on the shoulder of the beasts they swooped on, attracting sympathy and attention by picking at the food in their teeth and pampering any that would protect their disloyal flight.

Then there was the pride, the lions of the gang, only in this pride no females went out hunting, though many were laid as young and old males competed for the role of alpha male and king. But there was only one king, and to him all others were but mutton unless some affliction of family bond or loyal commitment commended a more forthright place at his feet. From his den he ruled, and from his den he sent all others out.

Dave Foley's reign was coming to an end and he knew it. There was a younger challenger to the throne whom he himself had groomed and nurtured, knowing that one day this boy would come for his seat – and that time was drawing near as he made his own preparations to step aside and retire to finer climates.

In the bedsit on Windmill Lane a young lion and a beast that was hard to describe, a mythical creature part Minotaur part chameleon part viper, sat and discussed a plan between them to overthrow the rule of the gang.

15

It was five years on, the year 1991, and little had changed in the arrangement of the bedsit except for its occupants. Fletch had moved out to grander more luxurious accommodation in a house further up the Windmill Road where he could straddle the boarder lines of the business across the Brentford/Ealing divide. He had shacked up with Samantha, a red head he'd befriended and subsequently rescued from a women's refuge after they'd gone hunting her wife bashing husband for a gambling debt he owed Foley; like many a victim of domestic abuse Samantha held a typical 'victim' mentality that had been ingrained in her from a constant battering down of her self-confidence, something that Fletch had taken advantage of as he kept her at his beck and call around the house fulfilling his domestic needs. He had other women, they all did, and there wasn't too serious an attempt to cover the fact; the women were an unnecessary distraction, certainly to Fletch and Jack, and not the biggest thrill in their lives as it were for others who thrived on the abundance of sex and porn that the power of their position bestowed.

Rooney too had moved out, this following an altercation with Frost two years previous when Rooney's liquid tongue had spoken out of turn in the presence of Rick in The Globe about a secret hoard of marijuana plants Frosty had been growing in the loft of the bedsit; the plants were young and as yet to make a profit and so Frost's investment was lost when word reached Foley that one of his houses was about to be turned into a cannabis factory, and so Tom Frost was forced to go grovelling to the big boss for leniency. Mercy granted, Frosty then took out his anger and frustration on the Irishman in a blazing row, the language of which could have sparked an explosion. From that moment on the atmosphere in the house had been tetchy at best and Frosty had remained, well... Frosty.

The incident had fractured, but not broken, the working relationship diverting the natural movement of events as the four friends began to move on in life. Fletch and Rooney now had their own pads, although Rooney had simply swapped one bedsit for another as his profits were always sunk behind the bar leaving him little with savings for a place of his own; to say he had an increasing drinking problem would be an understatement. Jack maintained his room at the bedsit, however he stayed there fleetingly as he travelled far and wide as he took on recondite tasks, occasionally for Foley but mostly for private contracts as his reputation built up and he devised a pattern of working: observe the subject, plan out a course of action, make it look like an accident, make sure it couldn't be traced back. He was trying to be smart and refused to tell a soul of any of his activities, even Foley daren't ask where he kept disappearing to. He figured that if he didn't tell anyone of the hits and made them look like accidents then there would be no one to dob him in; unless he screwed something up there was little chance anyone would suspect foul play.

And so Tom Frost had found that on most days he was left with the run of the house. He still grew a few plants up in the loft figuring that there was no one around to flap their tongue in Foley's direction. He tried to make the crop small so that the smell didn't filter out too far as it was easy to distinguish its sweet odour if you were familiar with it. He sold mainly to teenagers using the swimming pool, loitering at the front of the library before it and exchanging there so that he could see all incoming traffic and keep the transactions hidden behind the bushes that edged its garden where the boys would lock their bikes as he himself had done as a child. He remembered as a scrawny child riding there and parking his own pushbike outside before heading inside the swimming baths and dive bombing at the deep end with the closed blue shutter doors of the changing rooms lining the pool on either side, girls to the right and boys to the left, a widths length between the two sets of teeth with a rope of floss slapping the saliva separating the lapping floaters from the larking lingerers.

Although many bands had been and gone over the last few years Tom Frost, who reluctantly shifted away from vinyl to cassette so he could transport his favourite tracks out to the car with him (CD's not yet a standard feature in most cars), was also reluctant to move away from his Rude Boy image, still looking a disciple of the Two Tone Ska era and still playing The Specials, Madness, and The Beat loudly throughout the house uninterrupted as Foley left the two vacant rooms empty, presumably with some future designs on selling the place, although Foley suspected that the old man was just losing interest and was running various ends of the business into the ground. His drawn gaunt appearance along with his dated clothes and his tendency to loiter in the vicinity of the young gave him the appearance of a nonce, a predatory paedophile, rather than the hardened drug dealing criminal that he was; yet in his steadily absent awareness of all things around him and the lapse of judgement and common sense that was robbed of him by his growing taste of his own merchandise, he seemed blissfully unaware of how he came across to others.

A new war was raging as the Iraqi's invaded Kuwait. As ever war was a good distraction and kept people fearful and on edge, gossiping about the maybe's of what could happen and how it could affect oil prices and trade, and the bottom line of how much cash they had in their wallet. The wars raging overseas were no different to the war *'the boys'* perpetrated on the streets: it was all territorial and geared at controlling the assets of the region, only on the streets it wasn't oil but the small time commodities of back street peddlers. There was plenty to distract as the capital was still reeling from the Poll Tax riots. New business interests for the gang were computers and handheld games and the usual moody copies of films such as Terminator 2 and The Silence of the Lambs, along with soft pop tracks by Whitney Houston, Brian Adams and Phil Collins. Guns and Roses featured big but not as big as Queen would later in the year when Freddy Mercury bowed out the day after announcing he had Aids. The biggest music tracks to profit the gang though were the underground club tracks that fed the nightclubs, heavy beats that bellowed out from car speakers and many a teenage boys bedroom to the annoyance of ageing parents who didn't understand the attraction of repetitive drum and bass and the synthesized tuneless echo that appeared to exist without the need of vocals. The gang actively sought out up and coming local talent to feed into the genre as they set up a recording studio to ply the clubs and try to reap a profit from the sales; if they were really lucky one or two tracks might even brake from the dance charts into the mainstream (albeit with a substantial radio edit).

There was plenty happening worldwide but much was lost on the gang. Jack knew more of international politics and the decline of the Soviet Union as various states declared their independence, and then there was the release of Terry Waite and Terry Anderson from Lebanon. Jack's new found knowledge came in the guise of a new employer that had tracked him down and recruited him into the fold. It was this new employer that peppered his passports in ink as he adopted a montage of personalities as he became he characterised the people he dreamt up so that it was rarely the real Jack that got to carry out his assigned tasks. It was this new employer that would eventually lead him away from running with the gang as he embraced his true calling as a highly paid and reliable international hitman.

It was a James Conway who had approached him covertly for MI6 as a dispensable and expendable commodity. Of course MI6 had their own people so Jack had cottoned on quite early that not all the affairs Conway passed his way were legitimately authorised, this became all the more apparent as Conway in turn gave him over to an unofficial handler, somcone who was not on the government pay role: Derek Wahabi, a powerful and influential man, an Arab who had inherited his father's fortune, money that ran black like a thick flowing river. Wahabi seemed to have no end of contacts and influence and resources at his disposal though Jack couldn't understand the link between Wahabi and Conway, and in truth cared little for it. It hadn't taken Jack long to prove his worth having had his practice in the amateur realms of London's underground syndicates. He was no Jeffrey Dahmer but he did think the success to being a serial killer was not to let anyone think there had been a murder.

I wasn't here, it wasn't me
Look away then count to three
The guy you saw you'll soon forget
A face in the crowd you've never met.

I only held the bag, I didn't go in
It wasn't my idea, it's not my sin
The priest he'll tell ya I'm no mug
I'm no thief and I'm no thug
Just take a breath, keep shtum, keep calm
My feet'll run faster than you can raise the alarm

I wasn't here, it wasn't me
Just look away then count to three
(one two three)

Frost nodded upwards a greeting as Jack was pushed inside the bedsit with a gust of late autumn air that threatened to down the garden fence for the second time in as many weeks.

"Where is he?" asked Jack without a greeting to the wiry fellow before him who stood with a spliff in between his fingers.

"At the club," came the reply as his head bobbed to the loud vinyl track that he felt symbolised his life in the gang. "I see Robert Maxwell fell off his yacht!"

Jack didn't reply. Frost was fishing but was to get nothing for his efforts. Whether he completed the job on the tycoon or not would be something no one would know, but if Frost continued his foolish snipes and digging into things that didn't concern him then Jack had no qualms about adding him to his list of loose ends to be snipped off.

Jack placed his overnight bag in his room and then slipped out of the house sensing that the damage done between the four of them had wider implications on the gang as a whole, something he cared less for as the years went by yet still felt a bond of debt to his friend who had remained constant throughout.

The club was now the centre of Fletch's operations. Everyone called him that these days as though his parents had bestowed it on him at birth – Lee Fletcher being his Mr Hyde, his other persona through which he could encapsulate his sin and crimes and become that which did not exist and disappear and appear upon will, but to whom he had unwittingly become without notice or realisation until it were too late and had consumed him, not that he was unsure he had not willed it all along, unlike the unfortunate Jekyll; indeed he fought little of the gradual transformation that had become him since he were a wayward child.

The club was no longer the snooker club, although it was still owned by Foley and run under his command. Fletch now had moved his new *network* to the Top Hat. It had taken him an age it seemed to secure the finance and had to bribe the council planning department to fight off the plans to build a supermarket on the site, but eventually he had achieved his goal: the old cinema was his, his first step in a branch away from the establishment of *'the boys'* as he went head to head with his old mentor, not that publically they were rival gangs for Foley still accepted him as one of his generals, knowing the time to step aside was nearing ever closer.

Jack sauntered up to The Top Hat, its black and white sign adorning the top of the entrance where the black lettering of the movies used to show. He walked around to the side entrance and was let in by Clive, a huge brick shit-house of muscle, impervious as a tank and darker than the unlit stairwell he protected. There were a number of black guys in the new outfit, mostly hired in muscle who kept door at the various clubs and pubs, they with the others were of great custom to the horse steroids that were allowed to filter through to the bodybuilders and their gym contacts as the control of drugs and their own suppliers was regulated from the top. All the doormen wore suits, not cheap ragged things but smart black to mirror the boss' designer cut which he liked to wear. He didn't want to look scruffy in his command as he tried to separate himself from the gang Foley had set up, the suit making him feel powerful and in control; he wanted his staff to echo this as a professional operation, not the backroom smoke haze of a cave that the overweight Rick stood guard over, and there were no dogs here either, not that Jack had to contend with Rick's Staffy anymore as it had barked its last and been put down, sadly without Jack having to raise a finger against it.

Clive stood aside allowing Jack to descend the stairs

that led into the bar area.

"He's in the flat," Clive informed him, knowing who Jack was here to see. Jack nodded without saying a word.

Jack marvelled at how much work had been done on the place. The bar had been up and running before he left a month ago but even more had been done to the place since then. All the old red flip down chairs from the cinema had been removed to clear a space for the dance floor in front of the stage where now housed a bar at either side with seating in the middle. Under the balcony was a bar island with seating all around, a doorway led back out towards the main foyer which served as a separate function room with its own dance floor and restaurant, and upstairs on the balcony was another seated area that served as a restaurant come gathering quarter for the gang with TV's showing the sport hanging from joists above; it provided a good vantage point of the crowd and the activity whilst the club was in full swing.

Jack meandered through all this as though a ghost in motion. People looked at his pale features and dark attire and looked away frightened. They knew who he was and knew what he was capable of, though few had ever seen the effects of the damage he could cause. Even the most hardened of the gang were fearful whenever he showed his face unannounced in case it meant someone somewhere had crossed a line and upset the establishment.

He passed through the balcony and pushed open a door marked 'private' and ascended another flight of stairs. These stairs led to the flat, a home from home and a refuge for their leader away from a domestic life that was doomed to failure, it was a place where he could do as he wished knowing he was protected by those who marshalled his coveted walkways. He'd sunk a lot into this place, probably more than he could afford as he kept secret his personal layout and what he still owed on the place. He used every hidden room he knew off to the purpose of his business, and if the police came a knocking he was prepared; they could hide things in seconds, and if it came to it he had a secret way out from the flat.

There was a white brick of a telephone sat next to the white powdered residue of what had been a line of cocaine on the glass coffee table in the middle of the living room of the flat. A slim Chinese girl no older than eighteen and scantily clad in one of Fletch's long shirts which barely covered her bare thighs rose from her knees as Jack entered and the esteemed owner stood to his feet doing up his flies and his shirt buttons with a smile on his face. He gave a sideways glance to the girl and she scuttled off to another room out of sight.

There was a moment's pause to ensure they were alone and then the two men stepped forward and embraced in a short manly hug. When they parted Jack looked down at the coffee table but said nothing.

"I don't indulge in that stuff, it's for the girl − breaking her in," he said with a smile and feeling the need to explain himself to his visitor.

"I'm not judging."

"It's been a while," he commented on Jack's absence. The statement was posed questioningly but without expectation of a reply − he got none. He looked at the fresh scar on Jack's neck that began high up on his left cheek; it was healing but it would forever be with him. "Thanks for coming. I need your help with something."

"So I gathered from your message."

"There's a little situation that needs clearing up." Jack nodded. "But Foley doesn't want you to handle it." Jack raised an eyebrow and cocked his head. "He wants me to do it."

16

"How'd you get sliced?" Foley had asked as the boys stood silent in his office. Every man in the room no matter how old the age felt as a schoolboy summoned to the headmasters office following a classroom misdemeanour.

The three of them stood in the dock before the great desk sucking in the rancid air of their chieftain's breath.

It was Frost who needed to do the explaining, it had all been his fault after all, but he was spared by the sense of leadership that rose up next to him. Jack too fell silent, allowing his friend to place his feet in the boots he longed to fill.

"There was a scuffle in The Beehive after the match, guv, we all stepped in."

"Who drew blood first?" asked Foley snarling with disgust at the disfigured form of one of his soldiers. Jack had spent a night in hospital and had managed to give the police the bum steer when questioned about events by claiming he had been an innocent bystander caught up in the fight, something they no doubt didn't believe but had no evidence to contradict his story. Even beneath the maroon stained padding it as obvious there was a long gash on his face that would scar in time.

"They did," came the reply. It was the sort of reply that required further testament but none was forthcoming. None of the three wanted to offer up that the away supporters, who were part of a rival gang from

White City, had made themselves unpopular in the pub as they purposely tried to provoke a fight after Saturday's match against the home team at Griffin Park. The three of them hadn't been present to begin with but had been sent for by others when things began to look like they would get out of hand. They had gone in cautiously hoping to give a polite warning or two to the visitors of the decorum expected and to hopefully avoid any trouble, but as they entered one of the rivals had pulled a short flick-knife which raised the blood of Frosty. The knife had only been pulled for bravado and not for use but Frosty impetuously failed to realise that as his hand whipped round to the back of his trousers and with lightning speed withdrew and span open a butterfly knife twice the size of the opposing blade, which he then languished low and cocky for all to see like a flaming torch holding back a brood of hissing vipers at his feet whilst shouting a torrent of abuse at those opposite him. All were so captive by the show of flashing steel and vehemence in Frosty's tone that none had noticed that they had walked into the pub entrance by way of the crowded end occupied by their adversaries. As such Jack hadn't noticed the drooling bloodlust of the figure to his right until the beer bottle broke across his face.

All had gone black for Jack at that point as he slumped to the ground concussed and bleeding and the fight ensued around him. The battle was done and won in minutes as the outnumbered visitors were beaten black and blue with whatever the local boys could find, many of whom were unrelated to the gang. Blood was spilt on both sides but nothing fatal had come of it; each side had its wounded to attend to as both sides limped away before the police could arrive to attempt a round up. Two had gone to hospital: Jack and the one who had bottle him, Frosty had seen to him with a facial decoration of his own, not to mention the fractured ribs and broken arm inflicted by Fletch.

It could all have been avoided of course, but there was no point dwelling on it now.

Foley sat still in thought, knowing the situation was bad and that a lesson had to be taught to the other gang; he couldn't have them invading his patch and cutting up any of his guys, let alone one of his main guys; respect had been lost and respect had to be hammered back home. An immediate retaliation would only spark a gang war, and that was something he wanted to avoid.

"The one who did that, he was the other one in hospital?"

"Yeah, I took care of him boss," piped up Frosty a little too eagerly with too much of a relish of good cheer in his voice.

"So he's dealt with. Jack, are you happy with that?"

Jack nodded. He wasn't happy, not with the vengeance which he didn't get to enact, nor with Frost who had caused it and then robbed him of it.

"Very well. Leave it with me. It will be dealt with at another time. I'll send word to Rutledge to make sure his boys stay away or else." There was silence once more as they waited to see if that was all there was to be said. "Go on, get out of here," Foley barked as he dismissed the three.

The fight at The Beehive had been back at the beginning of summer and the scar on Jack's face had since had time to blend into his flesh with character.

It was another test; they both knew it but daren't say it. Foley was getting ready to roll over but before he did he had to ensure that whoever he handed the baton onto had the balls to do what was necessary.

There was an order to things, a procession of events that had to be fulfilled, something regal in its tradition of proving ones honour and might, something that kings of descent were ignorant of on their ascent up the ladder of enthronement.

Everyone had their place within the gang but everyone also knew that your place was decided upon whose faction of the gang you sided with. Rooney had likened the gang and its splinter network to David and Saul, with the latter set in his ways and growing bitter at seeing the uprising of his people siding with his favoured general who'd befriended his son. If this was so, who were to play the son? Rooney had suggested it be Jack who would don the mantle of Jonathan, he whom had often stepped in to parley on his friend's behalf. Jack certainly had grown into that beloved position of brotherhood held dear by his leader, even if it were to be for but a short while.

None of them held much for Rooney's drunken ramblings, which had worsened with age and the deterioration of his brain cells as his main food supply supplemented more alcohol in his system than blood. Still this hadn't ceased his discourse as he went on a confused holy rant to compare the gang to that of Christ's apostles, placing their enigmatic leader as Jesus and Jack as John his beloved friend, and himself as the loud mouthed Peter; jokingly he had placed Tom Frost in the role of Judas Iscariot, little knowing how significant his role would be to the downfall of their reign.

Even in his drunkenness Rooney knew his theology was a little more than skewed and his hypocritical stance on his religion was showing through his lack of understanding his blasphemy. A proud evangelist of the gospel he was not, but fortunately his confused words fell on deaf ears anyhow, for their message to the masses was far from the intentional evangelistic mission manifest of the twelve disciples, rather it was more akin to Satan's battle order than to God's, and they were less preachers and healers and more battle hardened and ruggedly vicious, more in the mould of David's mighty men; indeed they were in number closer to that lofty king's 300, yet shared the commonality in that they were all followers of grand figureheads of notoriety, some greater than others. It wasn't lost on Rooney (in his more sober moments) that Dave Foley's gang in its entirety were more on a par with the fortunate Barabbas and his zealot minions, running riot and causing a disturbance beneath the nose and authority of the Roman police force, quite in contrast to the holiness that had inspired and captured the generations that followed the great King David or the King of Kings who had taken Barabbas' place on the cross.

The theology of it all was too much that any of them could fathom in their ignorance of the scriptures, so they satisfied themselves with simply labelling Foley as Saul and Fletch as David, championing their victors army to the field, but when it came to calling to Barabbas or Jesus, even Fletch felt the discomfort of disrespect and drew a line against the blasphemy that was beyond his comprehension.

In all minds though, a time would come when Foley would be replaced and the new King David would sit on his throne. They all expected him to stand aside rather than be killed in battle.

Neither of them knew why Foley had chosen now to enact revenge on Alan Rutledge, he was sure to have his reasons. It was a long overdue lesson in respect that needed to be taught, but it was one that would be a tough one to carry out.

Killing to Jack had become common place. He cared not for the people, not for who they were or who they could be. He cared not for their family, nor did the pleading of their souls attach itself to him at the very last. He was bereft of emotion, unable to give himself to anyone in love. He could fake it for sure, but that's all it was, it pinned itself none to his heart.

Through all this Jack knew that his friend would struggle, for he had seen it in others that the killing was easy, living with it afterwards was the hard part. This was not to be an accidental death on the part of his friend, this was to be intentional, and for the message to get through it had to look intentional.

He checked his senses and felt it right. He had always relied on his senses, feeling when things were right or not; it had kept him out of trouble on more than one occasion, failing him only once, that one time leaving him scarred. He had known rushing to The Beehive had been a bad idea and had said so much as they'd run passed the police station next door to the pub. If he had listened to his senses then they would not be in the predicament they were in now, but the flow was right; he sensed no tension going against the grain, but if something were to block their path he would pull his friend out without hesitation. If the scar on his face had taught him nothing else it was to listen to his instincts and follow natures flow.

'Uneasiness is an instinct and means warning.' It was a quote from a Bram Stoker story, he couldn't remember which one, not that it mattered. His mind was good for remembering the fine details that mattered and that sparked his intellect and served a purpose, if only to him; all else was insignificant, like the stories themselves that he'd purged from his mind after having bled them dry from the library of the detention centre, remembering only what he needed. Oh, they had taught him well, a little too well maybe.

"Do you have a plan for this?" asked Jack of his friend who was reaching for the big buttoned square phone sitting on the coffee table, he pulled the cord knocking something off the breakfast bar that separated the kitchen from the room they were in. A head popped out from the bedroom as a swathe of long straight black hair swept round to see what the noise was. She was waved back inside the room and obediently complied. Numbers were punched and eventually a ringtone could be heard on the other end.

"Rick, can you set up a meet with Rutledge. Tell him I'm interested in that pub he can't shift on the Goldhawk Road. A private meet, yeah." Both parties hung up and the wheels were set in motion.

17

It was to be a short meeting. Jack had suggested the date for his own reasons.

"I don't know whether I can do this in cold blood."

Rick made a grunt at the comment and Jack turned in the car to catch the smug grin on his face.

"Don't give him the satisfaction," Jack retorted. "If you don't do this it's all over and you know it. You'll never be able to hold onto the club or anything else."

Fletch took a long hard nervous drag on his cigarette and then opened the car door flicking out the butt as he climbed out.

There were a couple of loud whizzes behind them as they walked across the road to the pub followed by cracking blows above a second later. The sky lit up in colour sparkles momentarily as Jack sized up Rutledge's driver parked solo in the broken brick laden car park. He made sure they made eye contact; it was a fearful signal, one that the driver wouldn't recognise till later when he reflected on his need to remain silent about what he had seen.

"Once we're through that door there's no going back. If you walk into that room without a serious proposal for the place he'll know what's going down and he'll be walking out and you'll be carried out in a bag."

The three of them stopped walking as the head man took courage and sucked in a breath, expelling it with a forward foot as his two companions followed him to the back door of the pub.

November 5th, Guy Fawkes Night, not that anyone ever cared about the penny-for-the-guy these days; kids didn't bother with it, most probably couldn't tell you the history of the event and what they were celebrating at any rate. All they cared about was where to get the latest and cheapest rockets and sky-bombs from the growing collection of shops that specialised in over the counter display fireworks. There was now not one night that lit up the sky but a selection of weeks as the period blurred into Diwali, the Hindu festival of lights, rolling ever closer towards New Year as the all too easily available fireworks were lit almost daily into the late hours with a lull on the run up to Christmas.

Fireworks – that's what it was all about now, not the families gathered round the bonfire to expensively entertain the little'uns with their 'oooh's' and their 'aaah's', all the family getting together on the night itself. It wasn't even about the youths reeling off the latest daring rocket pack from the estate playground or side street, hoping and laughing about the destruction that it could make if it struck a car, moving or still what did it matter so long as they moved quick enough not to be caught. Nor was it about the displays; the organised groups that spent thousands to light up the sky with their DJ's playing and their burger vans feeding the hungry as they stood around in the cold waiting for the official lighters, the organisers hoping that all would go smoothly and that the St. John's Ambulance crew on hand wouldn't be needed after all, their minds still reeling at the lengthy risk assessment that they had to complete on the run up to the event and the slightest hitch meaning that next year's event would be in question. No it wasn't about any of these things. What made this night special was plain and simple, it was the bangs. Something Jack Walters was highly attuned to.

He was sure he wasn't the only one of a criminal persuasion that took advantage of the fracas and audio chaos that confused and petrified the household pets and would-be guard dogs. Burglars he was sure planned their evening's nocturnal activities around the prime booming hours as those out at a friend's display or public event were obvious by the lack of sparks flying; yeah ok, maybe there'd be a few that would be grouch to the occasion and stay in and avoid the whole shebang, and if their doors or windows went in then 'oops', you'd kinda hope for a quick getaway. But either way it was a night for chancers and planners alike, and the opportunities were plentiful if you had a target in mind.

Bodies would never stay laid in situ for long obviously, another reason why Guy Fawkes Night was a winner – move a body and pretend it's your Guy, prop a body on a bonfire and, yep you guessed it, pretend it's your Guy. The smell of burning flesh was unmistakable but fortunately the wafting choke of smoking fireworks was also overwhelming, clouding the air adequately enough to disguise even the worst of the unpleasant odours created. Yep everybody (except the victim) liked Bonfire Night, or Fireworks Night, or Guy Fawkes Night – whatever you wanted to call it – Jack had his own name for it: 'convenient', it was growing to be one of his favourite nights of the year.

Jack was there for support only and to calm his friend's nerves and coach him through it, which he had done with great sensitivity. Rick was there to observe on Foley's behalf, to ensure the job was done properly, and not by Jack. They expected Rutledge to bring an entourage, which Jack was poised to fend off, but as they entered it seemed he was comfortable in the shell of the old decomposing brickwork of the abandoned pub, closed down by the council and the police for drugs and the continual onslaught of violence it brought to the area. Rutledge was so keen to be rid of the place that he jumped at any serious offer of selling the place and had been completely taken in by the ruse of Foley's champion and heir looking to expand his kingdom; it was after all no secret that he was vying for power over the gang.

He attended with only one other: Rutledge's personal bodyguard whom Jack had never laid eyes on before but whose stature and demeanour had been described to him. He was a brute of a man who wore a fresh scar above his left eye and into his scalp; the scar was the same age as the one Jack wore. Jack turned to his friend, their eyes meeting in a smile that only they could read.

There was a silence in the room as they each settled into a confrontational position in the room with a bare plain formica table in the middle across from which sat the foreboding figure of Alan Rutledge. Rutledge sat in an orange plastic bucket seat, a similar empty one waited opposite for the negotiations to begin. He was a stolid man without doubt, not so much in comparison to Jack but enough to be disconcerting to anyone trying to read his intentions and enough to give any man willing to do him wrong cause for second thoughts and to bow out from the room gracefully. He was an aging ex-rugby player with shoulders as broad as the posts and a jaw as straight as the cross beam. His eyebrows overshadowed his eyes which peered forever upwards out of sunken sockets so that only the slim section of white could be seen within the pit of murk.

If Rutledge was big then his bodyguard was a titan, a gorgon released from the depths by Poseidon to unleash terror on an unsuspecting community. No doubt he had done just that until he had been tamed by the god he now served. Jonas was his name; they knew it well by reputation and by encounter. Frosty had been lucky with the swiftness of his blade to have left such deep a scar of so formidable a target. Jonas was a man who would not, on any ordinary day, go down easily and no doubt had designs of his own on payback for his wounds.

Rutledge placed his hands palm down on the desk and waited.

There was hesitation to Jack's left, he could feel it. This was not going to go well.

Tic tac toe...

Rick stood by the door guarding it in case anyone tried to come in and disturb the activity, but also to prevent anyone from leaving prematurely.

...they're all broke

Don't take the cake...

'Toe the line soldier boy! Don't choke up now!' screamed Jack silently.

Rutledge turned his palms face upwards in an obvious show of impatience. They were only moments away from being rumbled. It was now or never.

Hands gripped the back of the empty orange bucket seat and for a moment the figure attached swayed back and forth with a nervous anxiety dripping from his brow. A hand pulled back from the chair and reached behind him barely feeling the gun that Jack had provided him, not knowing what make or model it was or even if it was loaded but trusting his friend to have seen to it that it was. When his hand pulled forward the gun was levelled at Rutledge's forehead, the shot ringing out before he had a chance to hesitate further and before Rutledge had a chance to lift his open palms in defence, his eyes widening slightly as his head rocked back as the bullet entered through a tiny hole and exploded in a spray that painted the wall behind.

The gun was still levelled horizontal over the desk, smoke wallowing from the barrel, a slight shake but barely noticeable. Jonas was slow to react, so unsuspecting had they been. He fumbled inside his jacket but Jack was too quick, he'd been waiting in preparation as his own gun pulled wide from his side holster and fired to the chest to stop him in his tracks, bringing him to his knees. Jack then stepped forward relishing the moment.

"Do you believe in an afterlife?" he asked solemnly before raising his gun to the trembling bleeding figure before him who clutched unbelievingly as the blood oozed through his fingers from the hole in his chest. A cold sweat dripped down the edge of the pale grime scuffed temple below the ruffled hair that was pulled back in a fist so that his chin was elevated for his eyes to stare down the barrel. But they refused, ignoring the hard steel by defiantly shooting bullets of their own into the eyes before him. The answer to the question never came, it was never truly expected, and no time was allotted for it as the second shot rang out from Jack's gun splaying blood across the beads of sweat as the head hung loose in the fist that now held it from the ground. The eyes were defiant to the end but even there the light of the titan grew dim.

They didn't dispose of the bodies, there was no time. Even if the driver in the back car park hadn't recognised the noise of the gun shots there was a good chance he had witnessed the flash from the guns through the thin veiled window. Their only hope of escape was to boldly march out with their heads low but glaring at the driver, who took the hint and quickly made his escape as the three headed to their stolen car parked across the street, Fletch automatically reaching for his cigarettes with shaking hands he felt barely able to control.

The bodies lay undiscovered for a number of days, the driver having vanished of his own volition. The record of a meeting had been made but by the time the police came knocking all tracks had been dusted off and reliable alibis that had been planned out in advance were firmly put in place.

Jack thought back to his first contract kill: how long ago it seemed that he had drowned Greg Dolan, and how easy it had been – it had surprised him, together with that feeling of unimagined power as when a teenager steps into a car and takes the wheel for the first time. But for his friend it had not been such a satisfying experience.

"I've not shaken like that since my old man bought a ticket to the devil's show of dancing flame," joked the tired looking shooter as they sat in the back of the car on the way out of Shepherd's Bush.

"Don't worry, the dead travel fast!" he had tried to reassure him in his own quirky way. It was a quote from a book, a largely forgettable one, however that line had stuck.

"Why'd you ask him? It's not like you care."

Jack hadn't expected the rebuke from his friend who seemed disgusted at his taunting of his victim before putting the bullet in his head. Jack just shrugged in response, he wasn't sure himself why he sometimes questioned his victims before he ended their existence, maybe part of him deep down wanted to know for himself whether there was anything else there, whether there was anything else to live for.

Rick dropped them off at The Top Hat that night without hanging about for any pleasantries, he seemed wary of hanging around the two murderers for he was now guilty by association.

When they had reported back to Foley the next day Rick had opened the door with a visibly new respect of the two men, nervously stepping aside and politely escorting them to Foley's office with an almost grovelling nervousness. Foley himself said little but his tone was low and resigned. He ended their brief meeting with a nod, a confirmation that this meeting was the last and that he would step aside at long last.

The two friends, the young gang boss and the hitman, retired to the club and the privacy of the Olympian flat to plan out the future of 'the network' where a bottle of whiskey was cracked open, the first of many.

18

Jack listened to the plans and gave advice where he saw it necessary, all the while knowing he had no part in the new venture of his friend. His path took him on a different route; one they both knew was ahead as the fork in the road loomed mercilessly.

He listened as his shaken friend poured drink after drink, expounding on his plans. He didn't want to be like Foley, lording it all from a pub, he wanted to lord it from a remote mansion, in the sun preferably. His ambitions involved dealing drugs, the hard stuff, something Foley had managed to get by without doing, but business needs were changing and you had to move with the times. No doubt their step up would attract more attention: the flying squad would take notice no doubt, not to mention other gangs that they'd be muscling in on as they shouldered for power; then of course there were the suppliers themselves, a cunning and merciless animal that would viciously rip the throat out of any it felt had the potential to undermine its business in any way. He knew the risks but had decided it was the only way to build further than Foley had gone. He wasn't satisfied with sitting on his laurels and controlling a small patch, he wanted the whole town, but to get it he'd have to get tougher; no more of the school boy antics and street gang marauding and planning small time heists, it was time to move up a level. To get there they would have to ditch the knives for guns, and for that he already knew who to go to.

Tony Cirrillo was a club owner in Soho he'd met on

the inside, he owned one of those seedy side entrance clubs where the girls stood pouting in the doorway with their cleavage hanging and their upper thigh on show, the sort of place you entered with your head hung low as you descended the stairs into its dark fiery depths to pay for pleasures of the flesh as your soul burned along with the wallet in your pocket; when you ascended the stairs again it would be with heavy steps laboured with shame and guilt, something you knew on entering, not that it would stop the craving of the temptation of the enticing feminine finger beckoning you forward with her slender painted nail.

Tony could provide the tools alright, better quality stuff than Foley could get his hands on at any rate. He wanted his gang protected and he also wanted them feared.

Bobby Sullivan was another that would be of use. He'd done a short stretch for dealing class A, he'd been busted at his flat in Pimlico with ten grand's worth of heroin. It was his first serious time inside and got released early on good behaviour. He would have served a longer stretch had the concealed drugs been proven to be his, but as it was he had maintained that he was just holding them for a friend, whose name he refused to give up, in the end taking the rap as just a middle man to the frustration of the police who no doubt had him on a watch list (another proud badge to wear along with the one that said 'I did my time' and 'I kept my mouth shut'). He would have got the respect for that and earned his place as a trusted dealer.

And did Bobby not owe him? A hard time inside himself he might have had, things he still refused to talk about, but he had overcome it and climbed on top in the end without the aid of a protector. Had he not stood up for Bobby when they came for him in the showers to make him their bitch? Had he not brought Bobby under his protection on the cell wing he controlled? Seeing back then that he would one day want to call on this weedy looking shrimp of a man, a sophisticated yuppy student type with more money than he needed yet seeking a thrill in life through running with the wrong crowd because he was bored with the pressures of being railroaded into daddy's import business, an action that had seen his allowance cut off and his Eton education wasted. He still spoke with his father but for appearances sake he would not be seen in public with the disappointment and embarrassment of his drug dealing son.

Yes Bobby could get him a meet with a supplier alright and he could promote his case for distribution across the south west corner of London. Tony would supply the hardware to keep everyone else off their backs, and his *'network'* would provide the muscle and the balls to carry it all out - and when necessary Jack would be brought in to tie up any loose ends.

Jack listened with itchy feet long into the night. His friend was compensating for the edge that still clung, gripping hard like a daemon hell bent on claiming him for his crime, his hand still shook slightly and Jack realised, not for the first time, that no matter how tough the man it didn't make him a killer. Jack wondered with sadness whether his friend would ever recover.

"Jack," he slurred the name as he struggled to focus on the words before his mind closed down for the night, like a computer slowly shutting down its systems before the screen turned black, "I want you to do one thing for me before you leave - Foley." His bleary eyes hung from his slumped head as he reclined across the sofa, the nearing empty whiskey glass drooped across the carpet an extension of his limp arm. He waited for a response before allowing himself to drift off.

Jack nodded, stood and left the room.

19

Jack had nodded his understanding. He didn't ask for a reason why, he didn't need one. He'd make it slow and painful. Jack's lip upturned at the thought, his mind echoing a favourite line from one of Shakespeare's plays that had long ago lost their context: *'Off with the crown, and with the crown his head! And whilst we breathe take time to do him dead.'*

This was personal. He would do it gladly for his friend.

Time was indeed allowed to tick by, for certain things needed to be in place first, but not for too long. A statement needed to be made, first by Foley and then by his replacement.

His friend already had a reputation for being a hard man, albeit as an occasional hot head with a tendency for being impetuous in his whims of violence and destruction, but his repertoire also consisted of being an ace safe cracker able to unlock anything, and also a sound leader who was prepared to take the fall to protect his boys, a quality that attracted loyalty and devotion and a growth in his membership as though it were a club everyone wanted to join but only the few were selected. This was something even Dave Foley couldn't compete with, it made him appear weak in comparison. Foley had always been selfish in his obsession for power in contrast to the generous lust for wealth that was already being bestowed to all working within the circle based out from the club in what eventually would be known to all as *'the network'*;

those loyal to their leader were already reaping the benefits.

The rivalry between the two gang lords was well known so it was essential that Foley made public his retirement and announced that his younger challenger had been handed his seat at The King's Head, a seat that was expected and accepted graciously, although Foley was surprised by the generosity of the man he'd brought into the fold as a boy as he was allowed to keep the pub.

Foley had probably thought that the boy had never known, or maybe he'd never been sure. The boy had known enough though, had known all along. Word had reached his ears, whispers from the grave as his father bled out, of who had set the ambush at the stadium setting into motion the hopeless events of his life that would secretly motivate his passions. He told no one in his life other than Jack. Jack knew little of neither revenge nor the satisfaction that was hoped to be gained from it and he doubted it would fill the vacant hole that so obviously needed filling.

Foley had basked in his retirement for a little under three weeks when the bold statement that had been passed to the new boss' confidant on the night of Rutledge's slaying was enacted.

Foley was found to have committed suicide, although for a long time it had quite rightly been treated as a murder investigation as his body was discovered slumped over his monument of a desk - the icon of a desk that Fletch himself in a fit of uncontrollable rage would later take an axe to as he personally trashed the den of his old boss, sealing the vengeance he'd asked Jack to carry out by destroying that symbol of power that Foley had rarely shifted his weight out from behind, like the pub itself that he rarely budged from only that was a little too precious, too valuable to destroy. Foley's his head had been sealed in cellophane, and deep clawing nail marks scratched into the table top as though he had struggled for a considerable amount of time before he died. The police suspected that Fletcher was responsible of course and hauled him in for questioning, but his alibi was rock solid. It had brought a smile to his face too to know that the police suspected that whoever had committed the murder had somehow managed to subdue his victim without leaving a trace of restraints and then torture him by suffocating him over and over again before finally allowing him to die. In the end there was no evidence, forensic or otherwise, that anyone else had been in the room and no suspects that didn't have a cast iron alibi, and an examination of Foley's depleted business interests and sudden debts which had inconceivably mounted up since the inland revenue had swiftly announced their interest in his affairs shortly after Fletch had handed him back The King's Head all led to an eventual, if unlikely, coroner's report citing suicide.

Fear spread through the gang rapidly upon news of the death. Not only did they have a ruthless leader, for only one person could have ordered the hit, but he also had his own personal hitman, for they all knew only one person who could have carried it out and his affiliation wasn't with the gang but with its leader.

20

It was ten years later, a different decade, a different war. There were many events hitting the global stage: natural disasters, political catastrophes, technological revolutions, but none came to being so heart stopping as what would forever be called simply 9/11 – the date the Twin Towers fell in New York City. Everyone you spoke to could tell you what they were doing at the time they heard of the dramatic attack on the US that caused the deaths of so many and the closure of US airspace. The 'War on Terrorism' was on and Al-Qaeda and its mastermind Osama bin Laden were the number one targets of the western world. All else paled into insignificance.

In the panic of instability and heightened security the gangs blended into the shadows as crime funding terrorism became the police focus, and people like Jack became ghosts in the employ of secret services who could eliminate targets that politically governments couldn't get near to.

On a personal level the pocket of the average citizen was being terrorized in a very different way as a fear of an altogether new crime was made available as identity theft became common place.

There was still a profit to be had from moody DVD copies of The Lord of the Rings and Harry Potter and the like, but it was miniscule and was a business now left to the Chinese who coasted the high streets with their bags loaded trying to turn a profit for the organised gangs that turned them out under threat of violence if they lost their stash. Others flogged their wares on the market stalls where police and trading standards rarely bothered to inspect the authenticity of the goods on sale. CD's were beginning to give way to MP3 downloads so the smart traders were already making a shift to on-line sales and illegal file sharing websites; in fact a new market was opening up for those willing to draw on the fresher younger minds capable of unlocking the keys to the ever changing labyrinth of computer programming and website design. This was where the new crime gangs were operating; this was what people now feared: being terrorised by a faceless enemy, information stolen, a whole life scammed from a computer terminal.

It was a wave of crime the leader of *'the network'* was slow to surf.

He'd been slow on the uptake of a number of things in recent years. He was still a formidable leader who earned the loyal respect of his diminishing followers. With the dwindling profits had come the dwindling numbers of hangers on as the flash cash lost a bit of its sparkle. To turn a big profit meant that big one off jobs needed to be planned and executed by those, and only those, that could be trusted, meaning that only a core group got to enjoy the rewards, so long as they managed to pull off the gig.

Some blamed Fletch's excessive drinking for the demise, some his greed for wealth, whilst others simply claimed he was too dim and set in his ways to change with the market; in essence they were all right, and yet the great man himself didn't see it as he blinded himself, so deluded was he of his own success of power and riches.

Gone was The Top Hat, that mighty old majestic cinema building, having only survived as a nightclub for only five years before he'd been forced to sell it, having lost control of the nightly brawls that spilled out onto the streets and its line of juvenile cliental that led to the stripping of its licence to serve alcohol. No longer did his proud sign hang on top of the foyer overhang but that of a growing black Pentecostal church, so far removed from the den of what he had achieved; Satan had been struck down and God had claimed back what was his.

Gone too was the snooker club, though it still operated it was no longer under the gang's control. Ground that they had conquered in the expansion of Foley's reign had now receded back to the humble boarders of their original turf as *'the network'* shrank back to *'the boys'* from Brentford, old style villains with scraped knuckles and hidden cosh's under their coats operating out of the local pubs and dreaming of the next best thing.

There were good with old time scams that they ran across the country like pikey peddlers moving from place to place and returning home for a well-earned rest from their holidays. He had taught many of his boys well, maybe a little too well as they mimicked his modus operandi across the nation scamming innocent victims of all they felt they were due. He had always been good with locks and working out scams such as renting houses under false names with fake references and not paying rent until they were eventually evicted, and living off the generosity of unsuspecting hotel guests whose room numbers were given at dinner, not to mention the seaside holiday homes identified as vacant through holiday advertising which were ripe for use with a little pre-planning and swift action with the locks. All these ploys he had taught readily not knowing that one day in the not too distant future he would be relying on these for his very existence.

Gone were the days when every job was sanctioned, when every job had to be run via Fletch (having adopted Foley's business method). If the job was approved the boss got his cut, and for this you got his protection, planning, equipment, alibi, a brief, and if you got sent down the family were looked after. So all in all it was worth handing over the 40% for the peace of mind and also to keep *'the networks'* goons from trying to muscle you off the patch. Only a fool would try to work the patch without his blessing. The security that came with being part of the gang meant that Fletch's territory had attracted not only the immediate local scrotes but had allowed him to expand through Isleworth into Hounslow, through South Ealing into Ealing Common and up as far as Hanger Lane and Alperton, and through Gunnersbury into the fringes of Acton and Chiswick (Fletch taking on Acton's heavy hitters had been a gamble as he sought to extend the hold he loosely had on the Ealing pubs along the Uxbridge Road that ran dangerously close to infringing on the Acton mob's territory, it was a gamble that had left him hospitalised with a machete wound to his skull and having been exceedingly lucky to pull through. It had been the first time he was forced to concede a fight, resulting in the beginning of the decline as his arrogance had shown him as weak against the heavily armed black drug runners who didn't take kindly to other gangs muscling in on their patch). In effect his team players were no longer loyal to the rules that had bound them as a gang.

There were few in the gang who hadn't done a long stretch inside, and of them all only Jack Walters had never been caught at all. 'Lucky Jack' they called him, the newer ones anyway, for he was seen only rarely and the older ones who knew him of old were too fearful of him now to even whisper his moniker of days gone by. He came occasionally to see his friend and to catch up on business, some even said he financed the dying crew for he was flash in a way that none dared speak of, a plinth of confidence that stood him upright yet always hidden from view as though his face were always carpeted behind death's hood with his scythe flung across his shoulder with only his steely eyes peering out.

Jack was always too switched on and alert to get caught, intuitively swerving away from capture. The police knew of him, his existence, his name and what he looked like, but having never caught him nor been in a position of rolling his thumb and forefinger in the ink of state ownership he remained a free man and out of the reaches of the prison system that would long to claim him should they ever find out his true identity. It was his friendship with the gang that held off the baying wolves from their door. It was his friendship with their leader that kept them from being overthrown.

21

He boarded the flight back to Heathrow under one of the alias' he often used, Lee Coyle, a name that shared a number of faces under the blanket of documents that had become easier to forge with the use of the latest computer technology. Hooky papers was something the gang still had a hand in but due to his dubious line of work he tried to keep from allowing the boys from being linked directly to him if he could, as a result he sourced his papers elsewhere and placed his orders direct through an unofficial government source.

It was a short flight thankfully; he hated long haul, he could never sleep on those flights and always arrived tired and ratty, not that he wanted to sleep for he dread to think what would happen if he had one of his episodes on a plane. On long haul he would spend his time reading, first the magazines and newspapers and then whatever novel he had picked up at the airport bookstore with the intention of getting through it by the end of the flight if possible so that he didn't have to carry it with him.

His heart was pounding, unusually with torn emotion. On the one hand butterflies churned his stomach with a nervous excitement over his unexpected encounter in Paris. On the other hand he'd received a text from Shirl, the latest house squeeze to polish Fletch's woodwork and fluff up his pillows. She'd been given directions to text a mobile number should anything happen to him. It was a set piece message that

Jack had worded himself and that only the two friends would understand.

As for Paris, well he knew her face but little else about her. Wahabi had shown him a picture of her recently explaining that she too was on the payroll. He hadn't expected her or anyone else to be at the ball in Paris and didn't quite understand why they had both been booked, although it wasn't uncommon for a prize target to attract the attention of more than one enemy employing someone skilled for such a task; on one occasion he had turned up to a hit in South America to find three others waiting in the wings; he had walked away from that one knowing it could get messy and not caring for the fallout.

They had danced together at the ball, a passionless tango, she in her muscle packed tall frame reaching over him straining to tear out of her dazzling gown, her pounding breasts squeezed tight against his chest as they both teased each other at knowing the target but each daring the other to make the move first. It was a surreal moment. There were few females with the callousness to carry out the job repeatedly and as competently, so when he did come across one he was genuinely struck in awe and admiration. But rarely had he crossed words with an associate of the same ilk in the field in the course of executing the task at hand, yet this vixen appeared to be purposely teasing him, flaunting herself at him in an attempt to put him off keel – and it had worked. He had the opportunity to seize his mark but passed on it, stepping back to allow her the opportunity to slip away up the stairs while he feigned a distracting collision with an unsuspecting party guest.

It was the first time he had met her in person. Other than what Derek Wahabi had told him he had heard only of her by her short lived reputation, being relatively new on the elite circuit of paid assassins. He was been curious as to who was writing her cheque for this outing as surely they hadn't been put onto by the same employer, but didn't lose too much sleep over it, being a government (ahem) paid job he thought that Conway would be happy with the hit no matter who had carried it out and so he was happy to forego the fee under such pleasant circumstances. The one they called 'V', or sometimes 'Vicki', and occasionally 'Viper', had slithered away into the deserted hallways of the upstairs bedrooms and carried out with more passion and panache the frenzied panic attack he had meticulously planned out, but that was okay, the job was done, and she, without saying a word had set his heart alight.

He knew he would see her again; they had made a connection, one he couldn't explain as the emotion tugged uncontrollably at his pumping heart in a way he didn't understand and had never felt before.

Jack had planned on getting straight into the car he had left parked at the long stay car park at London's Heathrow Airport and drive straight down to Brighton and the small one bedroom flat he had rented temporarily in the name of Jon Devereux. He had based himself down on the south coast for the previous six months whilst he hunted out a more permanent base. Brentford and its surroundings was more home to him than anywhere else in the world but to live there had its implications: too many people knew who he was and what he did; he was too traceable and would be easily caught out if he stayed there. He sought instead somewhere more secluded where no one knew him and where he could come and go unnoticed. He wanted in essence to disappear, contactable only by a select few (and in reality there were only a few he had any sort of relationship with anyway, friends he cared little for, and socialising came in the form of deviant hedonistic abandonment in backstreet clubs of vice where he would saunter in and out without anyone ever knowing his name nor caring for it), he took a risk with the couple of people who had his number but it was marginal and he was prepared for any eventuality should they wish to turn on him. He'd been hunting around Bournemouth and Weymouth before he'd flown out to undertake his most recent contract. He had a couple of places that he had planned on checking out upon his return but that looked like it would have to wait for the moment.

Under the circumstances he thought it wise not to stay at the bedsit, it no longer felt like home, and anyway there were better reasons to steer clear. He booked in at a hotel near the airport, The Radisson Edwardian on the Bath Road, and spied out his business from there without the gang realising they were under observation.

22

Two cars were needed for the job. Pete Dwyer had sourced one in the usual manner: a small cash payment after briefly looking over the old Ford Sierra which had been advertised in the local rag; sure it had rust and a small dent in the rear but the lights worked and the engine ran fine, and that was all that was needed. The second car didn't come so easily.

Lee Fletcher had introduced himself at the door in the usual manner having phoned ahead to inspect the Vauxhall Astra advertised. He was dressed smart in his usual attire, still liking the feel of his suits that made him feel powerful and dignified, classy even as he straightened his collar and cuffs and tucked in his tie to fasten his blazer at the doorway. He had waited a while for the young lad to answer the door and was about to walk away when the door opened and the snot nosed wide-boy quipped a snooty jibe at his suit. At this point he knew his friend Jack would have walked away sensing a bad deal, but he wasn't Jack. The lad was too cocky for his own good and clearly had no idea who he was dealing with.

It was dusk and the day had been long already. All he wanted was to get the car and go. For this sort of job he needed to purchase not steal, he didn't want them being picked up for the cars being reported lost or stolen, an untraceable cash buy was easier and the chop shop down in Hanwell would strip the cars afterwards and then ditch the rest at the breakers yard. It wasn't long to go before they executed the job and he was already on edge, the last thing he needed was some jumped up little prick winding him up.

The lad gave his sales pitch trying to make the Astra sound like a Ferrari rather than the battered run around that it was. The engine sounded a little ropey but well enough to last the night at high speed if needed. The brakes were a little too soft but he was sure the Coleman twins could handle the steering on it if they needed to swing its back end round a corner fast, as usual the two boy racers would be doing the driving; they knew every back road there was to know and had outrun the police more times than not. All was good except the money. The lad seemed to think he had a Roller parked in the driveway as he refused to haggle over his asking price. There was no way he wanted to pay more than what it was worth, especially as the car was a dead run by the end of the night anyway, but in hindsight it wasn't worth the argument and it was something that he would regret later on as his lack of patience made him too memorable than he needed to be.

The lad, no more than twenty with skinny arms under a white vest top, got in his face, 'take it or leave it, just don't waste my time!" he yelled before walking off towards his front door. He was out of time, he couldn't take it or leave it, he needed it now, tonight! Frustration got the better of him as he reached out for the lad, grabbing him by the hair and slinging him against the side of the car. Words of common sense were conveyed and a reasonable price was agreed upon as the lad suddenly seemed to come to a realisation of what type of person was buying his car and for what sort of purpose.

Fletcher stepped into the car putting on his black leather gloves as he did so, straightening up his tie as he looked into the rear-view mirror at the bleeding lad who stood in front of his house unsure of what his next move should be. He put the car in gear and drove it off the driveway, barely acknowledging that he had come so close to throttling the poor bugger almost to death.

It had started raining heavily again as the evening drew on, another sign that would have caused Jack to bail. They had waited out days of miserable grey drizzle, not wanting to contaminate anything as they all knew the rain made things sloppy, footprints were easily left, gloves were often stripped because they were too wet, and visibility was never too clear. The rain had its positives too: there were usually less people about and there was often a slower reaction from the public (not so from the police who seemed to have little else to do in the rain as the usual problematic anti-social activities went by the by) but that was little to compensate for their plans were set in motion. It had to be tonight, rain or no rain; the bank would reopen tomorrow and the vault code would have changed.

Grey days were coming, the omens were there, but he ran headlong into it almost welcoming the consequences.

Over the years they had joked about how The Sweeney would love to take down *the boys*. Not that they had ever done anything big enough back in the day to draw too much attention to themselves, not on their own patch anyway, they'd use the away games for that, mingling with fellow supporters, ants from distant nests only recognisable to each other as they crossed the trail and battle lines in pre-match drinks around the pubs and the wading crowds slow marching towards a game of two halves, only the goals scored weren't the ones going in the back of the net. They'd done a few bank jobs, mostly front counter hold-ups before the banks and building societies introduced the toughened glass and automatic shutters and self-closing security doors that trapped the would be robber inside until the police arrived. Cash in transit vans were a regular hit as they mapped out the drivers route and routine, hitting the van when it was thought to be carrying the most, but that too grew problematic as the boxes became tamper proof and the vans themselves harder to get into. Pubs, post offices, jewellers, and corner shops fell next in line as opportunities for a big haul dropped off. Every now and again they would get a sniff at a warehouse with a big hoard worthy of a rumble or a house set for an easy pickings (most burglaries were carried out by the doped up scag-heads desperate to find a measly earning to pay for their next fix which came courtesy of the gang, the burglaries permitted on the patch so long as they didn't exhaust the pickings and draw too much attention, burglars who didn't respect the lay of the land were paid a visit and put straight one way or another). In general takings were down. The big jobs were rare and the gang had failed to recruit the right talent to keep up with current trends.

They often laughed about the good old days and the simple disguises they used to wear and the time they'd served. They had played about with stockings and masks before moving onto stage prosthetics and wigs and hair dye, rubber fingertips to smudge the ink pad when they were arrested (before the days of DNA swabs in custody suites) swapping names between themselves and addresses they could manipulate so that they would get bail and disappear. How smug they had all felt at fooling the establishment on the times they had gotten away with it. It hadn't lasted though as they'd used it too often and the regular Bobbies knew most of them by name anyhow, and as with everything else procedures and technology moved on to combat their primitive methods. The gang's imagination had dried up, its leader had become a washed up drunk, and the road they travelled had run out of tarmac and had become an old and worn out dirt track in the desert full of potholes waiting to buckle their axle and throw them into a ditch.

Fletch had spent the last few years living the high life in denial. The drugs business was good but fractious and the profits were down there too as other more organised foreign gangs muscled in. Even the sex trade was being controlled by ethnic gangs who were trafficking their own girls into the country along with the heavy set Eastern European muscle to control them. The warning signs were there but he had fallen in love with the luxuries that his money had bought him to the point that he forgot he had to work for it. Despite having lost the club he still had champagne on tap, and a lock up of his favourite cars, and a string of houses that fell under the ownership of his *'network'*, and runners to fetch his mail and tie his shoe lace, and girls to wipe his arse if he so required it. He had become so disconnected and deluded by the power, but mostly the guilt fuelled drink, that he had forgotten the promise he had made to himself to be better than his father.

Of all the people to bring him back to his senses it had been Rick, that often silent figure that had remained loyal despite knowing what had happened to his old boss. He should have gone into retirement years ago but had hung on as a gloomy Lurch figure of a doorman now running The King's Head in his own right. He'd fronted the boss over his reputation, laid it all out on the line: the failing profits, the grumbling of his men, and the disunity of the gang. It was he who had suggested that they needed to do something big to re-establish themselves, to gain back some respect, to show that they still had it.

Rick had hoped that they would move into the realms of pushing back the other gangs by invading the lost territories they had at one time won over, but no, be it for lack of imagination or from being set in their ways, or from the drunken doped up stupor of the gang's leadership, who could tell, but in the end they went with a job that came from the loose lips of Rooney to the needle pocked promoting of Frosty to the blind leader who still saw these as trusted sources.

On paper it sounded like a good idea. They had an inside man who had given them the lay of the ground: the times the vault doors were locked and unlocked, the location of the keys, the camera positions, and the access codes for the alarm system. Some things like the vault keys were locked away but that was okay because he still believed in his reputation to be able to pick any lock. It was a night-time job when the bank was closed so no one was to be around which was ideal. On paper it should have been a quick in and out job.

They had got inside without a hitch, both getaway cars parked nearby waiting for the signal to speed up to the back door and collect those inside. The CCTV was disabled. The door alarm system too had been disabled. Fletch was true to form and picked the locks of the cupboard containing the vault keys. There was a combination lock as well and this was what was changed on a daily basis. They had paid a high price for the code but it was worth it – the vault opened. They had just started bagging up the cash within when the bank's telephone rang, once, they all froze, then a second time and cut off. That was the signal from the lookout – they'd been rumbled.

'I didn't mean to!' Tom Frost had exclaimed with a shriek as they all turned to him in panic. He had stumbled on a box as they were creeping around the desks and had fallen with his hand out to catch the underside of the table as he sought to support himself. He had felt his hand press against a button, but on no alarm sounding had shrugged it off and failed to mention it to the others thinking it was probably connected to the door alarm they had already disabled.

Hands grabbed at all the cash they could stuff into the bags they carried but their leader knew there was no time. For the first time in ages he sobered up as a moment of clarity washed across the forecourt of his mind like a bucket of water washing away the vomit from the pub doorstep.

A police car was at the front of the bank, it wouldn't take them long to circle round to the back. He had to distract them.

'Put the cash back!' he had bellowed, 'Take the empty bags and go! Now!'

The boys didn't like the order but they complied nonetheless. In the confusion they were all too dumbstruck to think for themselves so were relieved to have an instruction to follow. They fled out the back, out the way they came like rats shuffling back down the sewer drain. Once outside the rear door they each ran, star-bursting in different directions hoping to rendezvous with their pick up or find shelter elsewhere. As they made good their escape Lee Fletcher strolled up to the front window of the bank so that he was clearly in view of the police officers, keeping their attention on the front of the bank for those vital few seconds that his boys needed to escape.

'Hallo officers,' he had quipped with a cheeky greeting, 'come to make a late night withdrawal 'ave we?'

23

He knew he'd made some stupid decisions over the last few years but he found that he couldn't help himself. He would always be too quick to react and too slow to think. Had he been more academic at school then maybe he wouldn't have fallen in with Foley's crowd at all, but academia was never to be a card he could play. His mum had kicked him out when his was fifteen when he put a knife to her throat after she caught him stealing out of her purse, *'just like your bastard father'* she had said accusingly sparking him into a rage at being compared to the absent parental figure that had abandoned him and his baby sister when he was just two years old. He still spoke to his mother, visiting her occasionally, feeling that bitter tone of disappointment in her voice slapping hard with every curt comment about his gaunt cheeks and deathly sunken eye sockets that left him baying for a part in a zombie flick. He forgave her for kicking him out but not for allowing him to fall into the fold of Dave Foley and *'the boys'.*

He had always wanted to become something bigger and better but in the end had always found himself playing second fiddle to someone greater, always lurking in the shadows and never able to get out into the light. He had played up his part on many an occasion but he was never satisfied and always felt like a second rate standby for someone else.

"Hau's yer mum, Frosty?" came the voice out of the dark mimicking his own accent as his rake figure entered the alleyway hoping to score from one of his usual runners that operated out of the stone walled rat run that led down to the river. It had been not that long ago that he supplied the runners down here but now he was at the bottom of the food chain and they supplied him as a customer, a fact he hoped he had hidden from his friends although he knew deep down they had always seen him as a liability and were only accepting of him now for old time's sake.

There was a figure in the alleyway with him now hiding in the shadows where the street lights couldn't light his face. He knew the voice.

Tom Frost's mind flitted back to when he was a child, ten years old if that, standing in a queue waiting in line to pay for his McDonalds burger and fries with his cupped handful of pennies, two pence and half pennies that had been saved up in a tin can on the mantel piece in his bedroom. James Petersham was behind him in the queue and Richard Moss was in front, each of them held a similar trove of coins as the three of them had agreed that this was the best way to spend the hard saved tenure.

They were waiting patiently in line, the smell of burgers tantalising their nostrils, their minds a little anxious of the reaction of the staff who would no doubt be unappreciative of the hands full of shrapnel that would hold up the queue behind as it was spilled out next to the till to be counted. Tom felt his school pal James shunted aside and out of the queue behind him and so span round just in time to see a black arm sweep him aside also. His collection of coins escaped his hands as they parted in his attempt to stay balanced on his feet. Richard stood cowering next in line, physically shaking as four black teenagers, bigger than most others stood around who were shrinking back in the fast food restaurant, circled round Tom laughing as he scrambled to pick up his money. As Tom's fingers reached forward on the ground heavy feet kicked the coins aside and tried to stamp on his grubby paws. Tom saw red and leaped up at the biggest of the four, the one who had swept him aside. He cared not for their size, nor that he was outnumbered, nor that they were bullies looking for trouble, no matter how small a package it came in. As he charged forward a hand bigger than he could grasp with his ten year old fingers had caught him by the throat and had lifted him clean off the ground and had thrust him through the air so that his head was pinned between the vice grip of the hand and whatever wall had loomed up behind him. He couldn't see the face of the youth that held him, his eyes were too focused on the hand, and all else had blurred into insignificance. A trickle of urine seeped into his pants as all thoughts of the scattered money were lost and he had a growing sense of futility and impending doom as he was surrounded under a choking dark cloud as his eyes bulged and watered down his puffing flushed cheeks.

It had, of course, been broken up quite swiftly by the restaurant manager who had come running from behind the counter threatening to call the police, not that it had felt like a swift end at the time as he slumped to the floor vaguely aware that his friends were on their hands and knees collecting his money for him.

He felt that same impending doom now as he stood in the alleyway, only this time he knew there was no one bigger or bolder to come to his rescue. What had he done? Plenty he guessed, but what in particular?

There was the incident with Alan Rutledge's boys; he was largely to blame for Jonas getting the jump that left Jack scarred. Probably, he thought, it was his latest faux pas at the bank, and what a cock up that had been! It had been an accident but he knew he would never live it down; you didn't get the boss banged up for a five year stretch and expect not to face the consequences.

No one was talking to him except the dealers feeding off him and they were reluctant to be seen with him. It had all happened so quickly: one moment he was part of the inner circle of the gang, the next moment the gang was falling apart and he was to blame. He could hardly expect less than death lying in wait for him in the dark, and a large part of him welcomed it.

Tom Frost pulled his knife from its holder behind his back where he had always kept it and held it out openly so that it caught a glint of light off in the distance.

"Hi Jack," he said resigned to his fate and begging one last courtesy, "make it look like I put up a fight."

THE KILLING

PART THREE

C. P. CLARKE

But Faith, like a jackal, feeds among the tombs, and even from these dead doubts she gathers her most vital hope.

Moby Dick
Herman Melville

'For in the shade of death I shall find joy,'
King Henry VI, Part 2
William Shakespeare

"Everyone dies but not everyone lives."
Anon

Nothing seems to us changed. Out of the unreal shadows of the night comes back the real life that we had known. We have to resume it where we had left off, and there steals over us a terrible sense of the necessity for the continuance of energy in the same wearisome round of stereotyped habits, or a wild longing, it may be, that our eyelids might open some morning upon a world that had been refashioned anew in the darkness for our pleasure, a world in which things would have fresh shapes and colours, and be changed, or have other secrets, a world in which the past would have little or no place, or survive, at any rate, in no conscious form of obligation or regret, the remembrance even of joy having its bitterness and the memories of pleasure their pain.

The Picture of Dorian Gray
Oscar Wilde

C. P. CLARKE

1

He hummed a tune, one that always tottered on his tongue whenever worry plagued his mind; it was a silly song but one that was a product of too many years spent in the company of his best friend. He could hear Jack singing the words to The Toy Town Salute absentmindedly as he hummed along. He was heading back home unnerved, he couldn't believe he'd almost got busted for something as menial as shoplifting. It had been a while since he'd been caught for anything.

A couple of years ago he'd been arrested for busting a guy up outside a newsagents in Hammersmith, the guy had been in his thirties, a weasely looking chap with a pointed nose and a happy hand in his trouser pocket as he perved over a schoolgirl loitering outside the shop. The girl was no more than fifteen and in school uniform so there was no doubt that his conduct was inappropriate. He heard the comments as he walked passed, heard her rebuttal and saw her attempt to walk away, and clenched his jaw at the sight of the guy's persistence in following her and stopping her from walking off too far. Initially Fletch just watched, pretending to look at the hand written signs in the shop window advertising local massage services in comfortable surroundings. It was only when he heard the loathsome figure openly ask her for sex that he intervened. He gave him a good pounding, he couldn't help himself. Unfortunately the shopkeeper was also aware of the deviant loitering outside, he was known for it apparently, and had called the police upon seeing his antics who then promptly arrived as the last couple of blows were struck to the snivelling creature curled up in a foetal position on the floor. He got the sympathy of the officers who were very understanding (not to mention unofficially supportive) of his actions, along with the prompt backup of the girl who leapt to his defence declaring that the pervert had struck him first and that he was acting in self-defence. He was processed, for once giving his real name feeling that he had done the honourable thing under the circumstances, and was then released without charge.

The only other time he had been arrested of late was on one of his day excursions into the city, Temple was the area he'd been swanning around that morning when he spied a city suit who had made the mistake of placing down his briefcase on the ground slightly behind him instead of close to his feet as he used a cashpoint machine. It had been too tempting not to. He had got only a hundred yards with the case, attempting to blend into the milling crowd wearing his own suit, when a shout came from behind. He ignored the frantic cries of his victim as he coolly made ground away from the scene. He would have got away with it had it not been for the CCTV that was on every corner of the city like thousands of hawks perched high up on the window ledge of every building waiting to screech out and swoop down and attack its prey. The cameras were of course hooked up to a control room which in turn linked in with officers on the street who, as it happened, were loitering nearby on foot, his description still being relayed over their radios as he turned the corner and walked straight into them. He had given his name as Lee Fletcher then too but it hadn't taken them long to run it through the system and confront him with his real name. He was charged and bailed to return for a court date but, having given a false address, had then disappeared into the ether once more.

He hoped PC Lawrence wouldn't take it personally that he had given him the slip back at the department store, surely by now he would have realised who he really was and that there was an outstanding warrant for his arrest. The consolation for the officer being that at least it was an old pro that had shaken him and not some wet behind the ears upstart.

Shaken as he was at the turn of the morning's events he took a detour from his usual route home by scuttling around the back streets trying to avoid being noticed. His cough was getting worse and at one point he stopped to spit up a gloop of blood mixed saliva. He was feeling the cold and he wanted to get home and curl up before his day got any worse.

2

It was pure chance that Abigail Henderson had spotted him turning out of a side road as he headed towards the cut through to Gunnersbury Park. It was her day off; she'd had a dental appointment first thing and had planned to do some shopping this afternoon once the anaesthetic wore off. She was walking along Popes Lane with her mind in a world of its own, her tongue stroking at the proud filling as she tried to grind it down against her bottom molars. Had she been thinking about him? She wasn't sure, but her mind seemed to recognise him before her eyes fell upon his figure crossing the road in front of her.

He didn't look well. His broad shoulders were slumped forward and his head was bowing low as he skipped across the road with his hands in his trouser pockets aiming for the park. He coughed a little as he walked and had a bit of a sniffle, she figured he must have a cold; it was certainly getting into the weather for it.

"Now or never," she muttered to herself, wondering at the back of her mind how far she would let him walk this time. At least it was broad daylight and it was unlikely that gang of black youths would be around, even they had a school to go to as they pretended to be the innocent victims of society, an ethnic minority victimised by the masses. She thought that even if she lost him, as she had done previously, she would try and get ahead of him on the path and race round to where she thought he was likely to come out, cutting off the corner by the fishing lake by sprinting across the football fields to the gate at the far side of the park. She wasn't used to running these days but for him she would make the exception.

She was sure he lived over there where the houses pushed down onto the A4 and the motorway flyover just passed the Vantage West complex and the Mercedes Benz showroom with its distinctive logo emblazoned high in shining metal for every vehicle to see as it passed on its journey into the great metropolitan enclave of London. There were houses there squeezed in between Lionel Road and Clayponds Gardens, that patch of land that was neither Brentford nor Ealing but both. There was a chance that maybe that he lived further out towards the Texaco garage at the beginning of the South Ealing Road but she doubted it, certainly she hoped that she wouldn't have to follow him through that piss stinking subway that carried you down under the A4 where the gangs and druggies handed over their goods and chattel and where any self-respecting or street savvy member of the public knew to avoid out of fear of those who regularly used the underpass; she'd made the mistake of passing through there once or twice in broad daylight with some old girlfriends but even then in a group it felt intimidating.

Many times she'd tried to guess where he lived as she dreamily followed him home and fantasised about what they did when they got there.

As she followed him now she panicked as she almost lost him again behind the museum as he floated down into the trees away from the path. She thought about making a dash for the field and to wait for him to reappear on the path following round the fishpond but changed her mind when she heard his cough off in the distance. He was moving slowly now and not in the direction she had expected him to go. No wonder she had lost his trail before, for he had gone in the opposite direction off the path and had only given himself away by his uncontrollable cough.

By the time she reached him he was still hidden from view but the incessant hacking, like that of a strained cat attempting to spew out a gagging fur ball, left no doubt in her mind as to where he had stopped. She held her breath incredulous as she peered through the trees, then with her head spinning she turned on her heels and ran off before he could turn and see her.

3

Jack sat behind the wheel of the car, a frown of dilemma creasing his beaded brow. It wasn't that he was scared, just confused. His mind was awash with maddening anxiety. There was a mole of doubt digging about in his head blindly overturning threads in his life that he had felt unmoveable. His ideology and theology were being shaken, the soil turned so that thin beams of light poked piercing holes within to scare off the detestable and objectionable insects that had infested his way of thinking since a child and formed the adult that he had become. He had tried to outrun the niggling doubts of emotion all his life, but now as he neared the finish he had felt it creeping up on him, nudging his shoulder and now about to overtake him on the line. He didn't want to be defeated, least of all by himself.

He had driven around for almost an hour, circling his old haunts and sticking to familiar territory. Much had changed in the area with new buildings replace old familiar pathways. In places small red bricked gated housing estates and polished glass business fronts with obscure building names giving away little of what trade took place inside rose up as the changing face of the community. The occasional truant gave away that the school uniforms hadn't changed at all and even a few of the smaller old shops he'd frequented in his youth still existed. A number of the pubs had vanished from the landscape with at least one that he could see having been turned into a McDonalds and another into a Tesco Metro.

Occasionally he caught glimpse of a familiar face; he spied an overweight Jon Joe Mulrooney ambling towards The Globe in time for its doors to open, so certainly not all had changed, but he kept his own head down as he drove so as not to be seen. He didn't know anymore how much of a gang still operated, he'd had little reason to soil his shoes in their presence since Fletch had been sent down and he'd paid the courtesy, putting Tom Frost to bed for his stupidity, ghosting in and out like a rumoured spectre that no one was sure anymore existed, only living out in the stories passed down to another generation as an urban legend; in light of the job at hand the fewer people that knew he was around the better.

In any case he didn't stop driving until he was confident that he wasn't being followed. Normally shaking a tail was a five minute job, if that, but he was a little more than paranoid. The photo had done that to him. A hive of questions were buzzing about in his head and none would stay still long enough for him to grasp hold of and interrogate.

Who wanted his friend dead? He didn't know. The gang maybe? Probably not. Another gang? Possibly. But then why did the call come via the consortium? Why would they send him out here? Why not send her? She was capable; surely they'd danced off each other's jobs enough recently. Why torture him with ending his friend's misery? Let her do it. Unless she was already assigned to something.

He shook his head violently. Deep down he knew what she'd been assigned to, and deep down he knew why. Was he not a loose end that needed tying up? His last contract for Derek Wahabi's was a hash job and his abrupt end in blowing himself up had caused him now be a liability, and he had no one he trusted at the top to fight his corner. He was out of friends and had no one of influence commend him.

But then he thought about that day in the pub when she had let him go, toying with him like she had done that day they had tangoed in Paris. I f he was her target then she could have taken him out then in the pub, so maybe he was wrong and it was another he needed to look out for. Maybe she too, in letting him go before, was now a liability. Either way he had seen no one following him.

He took the picture, still sitting on the seat next to him, as his sign to check out, or to be checked out, however you saw it. Those high up in the consortium that he worked for, that incessantly corrupt and secretive conglomerate with its esoteric agendas that made the Freemasons and the Illuminati look like innocent boys clubs, of which its members included that bent MI6 chief James Conway, he assumed they at least had worked it out and knew who he had been in his former life, that life he had left behind as a child, the life that he had only ever talked about with the friend he had now been sent to kill.

All of this was wrong.

He now doubted everything. Had he been watched as he courted Trudi in the bar last night? Were they now uncovering evidence linking him with her murder so that they could expose him as a demented killer who finally came a cropper after having been on the run for decades? He thought this was probably so. It was now beginning to make sense. Have him kill the one man who could possibly know who he might work for, and then take him out also. No loose ends. Neat and tidy.

He thought about burning the picture, it was clearly part of the ploy to get him agitated to show how he was still that traumatised kid mourning over the family he had killed, and still after all these years on a killing rampage. He was supposed to be found with the picture, of course he was. They didn't want him known as a hired assassin. They wanted him known immediately as a public menace to distract from the truth that he was in fact both.

He sat parked up outside St John's Church just along from The Globe, he didn't know which priest took confession here now, he doubted Rooney did either but would have been happy to hear otherwise. He'd rarely been inside a church and cared little for them and had never even contemplated taking confession before. He remembered back to when he had tried to read the Bible and how Rooney had tried to explain to him what it had been about. He didn't get it back then, it was illogical, but then thinking about his life now and the predicament he thought he was in, was it not all illogical? Could anything be any more illogical than his own life? He had a sudden urge to want to make amends and to change, having grown tiresome of destroying people's lives, much like Dorian Gray wanting to make good the horrors of his life but unsure of himself and his ability to not give into the temptations of the cruelty he was accustomed to. That sudden need to confess his sins was yanks and twisted at his insides, but alike the fated Gray felt he had no one to confess them to and yet he had no portrait to stab the heart of – for that would have to be the task of another, and when it came he would welcome it.

A sudden flush of guilt and regret overwhelmed him as the tidal wave of a lifetime of held back emotion finally burst through the dam in a surge he was unable to stand against. His mind conjured up images of those he had killed, faces he thought he'd forgotten, lives he thought he cared little for, a myriad of morphing ghostly features, accusing spectres, some he could name straight off, they were friends or family, or in some cases lovers, but many he drew a blank on, only remembering the manner of their deaths but not their identity nor the reason why. His father was there, fresh in his mind, as fresh and as lively as the smiling figure in the photograph. So too was Greg Dolan, his very first contract kill, Jonas and Rutledge were there along with the parents of that little girl he'd never laid eyes on but had left orphaned, there was David Morse the retired army sergeant who lived close enough to his home to be called a neighbour, then there was Nigel West and Daniel Grimes from the job in Australia that hadn't quite gone to plan; Matt Bradley, one of the first to be blocked from his memory came flooding back, Tom Frost and Dave Foley, figures he'd run with for years, and there was a multitude of others, that flitted across the forefront of his mind, many were contract kills, but others like Trudi, he had done for fun. The conflict in his mind rose up again as he fought hard to control the welling in his eyes.

There was a huge part of Jack that didn't want to go on. His life was fruitless and full of sorrow. He had regret he had never allowed himself to acknowledge, loss he had prevented himself from grieving over, and love he had hidden from out of fear, but now at the end he found himself being berated by his own conscience that he had kept locked up in the dark cell of his mind, terrified of letting it out to scold him of the truth. It had tried so hard over the years to break out, and more so recently as he tried to smack it back down with a baseball bat at the knees knowing his wakeful mind was beginning to side with it and turn against him.

If there was a hell he was going there for sure for there was no way in this life he could make amends for his crimes. He thought back to Rooney once more, the most unlikely of evangelists, and wondered whether there was any truth to what he had said about the man Jesus. If he were God he could forgive, but would he? Surely not someone as defiled as he!

Jack shook his head, denying in his head what he felt in his heart. For if he was so sure that he couldn't be redeemed then why was he parked outside a church?

A tear trickled down his cheek, and for once he let it go. Then another rolled to join it. Within moments his eyes were overflowing and he found himself wiping away the dampness with the back of his hand as he failed to control the outpouring. He pushed open the car door still wiping his face dry with his sleeve and walked toward the big wooden arch doors of the stone building, the sound of cars and trucks thundering overhead on the flyover and shadowing his steps. He barely noticed the activity above and cared little now who saw him as he crossed the threshold and turned the handle of the door, hoping in part that it was locked. It wasn't and the door opened to a musty waxy coolness as he stepped inside and closed the door behind him.

4

She hadn't gone far. That was the beauty of having the park to walk through: her thoughts were calmed as she slowly meandered along the path watching the leaves fall from the trees onto the grass beside her, the wind gently sweeping away like a broom across the open lawn toward the main manor house. There was a grassed slope leading up to the back of the white walled terrace that ran the length of the museum, in the winter the snow would make a small sledging run for the kids, but there were none here now, all at school she supposed. That was good. Only a single dog walker distracted her thoughts, the stygian Labrador padding along beside its master stealthily with a stick in its mouth, dropping it every ten steps or so to readjust its grip and cocking its head for approval of its aging female companion.

In many ways the turn of events had been shocking, a revelation she hadn't been prepared for, but strangely she didn't feel that it was life shattering. If anything she felt more attracted to this enigmatic man that she had admired from afar. Whether it was through compassion at what she found or from a sense of connection at being tossed out and abandoned and alone she wasn't sure, but for the first time she didn't feel afraid of him. Up until now she had felt intimidated by him and worried of his reaction should she dare approach and utter a word of her feelings to him, but somehow his plight made him more approachable despite common sense telling her that such a man should be avoided at all costs.

There was a chemist along the parade of shops just by the train station, she had walked there and back all the while trying to piece together how she had missed the signs without reaching any conclusions. As she walked slowly back through the park to find him she almost felt cheery at the anticipation of speaking with him.

She broke off the path and through into the thick trees, hearing his cough before seeing the tent.

"Sounds bad," she said as way of introduction knowing that he had heard her approach. His head peered out of the green tent that was mostly camouflaged by foliage, his face not too surprised to see her standing there although frustration and irritation rode his face like a saddle sore cowboy, but she just put this down to his being under the weather.

"I bought you some cough medicine; you sounded like you needed it." His face softened at this and so she stepped forward and offered it out to him. He fumbled with something inside, putting on his shoes she guessed, and then stepped out of the four man tent and accepted the gift, tearing open the box and cracking open the lid and supping at the bottle without a moment's thought for the white plastic spoon inside the box.

"You need to see a doctor." He shook his head as he took another swig from the bottle, clearly glad for the instant relief it gave from the cough.

"You live here?" He cocked his head back at the tent and shrugged his shoulders. She huffed a breath of dismay. "I thought you lived in a big house and were some big hotshot."

He liked that.

"I was once."

"What happened?"

"I had everything I ever wanted, but it wasn't enough. I guess you could say chasing after the world drove me insane. So I turned my back on it, the riches, the desire for more. Now I just make do with the basics and live off what I can get my hands on."

She shook her head not quite understanding. "You mean to say you choose to live like this?"

He paused for thought and then nodded.

"You shouldn't be here, too many shit flies around."

She didn't understand his meaning and frowned at him.

"Black bastards from…, ah forget it, it doesn't matter."

She got it then, he was concerned for her safety, she felt reassured by this.

"What about family?"

"Got none, folks are both dead, and I never married, no one to leave my riches to so why bother hoarding them, right."

"But don't you want to live better than this?"

"No. I don't want to be tempted by that trap again. I chased that dream and it ruined me."

"I don't understand; you always look so smart and clean."

"Just because I choose to live in a tent doesn't mean I can't be hygienic, I know how to take care of myself."

"But it's such a hard life."

"Life is hard, lady. I've been through tougher things than this, things that at the time felt good but in reality just drew me one step closer to the gates of hell."

"You sound like you've been through the wars."

"Lady, you wouldn't believe it."

"Abigail, my name's Abigail." She put out her hand to shake his, a warming smile as she felt a relaxing of her spirit in his company.

"I know," he said simply without offering up his own.

"I'd love to hear about your life, if you'd care to tell it?"

He seemed to pause again for thought and then silently turned away back into the tent reappearing a moment later with a small folded camping chair which he proceeded fold out into shape and place on the ground in front of the tent. He gestured for her to sit as he climbed back inside the mouth of the tent and sat down in the entrance.

"I was just about to make a cup of tea, would you care to join me?" he asked congenially.

With a surreal flush of her cheeks she happily responded with a nod of her head. "Yes please."

5

It had been an eventful day so far as he sat on the blow up mattress of his bed within the tent pondering on his life. He had one earphone of his MP3 player in, the other dangling limply down redundant as he kept a keen ear outside his transient home. He had cause to move on a number of times: the park keepers (whom he now knew on first name terms), the council and the police had all tried evicting him from the park at various points but to no avail. He had simply packed up tent each time and moved to a more secure place, sometimes out of the park altogether for a few days before returning to his favoured defensible spot that gave him shelter from the elements as well as from unwelcome intruders. The music (he had access to plenty of mod-cons in the tent including a laptop, all of which he charged from the public area of the museum house with the consent of the staff there whom he had charmed with his polite yet commanding manner) had been shuffling through a mix of albums that he'd had loaded on the player, but he had stopped to replay one track repeatedly as it echoed an age of Tom Frost blasting it out from the old bedsit on Windmill Lane, the words now more apt as it parroted and reiterated his life.

Sweat on my collar worked from the night
Bruised an' battered from my daily fight
Hands scrubbed red raw
Blood drawn through to the tips

The lyrics of the Broken Bulb track had struck off from the beginning again as he thought about how beaten by life he felt and how even the act of cleaning himself was a daily trial as he washed and shaved within the tent from the large canisters of water he stored within the rear of its outer canvas. He took pride in his cleanliness; just because he slept rough didn't mean he had to live like a tramp. He shaved daily and washed his clothes regularly at the launderette and occasionally got his suit dry cleaned. His biggest trial was probably keeping the mud off his shoes and the hooves of his slacks, but it was a challenge he often overcame.

Tossing and turning the midnight hours
In a suffocating sweat
Fighting the duvet smothering me
Leave me be
Leave me be.

His fight with the new kids on the block yesterday came to mind and he drifted back to how once upon a time that had been him, the tough young cocksure jack-the-lad who thought he could take on the world with his mob in tow, the alpha male trying to dominate all around him, but no more, here he was alone and not really wanting to take on anyone.

Alarm goes off an I'm awake
Every muscle in my body aches
The day revolves the same mistakes
Sweat and blood of another day
Weak and weary bleedin' day.

He felt old, older than his years. His body was regretting the years of brutal punishment that he'd beat it with: the fights, the heavy weight lifting, the broken bones and scars that were part and parcel of gang life as he rose up the ladder and then had to continuously prove his strength to stay there at the top, and what for? For in the end he threw it all away, abandoned it for a life less complicated, less tempting, less secure.

I look mashed up
I look worn out
I rush through life
No one stopping me

He didn't mind so much the obscurity of it all; no one really knew who he was anyway. There were the odd occasions when he would come across someone he knew, he was after all still residing in the old patch, and he would pass his pleasantries and enquire of them the best he knew how pretending to either be still in the game or out of it and gone straight depending on his mood for a tale and a believable yarn. He didn't know whether anyone ever believed him, nor did he care.

I have to stop and grab my chest
Pull at my shirt and at my vest
No one cares where's my place
No one looks upon my face

Certainly this morning he had wanted to sink from the world, sneaking around the back streets trying to evade capture as the cold air hugged his lungs and caught them up in a tornado squeezing them dry and painfully choking the air he so desperately tried to suck in. The cough was a little better now, thanks to her. Never had he thought that she would end up being his saviour, but now he had spoken to her and shared a little of his life and she had listened without judging him, accepting him as broken, sympathising as one who had her own baggage, her own struggles in life. They had talked for over an hour. She had promised to come back; he hoped she would.

The song began to fall into repetitive verse echoing the *Tough Day* it had felt outside and the weariness he usually felt every morning, but his mind didn't feel as sombre as the lyrics as for the first time in a long while, probably since his last long stint inside when he took the rap for that disastrous bank job, he felt a tickle of purpose, of hope for a brighter future, and possibly having someone to share it with. He knew it was just optimistic dreams, but then why not?

A rustle of the fallen leaves between the trees pricked at his open ear causing him to pull the remaining earphone down from his lobe onto the soft surface of his sleeping bag. He was attuned to the difference of windswept leaves being blown or sniffed at by a light footed critter or padding dog off the beaten track, it was very different to that of a person trampling the crisp brown droppings that carpeted the green grass beneath. It was a heavy foot, too heavy to be hers, too direct to be aimlessly wandering off the path and no animal jogged along beside. It stopped at a distance away from the mouth of the tent, curiously watching he supposed, maybe unsure of what to make of the home hidden in plain view of the public. Plod maybe, or a

council worker? He reached for the gun he had taken
from the black kid yesterday; it was a small black
Ruger 9mm with seven rounds plus one in the chamber
minus the one that he had fired yesterday as a warning
shot to the kids, a cheap enough piece and fairly easy to
obtain on the streets if you had the right contacts. He
had emptied out the chamber and cleaned the piece
thoroughly last night and counted out the remaining
bullets; as confident as he had been as leader of his
motley crew it would appear that the youth had never
before pulled the trigger of his prized possession.

He levelled the gun at the tent opening, listening as
he slowly and silently counted to ten. As he reached his
penultimate number he was already shifting his weight
so that his feet slipped into a pair of white Adidas
trainers that sat on the canvas floor near the entrance,
their soles and three black stripes caked in mud from
his morning deposit to the 'sprinkling tree' as he liked
to call it. The trainers weren't slip-ons but he treated
them as such, rarely undoing the laces so that the heels
were folded down where he had walked awkwardly
without slipping his foot fully in; he did this usually at
night when the cold air around the tent intensified his
need to pee and his usual bottle for doing so was
already full: a warm bottle of urine was as good a hot
water bottle as any on a cold night. His feet rested now
in this uncomfortable position like a faun or an Essex
girl on a night out, calm muscles tensed and toes
agonisingly taking the pressure for the heel. He
propped himself into a crouch with one hand forward to
the curtain of the tent opening and the other held back
at his hip with the barrel of the Ruger pointed forward
ready to aim and shoot if necessary, not that he thought

he'd need to but nevertheless it was best to be prepared, and besides, old habits die hard.

He could feel the probing eyes outside the tent waiting as he slowly drew himself out so that he could see.

"You're a sitting duck in there," came a familiar voice as his head peeped out from the canvas.

He smiled and then went to tuck the gun into the seat of his trousers but hesitated as he did so, his smile falling short, his eyes studying the stern figure before him.

Jack opened his hands and held them wide from the overcoat he wore reading the mind of his friend.

The gun found its home as he stepped out of the tent and stood to greet his old friend.

6

They had driven to Richmond in Jack's Prius, the white trainers replaced by the smartish black shoes he wished he'd had the time to redeem earlier that morning, the tent having been padlocked as per usual whenever it was left unoccupied for any length of time. They had parked on a meter on Richmond Green and walked the short distance down to the river, careful to steer clear of the main roadways and the busy shops of George Street.

Both men were cautious. There was an unnerving flitter in Jack's eyes that gave little away except the weaving head of a snake still deciding a course of action. It wasn't the first time Fletch had wondered whether the tables had turned and that he had now become the target of his friend's lust for murder, not that he doubted their friendship, it was just that he knew Jack was capable of disconnecting the emotion from all who were close to him.

Their conversation was friendly enough as they walked towards the river, as it had been on the walk through the park and on the drive, talking around their conquests back in the day and the laughs they used to have as a gang as though nothing had moved on, each avoiding the topic of Tom Frost's demise and both seeming reluctant to broach the subject of where they were now in life. They had both moved on and it had been over ten years since they had laid eyes on each other (Jack had spied on his friend from a distance but daren't confess his observations for fear of panicking him), though texts and emails were still forthcoming between the two as they conversed and shared the briefest of details of their trails. But for Jack to show up out of the blue like this there had to be a reason, and his reasons usually ended with someone dying.

"Shoplifting now, really?" Jack had wavered disbelievingly as they drove across the Kew Bridge.

Fletch had admitted that his life had taken a turn for the worst and that his self-indulgence had been the downfall of the gang, accepting openly to himself as well as to Jack that he had grown addicted to the high life and stealing and bullying to get what he wanted, a kleptomaniac dressed in a suit of authority and disguised within a mission to attain and maintain leadership, promulgating his gospel of reign like an enthusiastic evangelist power praising the god to whom he thrashed his parishioners and potential converts with. As a result it had overcome him and overtaken him till all that was left was the desire to steal. It wasn't that he had lost it all but rather that he no longer wanted it all. The thriving for riches had sent him insane, coupled with the drink he had turned to to numb his senses from the very thing that kept Jack from existing at any level more alive than a stranded zombie marooned on an uninhabited island in the Caribbean. It had been the guilt that the grog had drowned, guilt being something Jack was immune to, but not Fletch - it ate away at him and starved his mind of the lust for power as he sat solitary in his prison cell. Upon his release and the klaxon of the cold steel slammer sounding fire in his ears for the very last time, he had vowed to bid farewell his vices: the alcohol, the drugs, the gratuitous sex, the violence, the stealing, the lust for riches, the drive for power, the vanity, and the guilt. All too many were his sins that extreme measures he felt were needed to cut himself off from the temptation he knew awaited on the outside and scourge his back with the flagellem of isolation. It was not that he'd had any religious experience within the confines of prison as he knew some to have, but rather that revelation had dawned that in the end he agreed with the writer of Ecclesiastes that all he chased was like grasping after the wind, totally and utterly meaningless. Like his friend he had never taken the trouble to study the great volume he found himself agreeing with, but had dipped enough into the prison chapel services to avoid the glares of the screws and to credit a positive mark towards an early release to hear the odd preach that spoke enough wisdom into the soul to cause him to search his, even if he missed the point the preacher had been making about finding the true path.

So admit he could that, yes he lived in a tent, and yes he had turned his back on the gang he had strove to lead, and yes he had conquered the drink and a great many other of his vices, not totally but mostly, and yes he fell to temptation on some more than others from time to time, or more regularly with the kleptomania, but in all he was a different person from the man Jack had once known.

Jack on the other hand had given little away as he had let his friend do most of the talking on route to the river. He lived on the coast still was all he would give away, other than to say he was not married nor spawning any brood of merciless young snipers. He would not answer as to any lovers, male or female, for he had been known to have both, not that anyone dared to judge him on it; pity the man to scoff at the barrel of

Jack's cocked finger. Working for *'the consortium'* still was a small fact he conceded to, not that he showered him with a baleful of information as *'the consortium'* was as little known to him as a line-up of sixteenth century Swedish politicians.

The most telling thing in Jack, the greatest difference in his persona having not seen him for so long it seemed, was his apparent lack of, or rather his diminished taste for his art. Like a bland curry his eyes no longer lit with fire at the mention of spilling the guts of another, though he was sure to do it without hesitation, there seemed to be an inexplicable lack of love for it.

He had put old Jack to the test trying to provoke his interest as they stepped out of the car. "It's getting cold," he had said, "soon be Guy Fawkes, guess you'll be busy, eh?"

Jack shook his head with disinterest bouncing the comment back, "As I recall you did a little breaking and entering on those nights yourself."

And indeed he had, chuckling in reply, "A long time ago my friend, a long time ago." Both avoiding eye contact to gloss over the night that had haunted Fletch over the years.

He had questioned him on other things directly but his friend's mind was preoccupied and sealed tighter than Giza's cavernous Tomb of the Bird's beneath the great pyramids, or the sealed entrance to Tutankhamen's tomb in the Valley of the Kings before Carter broke the seal to the curse, or the volcanic plug of Vesuvius before it blasted out and ripped from the mountain pouring its ash to become the buried roof of Pompeii. He dreaded to think what would erupt from the mind of Jack Walters when the flood gates came down.

"What's your cover these days, travelling kitchen salesman still?" Jack met the question with a dry look off into the distance as though a passing boat crossing the mouth of the path ahead of them were more engaging than the question posed.

"You still suffer at night?" with a shrug he recouped at least some margin of response but still not enough to put him at ease. He was beginning now to feel grateful that he hadn't left the Ruger in the tent and consciously pulled his blazer tight so that he felt the material push on the black body of the firearm, feeling its hard steel brush against the shirt that covered his flesh.

"I've still got it you know," he confessed as they stepped out onto the river path, the trees of East Twickenham opposite shedding their leaves in the wind across the murky grey expanse of water that flowed steadily with none but the familiar duck and geese to ride its current, "the speed and the sleight of hand. I can't help it sometimes, the craving just takes over." He hung his head in shame but deep down trying to find a positive to bring out of his confession. It was a day for it it seemed; first Abigail, now Jack, maybe he was damned after all.

"I'm getting old Jack, and I'm slowing down," he continued after a moment's thought to check the truth within himself. "I can't afford the simple mistakes I keep making lately, getting caught out pilfering the simplest and most basic of things from the supermarkets, and taking a battering from the younger generation, the new stars of the streets, these kids – they're a different breed these new gangs, Jack, they're not like us, we had a code, they don't even respect each other."

What was he doing, trying to make it easy for him? Yeah, he thought so. He was more than certain now that Jack was here for him, for whatever reason; he had a lifetime of enemies any one of whom would gladly stump up the cash to see him topped off, and did it really matter who? If anyone was to take him out he was glad it would be Jack, at least he wouldn't fluff it and would make it quick.

Jack was scratching at his scarred face, that lightning bolt strike through the timber trunk of a sturdy oak tree, fired and burnt black at the edges of its age, the slightly protruding stubbled jaw line from which the thin white gash beneath his left cheek, his scar that went deeper than his flesh, having severed his fractious self in two and bore the wrenched tissue of his mind to seep his sleeping self from slumber.

A small Yorkshire Terrier was barking at them on the path having scuttled away from an open gate leading to a private residence, it danced over to them like a dressage show jumper lifting its knees slow and high. Being the only two persons to be walking this stretch of the towpath they immediately caught the dog's attention as it yapped along-side them as they walked.

"You know why..." Jack began to say but he was cut off by the raspy voice, sometimes cracked from sleeping rough, sometimes coming out louder than expected like his old voice, of course the cigarettes didn't help, but at thirteen when he'd started smoking them no one had discouraged him from the tough guy image that would slowly eat away at his throat and lungs, silently mutating, their whispers reaching his brain but his hand of thought pushing them reluctantly aside as he slipped into denial with a refusal to accept his marble sculpture was cracking so swiftly, but at the same time prepared to strike the last match in the box and sit to watch the flame slowly die out. Recently he had thought the cancer would get him before the bullet and had begun to accept it, but now the gun was here before him in the flesh he wanted to delay it, if only for a few minutes more so he could enjoy the company of the man who would kill him.

"You know that church is still going?" he said quickly with a jerk of his leg at the terrier at his heels who seemed intent on following them desperate for attention.

Jack seemed to read his thoughts and played along. "The church? You mean The Top Hat? Yeah I saw that when I passed by there earlier."

"Yeah, who'd have thought a church would have a greater draw than the club, eh? Can you believe that?"

"So who's the girl?" Jack looked at him with no hint of emotion on his face plainly waiting for an answer.

"You saw that, huh. You must have been loitering around for a while. No one ever hears you sneak up unless you want them to. She's just a girl. You don't need to worry about her; she's not one of your loose ends you need to tie up."

Jack nodded seeming reassured.

They had walked a fair distance from the house where the dog had escaped yet still no one had come to claim it and still it drifted along the pathway as an irritating eyesore piece of bark floating away with the river current.

"I don't want to do this anymore, not you, not anyone."

"I…what…you…" His thoughts were distracted. Had he heard right? Surely not. Jack was Jack. He remembered the young Jack, before he became Jack the henchman, the hit man, the hired gun; there had been a boy once who used to laugh and chase the girls with the rest of them, he'd never been an innocent boy granted, and always slightly detached and a bit odd, but there had been a time when he was close to normal. "But you… Aaaargh! Shut up!"

The dog recoiled at the anger spat out in its direction as its incessant yapping stole the thoughts from his mind. It fell silent, but only for a moment.

"Jack, shut the damn dog up."

Without hesitation Jack reached down and coxed the dog closer and as it came in to sniff at his hand he sharply twisted its neck and tossed the limp body into the river with a splashless plop. It was done with a casualness that anyone watching would have thought he'd thrown in a stick or a large stone or maybe had previously thrown in a stick and that the dog had jumped of its own accord after it, but no one had seen, so swift was the action, so instinctual.

Fletch laughed. "You want to give up, eh! Jack, it's part of who you are."

"Maybe, but I don't want to do it anymore."

"Level with me, am I your target?"

"It's not just that," he admitted to no great surprise. "I'm being set up. They've lured me out into the open using you as bait."

"Well whoever you've pissed off knows you well enough. I'm no one. No one cares about me. I'm not a threat to anyone, not anymore. I'm a ruined man, just like you. I guess we ruined each other, and we've both got our day coming. We're not gods, Jack. My father was no god and neither am I, and neither are you. Neither of us are going to live forever."

"What are you saying, that our time is up?"

"Not necessarily, but you do what you've got to do. If they're using me to get to you then what the hell are you doing standing here? Get the hell away from me. Or are you, like me, just getting tired of the game?"

Jack laughed at that as they walked along towards the bridge with the intention of climbing the steps back up to the main road. He had given up searching the faces of passers-by and checking the reflections in windows, and assessing the threat of a sniper from the bridge and across the river; he had done it more out of instinct than out of a care for his own safety.

"So where do we go from here?" Jack asked honestly seeking the council of his old friend.

They reached the stairs and began to climb, the hub of the traffic reaching their ears as the sounds and smells of the river hit an imaginary wall behind them and followed them no further.

"I think you go back to Portland and I go back to the park. Disappear Jack, for your own good. Get out while you can, if you really want to, if you think you really can. You must have enough cash stashed away to get lost somewhere. Use it! But I know you Jack, I think you'll find it hard to resist the temptation. I've got my vices and you've got yours, and that temptation's always there."

"How do you overcome it?"

"To be honest, you can't do it alone, believe me I've tried. And when it comes to our vices, well let's just say that life has enough headaches of its own without having to deal with self-induced ones!"

They broke free of the bridge onto the rumble of vehicles congesting the one way system into Richmond's main shopping area. The footfall of traffic was getting heavier as people weaved in and out of each other at different speeds like fish, every now and then one dipping into the colourfully decorated coral and leaving the flow to be joined by another from another dazzling window display.

Behind them rolled a 65 bus, its red double decker towering above the shop signs and obliterating the view across the street looking an archaic icon in the modern high street where all the new buses seemed to be single deckers.

"This is my ride," he said glancing back up at the oncoming red carriage that rumbled along the tarmac swerving into the unsheltered stop where a few others were gathered patiently.

Fletch struck out his hand to his old friend and the two firmly shook for what they both knew was the last time. Whether there would be any other interaction between the two neither could say for sure.

7

Jack was quick to get back to his car and drive the short distance across the busy roundabout to park up with the engine silently idling awaiting the few seconds on the Kew side for the 65 to make its slow trundle passed having loaded up at the various bus stops along the main road outside the shops and the train station. He didn't have to wait long before he spied his friend's low hung head near the back seat taking in the passing view as one does the sweeping blur of a vast and rapid journey not cared for as the mind settles on a scene elsewhere already played out.

Jack not only waited for the bus to pull out from the bus stop before him but patiently watched it as it curved into one further ahead, it stopped for a moment to let passengers on and off, and then resumed its journey, only then did he pull out into the traffic keeping a watchful eye on the vehicle far ahead.

He knew where Fletch was likely to get off the bus but he didn't want to lose him at this stage. Things still weren't settled in his mind and until he figured out all the angles he didn't want to lose sight of his mark.

Fletch had said they weren't gods, indeed they were not even demigods. In the guise of Hermes the god of business and patron of thieves they may have been cast, and too Dionysos for their revelry and wine, and Ares for their war-like attributes that left them so hated too alike the god, but for Jack too moulded in the void of Chaos was he, too enraptured in the darkness of Erebus and too ready with the hand of Thanatos had he become so that to Tartarus he felt he already belonged. They may have overthrown the great titans that went before them to become as demonstrously feared and as unperceivable to destroy, yet they were not myths but men, legends in their own imaginings, as proud and as stubborn as Achillies and as territorially aggressive and possessive as Agamemnon, sacrificing all in pursuit of their goal, even family. Men like them were forged in the fire by Prometheus, the maker of men, and so into the Phlegethon fire of Hades they were destined to return.

But not so set in the ancient's archives was he for something had cracked the marble mould that cast his immortal statue; since visiting the church he had changed. He didn't know what had changed exactly, but the song... the song was gone. No longer that underlining tune echoing in his mind like the hum of traffic' always present yet unawares, with it gone there was a silence of the mind overtaking the crashing waves of music and nonsense words creating a clarity in which to think and feel, it was a disconcerting, but not unpleasant, sensation as it made space for a new song to fill the void.

He followed the bus as it made its way through Kew towards Brentford, weaving its way through all their old haunts on route to its final destination of Ealing. Fletch was likely to get off on the South Ealing Road and amble along Popes Lane back into the park. He would follow him all the way, disembarking for the final journey on foot as he shadowed him to his lair. He knew all this, the motions of actions he would automatically carry out without purpose that made sense as somewhere in his mind screamed a question as to why. He didn't understand his own motives, nor could he see an outcome as he succumbed to the unyielding search for intervention that would bring sense and clarity to his life.

What dinosaurs they were, he thought as he parked up the Prius outside the King Neptune fish and chip shop on Popes Lane and waited for his friend to pass through the park gates before getting out of the car and following him. They two were both a dying breed, superseded by the evolution of technological advances; gang crime had moved on, it was less organised and controlled and more recklessly violent for violence sake, and as for wiping someone out, well a person could be all but deleted by the internet, the blood may still run through their veins but their capability to exist in the world would have been severed like a main artery left to bleed out. Such were they the Tyrannosaurus Rex and the Velociraptor; in the end all big beasts had to die for there was no room on the earth to keep them all. He wondered whether he would be doing a justice to his friend by terminating him, surely he had lost the greatness he once had and now ambled along without the keen watchfulness he once would have been instinctively attuned to, now moping along as a grandfather of a terminal beast.

He heard the cough far up on the path out of sight, almost as a signal allowing him to know which direction he had taken and to hurry up and get it over with. For the first time Jack realised that his covert activities were not so subtle and that he had fallen into too primitive and predictable a patter and that he was doing all that his friend was expecting, maybe even hoping for; confirmation maybe that for both of them they were reaching the end of their game.

Jack stopped dead on the tarmac path and allowed his friend to walk ahead alone. He needed to think without his target in mind, or at least not in view. He broke off from the path and cut across the open field towards the far gate way passed the hidden abode of his friend and out onto the road where only yesterday he had stood staring in at the gang of black youths who had stolen away from their confrontation in the park.

8

He waited for a long while for the sound of the crunching leaves, not expecting the tent zip to open but for maybe a sudden jet of light to pierce the canvas as a bullet whizzed through the air, or maybe he would wait until he cocked his head out through the opening and then strike him blind, quick and painless. He expected the tent to be torched afterwards and somehow for it to be made to look like an accident, his body charred beyond recognition to save him the humiliation – Jack would do him that honour at least.

He expected much from his friend for he knew what kind of animal he was and knew that he felt as compelled towards this gaping iron clawed trap as he was repelled to flee. He had thought for a moment as they had talked by the river that maybe Jack would spare him, but it was a fleeting thought, and a sense of relief almost flooded over him when he had caught glimpse of the black Prius humming almost silently as he stepped off the bus. Jack was a cunning fellow and as stealthy as any snake so he had not been surprised to have lost his scent as he made his way back to the tent. He had tensed in anticipation the whole round trip along the path that circled the park, taking his last stroll at any easy pace to suck in the damp frisk air and observe the skip in the step of a group of toddlers reined to their mothers on route to the playground, and a half team of school boys having shed themselves of the unnecessary jackets and ties of their uniform with bags slung over shoulders and a single ball bouncing between them as they jogged along to the open field and the goal posts that awaited them. It all brought back memories of his own childhood and for once understood the old saying about your life flashing before you at the end. Only it wasn't quite the end, not yet.

He'd coughed loudly as he approached the tent in case his approach was missed, half expecting to be clumped across the back of the head, but nothing came.

He sat impatiently in the tent waiting until his thoughts turned to Abigail. He didn't want her to be the one who found him. He was glad he had met her and talked to her, and yes even connected with her, but his fleeting dream of rebuilding his life and a new relationship had come too late and he now wished he'd never met her for the damage it would do to her. He hoped she wouldn't return now, not while Jack was still out there, for he would have no pity in his heart to spare her.

9

Jack had left the park, far from the car he had abandoned on the other side of the vast patch of urban green space. He had jogged, almost sprinted from the yellowing scene of shedding trees that waved a gentle farewell in the lofty breeze that swooped down to usher him on across the open trimmed grassland as his feet kicked back the mud and his knees pumped to his chest. He wasn't sure why he was running, he just felt a need to be free of the place and to exorcise the demons that clung to his back and chased him the short mile or so to the other side of the park. It wasn't enough of a run to be enervated physically but mentally he felt drained and confused. Nor too was he dressed for the activity, his basic loose fitting combat trousers, dark hoody and trainers gave the appearance enough to pass for a late afternoon jogger, but a closer inspection would reveal the bulging bounce of a gun holster strapped across his shoulder and a knife belt wrapped around his right leg.

He stood aside the roaring traffic beginning to build up on the homeward march of the axle that drew between the two wheels of the A4 and the A40, his chest heaving as he drew in the costly exhaust fumed air around him. His mind was in turmoil. He had fallen into a trap that he should have seen as soon as he discovered who his target was yesterday, but his mind had been clouded by a distant emotion for his oldest and his only friend, something that whoever had set this up had counted on, and he had played right into it, giving way to predictability rather than caution. Even stood here now he was vulnerable; they hadn't needed to follow him everywhere for they knew where he would gravitate towards. All they had to do was wait him out.

He had already decided not to go back to the car; he was done with it and would acquire another to slip out of the area, or maybe even stray further afield by public transport hoping the proximity of a crowd would secure him some breathing space until he had re-gathered his thoughts. As for the target, well maybe he was right, maybe it was time to move on. He had given his confession and said his prayers, for all the good he thought they'd do him. If there was a god he hoped he had heard him, hoped he knew he was authentic in his heart felt sentiment, even if he still succumbed to temptation he felt he needed to turn away from the life he'd been leading up till now, if he could, but if not he would die with the hope that God had heard him anyway.

He broke through the gates of the park as his senses were bombarded by the sound of heavy traffic flashing horizontally across his eyes. He wondered about making his way north towards Acton Town Station but figured that route had already been compromised once already today and so turned south out of the park towards Chiswick, the decision sparking the oddity of the photo back into his mind. He had left the photo back in the car having placed it out of sight in his sizeable kit bag in the boot, someone would get a shock when they finally popped the boot, at least it was likely to be the police and not some trigger happy crazed maniac who'd find his hoard once it was noted that the tax disc and chassis number didn't match with the licence plates. Damn he'd forgotten about the bag. The photograph and the bag were the only things that were identifiable and could link to him; with his DNA from the bag and his face in the picture plus the specialised weapons tucked snugly in a way so that it wouldn't take a genius to figure out he was no amateur the find would likely spark a nationwide manhunt.

He pulled up short in hesitation thinking he would have to go back for it and wondering which way to turn, back through the park or away towards Chiswick, hoping a sensible alternative choice would present itself, but none was forthcoming as his head span on the edge of a hurricane being buffeted by spiralling whipping winds that wanted to lift him from his feet to carry him up and away to someplace where he could float off into an unknown direction he cared not to dictate.

A youth nudged his shoulder as he walked passed, Jack having blocked the walkway with his indecisiveness, so that he span a half turn barely acknowledging the other passing pedestrian as Jack muttered a half-hearted but sincere 'sorry' which rang discordant with the thundering lorry that passed just at that moment, the word lost to the air as Jack was lost to the direction of his travel as he tried to refocus on his compass and spy out the way ahead.

So there he stood and looked at his direction beyond the old Catholic secondary school, the building, now tired looking but still in use having been turned into an academy for foreign students, to the small Catholic church beyond which stood along his path of freedom between the park gates and the road that opened up into the Chiswick roundabout and the B&Q Warehouse store on the corner. There in the doorway of the church stood a woman of height, her head clearly visible above the gates and hedge of the front of the church grounds, and through the distance there was no doubt that she was staring back at him and waiting, for he knew her instantly for there was no doubt that it was her and that she was waiting for him to join her.

10

Finally there it was. He cocked his head and listened intently as he sat fully dressed, shoes and all, as smart as he could be for his final send off, legs crossed awaiting the inevitable. The footsteps circled slowly, not too close, inspecting the camp from a distance, treading carefully so as not to alert him. There was no four legged patter to accompany the crunching leaves, no lapping tongue or pant or sniff of a mutt so he was reassured it were no dog walker – but his mind wasn't totally at ease. The steps were too hesitant for Jack, and too light. He let out a sigh of frustration as he heard the slow approach that seemed to stop a few feet from the entrance to the tent.

"Abigail, if that's you don't come in." She took a step back at the sound of his voice but her uncertainty of his command had not sent her away. He needed to be more direct. "Abbi," he sucked in the words not wanting to say them and certainly not meaning them but wanting with his heart to keep her safe, "I don't want you here. I don't want to see you again. Stay away from me!" He put a vicious bite onto the end of the last comment to make her think he was angry with her, hoping she would think he was a violent bastard or mentally disturbed, aware that she didn't really know him from Adam, in truth he was both to a certain degree but he wanted to change that image of himself and make amends.

There was a sideways step, then a backward step, then another. He hung his head low in regret as she backed away knowing he could do with her comfort right now, stranger though she was.

Then she rushed forward to the entrance of the tent and before he could unfold his legs to reach forward for the zip it was pulling down rapidly from the outside but the hand that pulled it wasn't the slender white hand of a female and nor was the face that leapt through the smooth pale cheer of Abigail.

Mohammed Abdi had seen the tent and knew its occupant. He knew the park well enough to know that he wanted control of it and that no homeless tramp was going to keep it from him. He had only one way of saving face after the humiliation of being sent running in shame in front of *his boys* yesterday. Sure the old tough guy had his gun, and yeah to give him credit he had a few tricks up his sleeves that put him a cut above any other bum sleeping rough on the streets, but he was still a bum, and this was his turf and he was the boss around here now.

He rushed into the tent sideways protecting his broken wrist, his long kitchen knife poised at his side ready to thrust out. He'd hesitated enough. Anger and hate and a drug fuelled haze widened his eyes as he let out a manic cry as he forced his body into the small opening of the tent.

The cimmerian figure that burst forth took him by surprise, so much so that he fumbled backwards searching for the gun he'd put aside when he'd taken off his blazer but not immediately knowing where he'd placed it. By the time his predicament had fully registered he had lurched back grasping for the misplaced firearm leaving his body exposed. Had he not been so certain of his death at the hands of Jack he would have reacted more instinctively by closing the distance and blocking the sway of the knife held clumsily in his opponents left hand, but he hadn't and the long blade had found its target, piercing through his shirt at the ribs and plunging deep into his chest.

This wasn't the way he wanted to go, not like this, not at the hands of a jumped up little shit fly gang leader who thought he could control the manor. *Jack, it was supposed to be you!* he cried in his mind as the knife pulled out and in a frenzy cut in a second time into his gut and then a third into his chest again as he doubled up, half in pain and half in a futile attempt to protect himself. The forth strike sliced into his left shoulder piercing the muscle so that the point of the blade protruded through the back of his neck. He let out a feeble cry of pain that barely registered between the two as they both succumbed to the intensity and rush of the situation, their senses escaping to a distant fairy tale land to detach themselves from the horror and the crimson tide that flowed.

The final blow entered through his left jaw and dug deep under his tongue and up through the back of his throat. His assailant had felt that was enough it seemed as he backed out of the tent not even bothering, or most likely too adrenaline hyped, to wipe the blood from the blade as he made his escape.

The pain wasn't so bad now that he was in the death throes of his life. It was uncomfortable but a fog was falling on his remaining senses that would cover over his misdeeds soon enough. She would find him no doubt, and for that he was sorry. His last thoughts as his eyes fixed open were of how he had tried to not make the same mistakes as his father and how he had failed in every way.

11

The door to the church creaked open, its little used hamstrings straining under the heavy wooden weight as the fixed hinge cried out for liquid refreshment to oil its fibres. The interior was small and basic: a dozen wooden pews lined the open shell with aisles at the wings and along its sternum; the walls were pale painted stone with undecorated lead lined glass arches broken by the small carved wall hangings of the Stations of the Cross; at the stone altar lay a white cloth with a golden bible stand and a golden eagle lectern to its side; there appeared to be no confessional box, however a closed door in the far corner told of a private room hidden from view.

He dipped his fingers in the font by the front door and signed his forehead as he entered, he didn't know why, it just seemed like the right thing to do.

She sat midway along a pew in the centre of the church. She was tall even in a seated position, her long straight dark hair as still as the stagnated air within. There was no attempt to hide; she didn't even look around as he entered.

He closed the distance and settled as best he could into the hard surface of the dark wood, his heart beating slower than he thought it should. She didn't turn to look at him as he slid along the smooth bench, not taking his eyes off her as he left a gap that even Rooney's wide frame could have fit comfortably between.

Rarely had he had a chance of studying her appearance as his glimpses of her over the years had been merely that as they circled each other in the field, moving always with a bond of uncertainty. She was athletic beyond doubt, in a slender reaching tower of strength embodied in strong arms and stolid legs, yet she maintain genuinely attractive facial features with strong cheek bones that were smoothed over with glisteningly buffed marble skin drawing round to slender ears and a firm unbreakable jawline that carved beautifully beneath bulbous puckered lips that most men would die for and most women would swear were enhanced.

He remembered her smile at the bar when he'd last seen her, when she had let him escape, that toying taunting smirk that left him pondering as to her intentions and the game she played. There was no smile now as she finally turned and made eye contact with him.

"This is the second church I've been in today," he offered awkwardly to break the stillness between them, allowing the finality of his resting place to jokingly titter on the crest of his mind.

"Name not religion, for thou lov'st the flesh, And ne'er throughout the year to church thou go'st, Except it be to pray against thy foes."

He smiled at her reply. She truly was a woman after his own heart. If only she would stay her weapon and escape this life with him… he almost allowed himself to dream before cutting off the emotion and the hope that came with it.

"Henry VI?" he asked with an uncertain cock of his head, and at last she smiled, and he felt the warmth of it through to his heart.

She had an envelope on her lap, one he recognised as the sort that usually contained the particulars (name and photograph) of a target, it was the same size as the picture he had found in his car. She passed it across the seat and left it within his grasp between them. He picked it up and opened it and withdrew the photograph inside, not a photocopy as he had seen before but the original.

"A happy family don't you think?" she asked watching closely as he studied the family photo. "So why, Jonathan?"

The question wasn't as to why he had done it but as to why she should let him live, and he'd almost missed its relevance and would have done had she not used the name she had once called him.

He stared at the photo and then back up at her, studying her features, her similarities to his own. How had he missed it? He looked back down at the photograph and at the smiling nine year old girl in the picture stood next to him in between their proud parents.

He took a deep gulp and looked up once more. "Lisa?"

She had a gun levelled at his chest. She had spent the last decade studying him and second guessing his behaviour, getting him to crack a little here and there to make him a little more approachable, getting him to lower his guard enough so that she could spell it all out for him.

"I thought you were dead."

"You thought what I wanted you to think. You didn't honestly think I was going to wait around for you to come and get me in my sleep did you?"

"No, I wouldn't have…I…"

"Why Jonathan?"

He didn't have an answer. He couldn't explain why he had killed their father, nor why his dreams of death had overtaken his waking life and carved out a living nightmare for all he came into contact with. He had no answer for why, but he knew now that it was wrong, even if it were too late to take it all back and too late to prove he had changed his heart. What was done was done and he had to face the consequences.

He hung his head in shame, fitting that it would be his sister to exact judgement. "Lisa, I forgive you for what you're about to do, and for what it's worth I'm sorry."

She snarled a huff, scoffing at his attempt at an apology and caring little for how genuine it sounded. "The devil can cite scripture for his purpose. An evil soul producing holy witness is like a villain with a smiling cheek, a goodly apple rotten at the heart. O, what a goodly outside falsehood hath!"

He listened intently as she slowly recited the familiar passage, seeing clearly now how she had studied him over the years and knew his likes and dislikes, his hobbies and tastes, his patterns and behaviour, his thoughts and intentions.

"Touché. So eloquently put, no more befitting The Merchant of Venice than the Merchant of Death. Do what you must, but I am sor…"

The shot rang out loud and clear, it echoed around the walls of the building, dying there under the thunder of the traffic outside and never reaching the ears of life, but be there souls still lurking beneath the stones of the graveyard alongside they may have shifted the earth around them in a shudder as the toll of death himself rang for his turn to join them as his roam of the world drew to a close and a door was unlocked to his bright gleaming room in the afterlife.

His words were never finished as she stood, leaving the photo by his side as he bled out, his eyes watching her go as he struggled to draw in breath to a heart that was rapidly failing. His mind focused on that exasperating last breath, often dreaded, sometimes longed for, fearful of pain yet a blessed relief as the last expulsion of moist air escapes across the tongue over a drying mouth from a gully left lifeless and relaxed, knowing no more is it needed, the chin propping open to allow passage as the eyes visualise, for the last time, that valuable commodity of life ebbing away from its mortal shell, the still conscious soul longing to flee its entrapment to wherever, whatever, the journey should lead on to…

12

As Vicky Rivers, the Lisa Rivers as had been, she who had adopted the name of her late mother, left the church into the wind swept chill of the darkening day outside, she gave little thought to the poor parish priest that was to stumble upon the body of her brother slumped across the centre pew of his church, nor did she give a thought to the agony she had left him in as his dying breath permeated the otherwise serenity of the church's interior. For her it was over. She had hammered in the final nail in the coffin of the life of Lisa Rivers, that little girl, frightened and alone, no longer existed.

Vicky Rivers was bolder and sharper and more dynamic and more creative than the shell of the girl she had killed off all those years ago, and she had ambitions greater than those of her brother, and with him now gone and out of the picture she had less to contend with and the playing field was wide open.

As she did up her coat to walk away she felt the comforting steel, still warm from being fired, within its holster and smiled insanely.

THE END

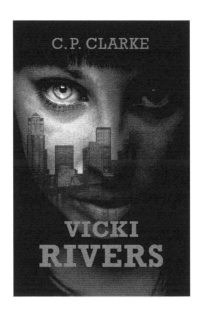

Vicky Rivers is a troubled woman, scarred by a violent childhood trauma that had turned her into a killer, but not just any killer, she is a highly skilled assassin in the employ of a powerful and secretive organisation, an organisation that harbours a deadly secret.

Vicky has her own secrets and her own obsessions, obsessions which will set her on a direct collision course with her employers as she seeks out the dangerous truth behind their secret research and the hunt for immortality.